ANASAZI EXILE

Borgo Press Books by ERIC G. SWEDIN

Anasazi Exile: A Science Fiction Novel

ANASAZI EXILE

A SCIENCE FICTION NOVEL

ERIC G. SWEDIN

THE BORGO PRESS

MMXII

ANASAZI EXILE

FIRST EDITION

Published by Wildside Press LLC

www.wildsidebooks.com

DEDICATION

For my Mom,

Who gave me a love of reading novels.

ANASAZI EXILE

PROLOGUE
1241 A.D, WESTERN EUROPE

Hans swung the ax with quick blows, cutting away a strip of bark around the tree. Like the other men, he had removed his grey woolen shirt, folded it neatly, as his grandfather had taught him, and laid it on the grass. He enjoyed the cleansing feeling of sweat pouring down his bare back. Just as he had cut down men on the battlefield, this tree would soon die. The death of the tree would take longer as its sap slowly leaked away, the leaves wilted, and the wood grew dry. Baron Henri had chosen this place, near the river and a large meadow, for a new village. The people of his manor were fertile and the prayers of the priest had kept sickness at bay, so he needed the new village.

Hans loved the baron as only a loyal man can. He had served his baron for his entire life—working his fields, tending his herds, following him into battle. The baron had always treated him well, even blessing Han's marriage with a gift of two horses. True, the horses were old warhorses and one was almost lame, but they were horses nonetheless.

He moved to the next tree, examined it for a moment to select his cutting place, and began swinging. Six other men from their village sliced at the trees. Two were his brothers, another his brother-in-law, two were cousins, and the youngest was a nephew. Just as he knew everyone in the village, he was related to most of them. Even the baron was a distant relation, a third cousin.

At one time, Hans would have been in charge of this small

party, a trusted lieutenant of the baron, but a blow to the head in a battle two summers ago had left Hans with chronic headaches and a sense that he had lost something. He could not even remember the details of the battle and sometimes wondered what had hit him. The haft of a spear? The flat of a sword? A rock? His wife told him that he spoke more slowly and didn't always make sense. He no longer led men.

The baron had decided that before the new village could be built, he wanted the trees removed and burned into charcoal. Killing the trees this summer would dry them out. Next summer the villagers would fell the trees and place them in a large hole to burn.

A thunderclap shook the air, rustling the leaves of the trees. Hans looked up, puzzled; there were no clouds in the sky.

"Come, come quick!" his younger brother yelled from the meadow.

The cry did not sound like fear, just surprise, even wonder. Hans jogged with the other men out of the trees, taking care to keep the blade of his axe turned towards the ground. He had seen too many accidents to not constantly respect the ability of tools to hurt a man.

His brother pointed to the sky. Hans squinted, surprised to see a thing in the air. He had only ever seen birds in the sky, so this must be a bird—but what a strange bird, all square, with short stubby wings that did not move.

The thing grew larger as it came closer. Much too large to be a bird. Hans felt no shame as he joined the others in running back to the trees and crouching down behind a trunk.

"What is it?" his cousin asked from behind a nearby trunk. His cousin crossed himself, lightly touching his forehead, chest, and both shoulders.

Hans shrugged and looked back to find his fourteen-year-old nephew burrowing into the leaves and detritus of the forest floor, sobbing a prayer. Hans could understand the terror that dominated the youth—his own heart fluttered with the same fear—but six seasons of campaigning had taught him that fear was a tool, to be used, not to be surrendered to.

The bird circled down to the center of the meadow, making a whispering sound no louder than an arrow in flight, hovering just a few feet from the ground. It was big, as big as the great hall of the baron, where a hundred people could squeeze themselves in. The air smelt funny, tickling his nose in an annoying way.

A tongue dropped from the bird to the ground and a naked woman tumbled down it onto the grass. Hans was vaguely aware that his mouth was hanging open like that of an idiot.

The bird lifted up towards the sky, leaving no sound in its wake. His fear rapidly subsiding, Hans ran into the meadow to watch the bird go. It faded into the blue sky faster than it should have, as if turning invisible. This was powerful witchcraft, a magic beyond any that he had ever heard of told by bard or priest.

The men of the village followed Hans as he approached the woman. They fanned out, instinctively avoiding the error of clumping up. If they had to use their axes as weapons, they needed room to swing.

The woman lay sprawled in the thick grass of the meadow. His wife was the only naked woman Hans had ever seen, and what lay before him was the most beautiful creation that he could imagine. Her flawless skin was pale white, and he wondered if she had ever been out under the sun. Had she lived her entire life in the strange bird?

"What do we do with her?" a cousin asked.

"Take her home."

"No!" shouted his nephew. "She's a witch. She will curse us. We must destroy her."

A murmur of agreement swept through the collected men. Hans pressed his fingers to his temple. Another headache was coming on, the kind that left him half-blind and whimpering. He groped for words. "I think that maybe we should ask Baron Henri what to do."

The woman moaned and opened her eyes. To a man, every

villager jumped back.

The voice of his nephew grew ever more shrill. "We don't have time. She awakens. We must kill her now."

The youth's father stepped forward and raised his axe. He screamed to give himself courage and brought the axe down with all his might. The woman rolled to the side, her movement too sluggish to avoid the blade slicing into her side. Red blood stained the grass.

Do witches have red blood? Hans wished he had paid better attention to the stories. One thing was certain: if she had blood, then she could die.

Hans raised his axe and stepped forward, his kinsman joining him. A pang of sadness briefly crested in his consciousness; to destroy something so beautiful must be some sort of sin.

He saw the fear in the woman's eyes change to determination. She suddenly seemed energized and sprang to her feet. She lashed out with her fist at Hans, catching him in the nose. His face exploded in pain and he dropped his axe as he tumbled backwards. He was dimly aware that she had leapt over him and run for the forest.

The other men cried out in frustration and chased after her.

Struggling to sit up, Hans felt his gushing nose and noticed that it moved underneath his clenched fingers. It was broken.

His kinsmen returned, the youth whining, "The witch got away."

The Center Place, 236th Year of the Master

The sun had almost reached its highest point in the sky, during this, the longest day of the year. Kartvi lay prostrate on the ground, his nostrils filled with the scent of sand. Three days he had fasted and prayed—his empty stomach craved food, his mouth felt as dry as the sand, and his skin felt hot and brittle. He mumbled the prayer again, searching for the strength from the old gods to do what he must do. Kartvi worshiped the old gods, not the Master.

The old gods lived in the lower world. They had made the animals out of clay, molding them with their hands. The world of darkness had only animals in it until Spider Woman created all the peoples of the Earth out of clay, a man and woman for each tribe, molding them with her own hands, and teaching them their own languages. Then the Two Brothers led the animals and people to this land of desert and sky, the Fourth World, and the People spread across the land, planting corn and making families.

Death also came into the Fourth World and the people knew sorrow. The dead went to a new world, except those that stayed as ghosts, too miserable to find their way to happiness. The people honored the old gods, giving them the worship and honor that was their due; then came the Master.

The Master was a god on Earth, more cunning than any of the old gods, stronger than any man, able to run faster and further than any youth, who saw things in the distance with the eyes of a hawk, and possessed the hearing of a coyote. He was older than the grandparents of the grandparents of any of the People. By his command, the palaces of the canyon had been built, some of them hundreds of rooms large. Few people lived in the palaces. Most of the People lived in huts of sticks and mud and spent their lives laying stone upon stone to build the palaces.

The Master loved to honor Death. He led his own people on raids against the surrounding villages. The slaves he captured worked until their hands and backs were raw and broken, and then they were sacrificed as food. The Master called it man corn. Kartvi had eaten this flesh, ignoring his stomach's objections at such obscene meat, and prayed that the old gods had not noticed, or that they would welcome him even if they had.

The Master often challenged Death to a personal dance. Even Kartvi had seen the Master cut into his own arms and stretch them out above his head, the blood flowing down his arms and staining the feathers of his cloak. Before the astonished eyes of his worshipers, the wounds closed themselves. No man could do that and no stories of the old gods told of such powers. That is why the people obeyed him, built palaces of stone and roads that ran for days to connect the palaces, and willingly offered themselves up for sacrifice.

The old gods did not ask for sacrifices. The old gods promised a better place for those who died with honor. The Master offered no such salvation—just work—and the opportunity to worship him.

Last winter both of Kartvi's sisters had been taken to serve the Master. His sisters, the prettiest girls in the entire village, full of life and laughter, had died worshiping the Master. No one knew what had happened to their bones, so his mother had lain down and refused to eat. Her grief drove her into the embrace of Death.

Only Kartvi was left; only he could make it right. He and the old gods.

Finishing his last prayer, he pushed himself up from the ground. He drank water from a pot that his mother had made with her own hands, choking as the fluid stung his parched throat. Fresh squash and dried venison made his last meal.

From beyond the bluff, he heard the call to worship.

Kartvi crawled to the lip of the hill. Below him sprawled the Palace of the Master, with a large plaza beyond. Thousands of people from all the palaces and from the villages in the canyon were assembled in the plaza, dancing and chanting, making the air throb with power, asking the Master to honor them with his presence. Over and over, "Master, Master, Master..." The sound was amplified by several muscular youths working on foot drums, like those traditionally found only in kivas, tapping in time with the words.

The Master had not made his appearance yet. Even though his own village was three days' walk away, Kartvi had been to two of these celebrations and knew that the Master only emerged when the crowd was completely soaked in sweat from their dancing and their voices grown ragged from the chanting.

Finishing the last of the water, Kartvi pulled on his sandals, slipped a knife into his belt, and picked up two spears. He was the best hunter in his village and had even taken down a buffalo and a cougar. The white streaks of scars along his rib cage reminded him that a trapped cougar is dangerous prey. But today's quarry was the most dangerous yet.

Picking his way down the hillside, he approached the rear of the palace. The curved wall of the building before him reached up five stories. Normally someone would be around at this time of day, even if just children playing. As he had expected, there was no one nearby. Picking up a log that he had placed behind a bush a month earlier, Kartvi placed it against the wall so that it reached a narrow second-story window.

Juggling his spears, he shimmied up the log, tossed the spears into the room beyond, and wiggled in behind them. The room held baskets of corn. One spear had ripped open a basket, spilling ears of corn onto the rough wooden floor.

Kartvi listened for a moment, finding only silence beneath the throbbing of the chanting. No hanging covered the door to this room. The room beyond it was dark and smelled of old wood smoke. Using the same skill that helped him remember the intricate twists of thousands of game trials, he had memorized the maze of the palace and its hundreds of rooms. Of course, the group of rooms and great kiva that the Master used for his personal quarters were unknown to Kartvi, and to all but the most precious servants. Those servants and the other members of the household were now out among the chanting crowd, leaving the palace empty.

Counting the doorways in other rooms with his hand, Karvi moved deeper into the palace, feeling his way in the dark. Sometimes faint light filtered down from ventilation holes set high in the walls to let out smoke, but that was all. Everyone knew that the Master could see in the dark.

He came to the sixth room and crept inside, where an opening in the wall led to a ladder. He climbed slowly, careful to not bang the hafts of his spears against the ladder. The room above was filled with pottery received as tribute. Kartvi did not need more light to know that these pots were the finest that the people could produce, with the most vivid colors. His mother always had devoted the most lavish care to those pots that she knew would be sent to the palaces.

The Master disdained the use of guards; tales of his ferocious ability to defend himself kept potential assassins away. A completely empty palace on this holy day only showed how powerful he truly was.

Karvi passed through dozens of more rooms, some with only two doorways, others with three or four doors—a trail more obtuse than any animal had ever left—and climbed two ladders, one up and one down, before he finally reached a corridor. The soft stone of the floor was well worn from many sandals. The end of the corridor led outside to a large balcony overlooking the plaza; the bright sunlight caused Kartvi to blink rapidly. The chant thundered in the corridor, as if the sound was being channeled down towards the Master's chambers.

Moving quickly down the corridor, concerned that his timing might be off, Kartvi stopped a bare dozen paces before its end. The walls here were no longer dressed sandstone, but covered from floor to ceiling with hangings, woven from yucca plants and painted with bright colors. The Master dominated each picture, showing him at repose, at war, slaying his enemies, feasting on them, receiving the worship of the people, taking their daughters as temporary wives to be cast aside and slain.

Removing his sandals, Kartvi concealed them behind a hanging. He then approached the entrance, confident that no one in the blinding sun of the plaza could see into the dark cave-like opening. Two months ago, while bringing an offering from a fresh deer kill to the palace, he had noticed that one of the hangings covered a small alcove.

He slipped into the alcove and stood straight with his head turned to allow the hanging to lay flat against his face, chest, and thighs. He clutched a spear tightly in each hand. The tip of the spear on his right pressed ever so slightly against the hanging, creating a narrow gap to see through, and allowing a sliver of sunlight to touch his face.

He carefully slowed his breathing, summoning the patience of the hunter that he had learned from watching cougars lying in wait for their prey to approach closer. Animals and the gods had taught him well. His eyelids dropped as he waited—totally motionless, completely alert, but almost sleeping. Antelopes in the mountains, normally so skittish, had actually approached him while he waited in this state.

He stilled his thoughts, as if the very dance of his mind could be sensed and give him away. Time passed, slowly or quickly, he could not tell.

The chanting grew weaker as the crowd tired. Suddenly the Master was striding past Kartvi's hiding place, completely naked, as was his habit at all ceremonies. The god moved with confidence. Kartvi's eyes widened; then he lunged from behind the hanging with the speed of a striking rattlesnake. Despite Karvi's stealth, the Master heard him and had started to turn when one spear plunged into the small of the Master's back, where the sensitive kidneys lay. Any other man would have screamed in great pain and gone rigid from shock. The Master only exhaled a little sigh and continued his turn.

Katvi thrust with his other spear, seeking the spine, and grunted with pleasure as he felt the shock of obsidian meeting bone. The Master fell to the floor and Kartvi paused for a moment as he reached for his knife.

Kartvi watched in astonishment as the Master heaved himself up on his hands and quickly dragged himself down the corridor and out onto the balcony, leaving a trail of sparkling blood, the two spears still protruding from his body. Kartvi sprang after him with a cry of rage.

The chanting turned into a single great gasp as the crowd saw the Master emerge, not in glory, but in the gravest distress.

Kartvi had rehearsed in his mind the many ways that this fight might go and did not hesitate. He plunged the knife into the back of the Master's neck, breaking the vertebrae and severing the spinal cord, just as his spear had done to the lower back. The Master's arms and body went limp. The obsidian broke from applying too much pressure, leaving Kartvi with half of his weapon and the rest trapped by the vertebra. Moving quickly, fearing the Master's proven ability to heal quickly from any wound, Kartvi yanked a spear free and used the head as a blade to saw at the Master's neck. For a brief moment, he looked into the Master's eyes, and the look of pure hatred chilled him. He also saw fear in those eyes and it filled Kartvi with the sweetest sensation he had ever felt.

The head came off and Kartvi stood—covered with gore, dripping blood that glistened in the sun—and held the head high by the hair, showing it to the crowd.

"This is the Master and he slew my sisters! I am Kartvi of the Cougar Clan! Know my name and remember me!"

The crowd surged forward. And Kartvi died.

CHAPTER ONE
PRESENT DAY, NEW MEXICO

The day they found the tomb began like any other day for Harry Deacon. He usually only needed four or five hours of sleep a night, so he woke before dawn and, as was his habit, he climbed a nearby bluff. Laying his jacket on a sandstone outcropping, he went through three Kenpo forms. The last dregs of sleep faded before his disciplined breathing and the controlled sharp thrusts of his feet and fists.

Born in Puerto Rico, raised on the cold streets of Minneapolis, Harry had spent much of his adult life in the desert. He knew five deserts intimately: he had trained in the Mojave and the Sahara, fought in the rocky sands of Iraq and in the high desert of Afghanistan and Pakistan, and now he dug for pottery shards in Chaco Canyon. A thin sheen of perspiration meeting the morning air sent a chill through him.

He finished his last form and automatically reached for his jacket and weapon. Only the jacket was there, of course. Even after five years of retirement, the ingrained habits of twenty years popped up at the oddest moments. He tossed the jacket across his shoulders and sat down on the outcrop. He was proud of his service, but the memories still tormented him. Maybe that's why he never slept the whole night through. He usually didn't dream of what he had done, but of what he had seen, and what he had failed to do.

The sun peeped over the horizon, sending slivers of light searching among the ruins of Chaco Canyon. Casa Ángeles, the house of angels, stood near the dig. Two large walls met in a corner, sheltering the ruins of what must have been fifty or sixty rooms and the foundations of two kivas, large circular rooms that served as sacred clan centers. As a great house, Casa Ángeles was smaller than most in the Canyon, but it was the ruin near where they had a permit to dig, so Harry thought of it fondly as their house.

Harry rested his hands on his knees, palms up, closed his eyes and let the sunrise wash over him. In a sense, he prayed; not to the God he had learned to love in Sunday School, or to the vague New Age paganism that his ex-wife embraced, but simply to a higher power, one beyond the mundane concerns of everyday life, one who cared about him. The prayer had no words, just a sense of calm and at peace.

"Room for two up here?"

He recognized the familiar voice of Brenda Finnigan and was surprised that he had not heard her approach. He must have truly been someplace else.

"Cost you twenty bucks," he said, not opening his eyes.

He felt her sit down next to him.

"I'll have to owe you on that. I'll pay you when I become a famous archaeologist and the money comes rolling in."

"I'll add it to your tab."

She fell silent and he imagined that she too was sitting peacefully, eyes closed, welcoming the sun and the morning. She didn't usually join him; like most college students, she found rising early an ordeal. He felt her hand settle gently on his hand. Even after a month of digging, her skin still felt softer than his roughened calluses. She lightly held his palm, her fingers wrapped around his thumb, like a small child.

She was a short woman, only twenty-one, fair-skinned, freckled, and blessed with the red hair of her Irish ancestors. When he first saw her, he was attracted to her vitality, quick energy, and voluptuous hips and breasts. He was twice her age, so he did nothing but look—not like a lecherous old man, but with subtle appreciation. To his surprise, they became friends, without even the subdued sexual charge that often underlay friendships between men and women. Theirs was the friendship of a father and daughter.

She had once even called him "Dad," a slip of the tongue that would have delighted Sigmund Freud. He had pretended to not hear, not wanting to embarrass her, but it reminded him of calling his second-grade teacher "Mom." He knew that Brenda's own father was often gone from her life, and he himself had never had a daughter. His own son was sixteen years old and living in Chicago. At least Harry thought it was Chicago, maybe James and his mother had moved back to Minneapolis.

The sun rose higher, warming his face, creating a golden glow behind his closed eyelids. He prayed to be a better person, to improve himself each day.

"Okay," she announced. "I'm bored and hungry. Let's go eat."

"You've been here, what, five minutes?"

Her hand left his palm. "Four minutes, twenty-two seconds."

Harry turned his head toward her and opened his eyes, blinking to adjust his vision. Her hair was pulled back into a ponytail and her face had that aching smoothness that came from youth. In another few years, especially if she spent enough time on digs or other outdoor activities, lines would start to carve their way over those freckles.

"Okay, let's go," he said. "It's your turn to cook and mine to clean."

"Wheaties, then."

"I think that cooking means that you actually have to turn on the stove. Besides, we're out of milk."

"Okay," she said. "Dry Wheaties and sausages."

"You're lucky that I remember too many MREs. Wheaties and sausage are good enough."

* * * * * * *

Their camp had five tents: one for Dr. Bancroft, one for Harry, one for the three male graduate students, one shared by

Brenda and a female graduate student, and the last—a huge ten-man Army surplus tent with floorboards, used as a common area for eating, meetings, and work. The green canvas sides of the main tent were rolled up to let the breeze pass through. No one complained about the camp, or how sand and dirt got into everything, since everyone but Brenda had already lived in worse conditions on digs, and Brenda was not the type to complain.

This dig was a curious affair. An obscure foundation from New York had paid for an earlier survey team to take soundings using ground-penetrating radar all over Chaco Canyon, seeking buried formations and larger objects. Dr. Bancroft had been hired as the principal investigator to dig at the more promising soundings. She was the grand dame of Chaco Canyon, having scraped at the ground and dutifully cataloged every detail ever since arriving in the 1950s as part of her father's team. As always, the dig served as a way to train her students. Harry was the only post-doc on the dig and acted as supervisor.

It was obvious that her heart was not in digging at the whim of some distant foundation and Dr. Bancroft had used some of the grant money to fly with the other students to a conference in Scotland. Harry could have gone, but then they would have had to shut down the dig. Harry had spent two tours in Europe and only slightly envied the sight-seeing of castles, grassy highlands, and the like that the professor and students were certainly touring between conference panels. It would have been nice to look up some old pals, but if he had gone then Brenda would have been forced to return to Maine because she had some odd passport problems that prevented her from flying to Europe. So he had chosen to stay and keep Brenda working.

The first hole that morning was a bust, just a rocky outcropping buried under two feet of dirt. Brenda tossed aside her shovel and sat down to suck on her water bottle. Harry bent to shovel the dirt back into the hole. The Park Service demanded that their digs be as unobtrusive as possible, and that meant not leaving holes everywhere. Briefly he envied the great archaeologists of the past who had excavated places like Troy and Assyria, hiring native laborers for pennies a day to do their digging for them.

It was only nine in the morning, so they moved to the next spot on the list. The radar had revealed a large mass with no protrusions. Not promising, but the grant contract required a visual inspection of every possible object.

An hour crept by as they dug down three feet. Though they weren't passing the dirt through a sieve to make absolutely sure, they found no artifacts. No pottery shards, no obsidian flakes, and no rocks that might have once been some sort of tools. The sun had risen far enough to make digging an ordeal in sweat and dust. Brenda's shovel hit the rock first.

They both dug in rhythm, avoiding each other's shovels as they widened the hole. Harry exhaled in frustration. Just another damn rock. An annoying piece of basalt, black and porous with gas bubbles formed when it had cooled from lava millions of years ago. Sand was firmly embedded in its pores.

Brenda announced the obvious conclusion. "This shouldn't be here. Almost all the rocks around here are from the Menefee Formation and the Cliff House Formation, mostly sandstone, some shale, a bit of coal. All seashore deposits. No basalts at all. That requires volcanic activity."

Harry was weak on geology, preferring to read history books and science fiction novels. Brenda often sat up late and pored over textbooks by lantern light, marker in hand, hair hanging down, lips moving as she crammed every last scientific nugget into her mind.

"So it doesn't belong here," he said, encouraging her, remembering that this dig was part of her education.

"That means that it was brought here by someone. Probably the Chacoans. That makes it an artifact."

They dug all day, taking time out for a siesta during the hottest hours. By sunset they had enlarged their three-foot-deep excavation to the edges of the square-shaped dark rock, about six feet on a side.

Brenda was excited, and even Harry was intrigued. The

shape was not natural. Why had the Chacoans taken the time to chip away at a piece of basalt and form it into a square, and then buried it?

"Maybe it's a tomb," Brenda suggested as they ate their dinner. "Though it's not like anything else the Chacoans ever made." She had taken the time to cook hamburgers for them. Harry lathered enough mustard on his to make small beads of perspiration break out on his forehead as he ate.

Harry shrugged. "Maybe. If we were somewhere else, like Egypt, I'd agree that it was a lid to a tomb."

"Very curious. I've always been disappointed with how the Chacoans buried their dead. I mean, they apparently didn't fear their dead, not like the Navajo, so we do have some burials. But they usually buried the dead in shallow graves in the midden, as if they were part of the other garbage. Does that mean that they saw the flesh as not important, once the spirit had flown?"

"Not all burials are in middens," Harry said. "Some are in cists. Those chambers were normally made of stone and used to store food. It cost them something to give up that sort of useful construction to make it a burial site."

"There must have been social value to the burials. They were often buried with everyday tools." She pursed her lips in annoyance. "And we see gender boundaries there—food preparation items for women, hunting tools for men."

"Would you prefer to be a hunter or a gardener, Brenda?"

"I don't like hunting, so I guess a gardener."

"But you object to Chacoan women being gardeners, not hunters?"

"I object that they didn't have a choice, not what they did. They provided most of the food through their farming."

"It's true," Harry said. "But we have only artifacts, so we can only guess about how their social structures actually worked."

"Women have always gardened, and men have hunted. That's the way it's been for thousands of years."

"True," he said. "But back to the main topic, which is Chacoan burial customs."

"Okay. No tombs have ever been found. And few graves have been found with valuables, like jewelry, or what we would recognize as high-value items."

"Do you buy into the interpretation that this means that the Chacoans had a relatively egalitarian society, with shallow social classes?" Harry asked.

"No, I don't. I mean, it could be true, but most societies have a strong hierarchy. Maybe we just don't see it in their burial customs."

"Maybe there aren't so many graves because they just ate 'em."

She slapped his shoulder. "You always have to bring that up, don't you? It's disgusting."

"There's been lots of evidence of cannibalism found," he said. "And we know that the Aztecs practiced it."

"It's racist to think that the ancient Indians ate each other. Besides, that evidence is all disputed."

"Calling something racist just shuts down the conversation."

"The Pueblo people think cannibalism is one of the worst sins that anyone can commit."

They had argued over this same topic so many times that the conversation had taken on the nature of a script. "Yes," Harry said, "but maybe they think that because they are so horrified by what their ancestors did, and they just want to keep it a secret."

"That kind of argument can't be refuted because you want to have it both ways," she said. "If the Pueblo people thought cannibalism was okay, then you would use that fact as evidence. Since they despise cannibalism, the exact opposite attitude, you use that fact as evidence instead. What would convince you that the Chacoans and other ancient Pueblo peoples didn't eat each other?"

"I don't know the answer, but I try to not love the people of the past so much that I blind myself to their more unsavory aspects."

The argument continued and they both enjoyed it immensely. The moon rose, half-lit by the sun and half in shadow, and

Brenda finally announced her intention to go to bed. Harry quickly cleaned the dishes and the conversation wound down.

"What are we going to do now?" Brenda asked.

"First thing tomorrow, drive into Bloomfield and rent a brace and hoist. We're going to lift that sucker up."

CHAPTER TWO

When he woke the next morning, Harry went through the simple ritual that pushed the fog of sleep away. He sat on the end of his cot, shook his boots to make sure that no scorpions had found the residual warmth of the leather too tempting, and shrugged on his clothes. He appreciated the simple things of life, like clean socks, a warm cot, not being shot at.

He brushed his fingers along his scalp. He had shaved two days ago and the fuzz was not long enough to justify the razor again. When his hair had started to thin in his late twenties, he decided to shave it all off, since the military liked his hair short anyway. It helped with vanity, too. He usually wore a hat to protect his scalp and ears from too much sun. He favored one of his old camo hats, painted in desert camouflage.

Brenda did not join him as he welcomed the sun and worked his muscles. Relishing the feel of thrusts and blocks, ingrained in muscle memory from long practice, he reviewed in his mind the physics of moving the stone, which weighed at least a ton. In Kuwait he had worked with a combat engineering battalion and had learned a lot from them, impressed with how human ingenuity, levers, and pulleys could be made to move anything.

As the sun painted the land with its early morning colors, he went to Brenda's tent and clapped his hands. "Wake up, sleepy-head!"

The mumbling from inside encouraged him to stick his head inside the tent, a three-man igloo type. She was still in her sleeping bag, showing only a mop of red hair with earphones attached to a battery-powered satellite radio. He could hear the faint sounds of '70s folk music.

"I'll be back in about two hours. I may have to go all the way to Farmington if I don't find what I need in Bloomfield."

He took another mumble from Brenda as an answer.

* * * * * * *

His wife had gotten half his military retirement in the divorce, and he still paid child support, which left him on a lean budget. Unlike many of his fellow retirees with a divorce and kids, he did not begrudge her the money—his years of service had been hard on her. He tried to save as much money as possible, to fund travel, and refused to buy a new truck. Besides, he liked his ten-year-old full-size Dodge pickup; it fit him like a comfortable glove and he knew all its quirks. A shell on the back gave him a large cargo space where he sometimes slept on a foam pad. He usually spent summers at a dig, keeping most of his gear and mementos in a storage garage in Salt Lake City. For the last five years he had only rented apartments during the winter while working on his doctorate at the University of Utah. Now that he had earned the degree, he would have to move to wherever archaeological projects took him. He had already decided that he didn't want a faculty position, being much too adverse to academic politics. He just liked to dig.

Twenty-four miles of gravel roads led to Nageezi. According to the map, Nageezi was the nearest town to Chaco Canyon, really no more than a collection of houses and a Navajo chapter house, a kind of town hall for the locals. A new four-lane road, US 550, led north to Bloomfield. An occasional ranch house or trailer was pretty much the only human habitation, other than a solitary trading post with some gas pumps. Closer to the San Juan River, the rolling desert gave way to steep hills covered with sage and some juniper trees. Small oil and gas wells dotted the landscape. A large power plant outside of Bloomfield spewed smoke and prosperity.

Along fifty miles of the northern bank of the San Juan River, the whole stretch from Bloomfield to Farmington to Shiprock formed an erratic sprawl of houses and businesses. Driven by the gas and coal business, the area was booming, with all the big box stores you would expect to find anywhere else in America, along with a mall, car dealerships, pawnshops, liquor stores, and the Sunray Park & Casino, built on Indian land to avoid state law.

Harry pulled into a favorite strip mall. He started two machines at the laundromat going with Brenda's and his accumulated laundry and bought two bagels for breakfast at Marie's Café next door. Some of the local customers directed him to a commercial rental place in Bloomfield.

By ten he was back at the dig. The tents tended to act as mini-greenhouses, so one could not really stay in bed too long; apparently Brenda had roused herself and joined the world. Her usual ponytail again tamed her red hair, and a retro Joan Baez t-shirt tugged at her breasts.

"What ya got?" she asked as she helped him unload the pipes and chain.

"It's a tripod hoist, used to lift out car engines. And this is a brace bar, which we can use to hook under the sides of the rock and lift it. We're going to lift up one edge and see what's underneath."

"Sweet. Just like Indiana Jones." She winked at him.

"Yes, Indiana Jones. Archaeologist extraordinaire, treasure-hunter at heart, willing to destroy everything that gets in his way. That scene in the first movie still irritates me."

"Which one?" she asked as they hauled the heavy pipes over to the dig.

"When he and the girl get trapped with the snakes in the underground room. They are surrounded by the finest collection of ancient Egyptian artifacts in the world, but to escape he destroys everything. It made for nice eye candy, but any archaeologist worth his salt would have died rather than do that."

"I wasn't even born when they made that movie," she said.

"But didn't they need to stop the bad guys from using the Ark of the Covenant and save the world? Wasn't that worth busting up a few artifacts?"

Harry felt old at her comment. He had first seen the movie as a young teenager. "I guess that the story demanded that he destroy everything," he admitted. "But it still irritates me."

Harry showed Brenda how to set up the hoist and secure it. They attached the hooks of the brace bar across the rock at one end so that they could open it like a lid. Harry made sure to fasten the bolts on the hooks as tightly as he could, then stood on the rock and set the hoist. He pulled up the slack on the hoist chain and, through the wonders of mechanical magic, worked the lever back and forth, using only his muscle power. The basalt rock twitched as it broke free of the surrounding dirt and slowly rose several inches into the air.

"Want to give it a try?" Harry asked.

Brenda was game and traded places with Harry on the rock in order to reach the hoist handle. "It moves so easily," she said, slowly working the chain links through the hoist.

Harry peered under the rock. A space was opening up, but the sun was too bright to see anything in the cavity. "Can't see a thing. We need a flashlight."

Brenda stopped the hoist. "I'll get one." She scampered off the rock and raced to her tent.

Harry admired her enthusiasm, though he knew that there was probably nothing more than dirt or rocks in the cavity. He stepped onto the rock and worked the hoist to raise it a few more inches.

She returned and knelt down, shining the flashlight beneath the stone. "Ohmigod!" she exclaimed. "It's stairs!"

"What?" Harry leaped down next to her.

Damned if she wasn't right. There were stairs underneath the rock, made of smaller pieces of basalt, laid edgewise to their vantage point. The beam of the flashlight acted as a strobe, showing pockets of dirt on the stairs that must have drifted in over the years, particle by particle. A musty smell combined with the irritation of dust in his nostrils.

"This is extraordinary," Brenda breathed. "This isn't like the Chacoans at all."

Harry grinned, feeling foolish and giddy. This is how Howard Carter must have felt when he discovered King Tutankhamun's tomb.

Brenda threw her arms around him in her excitement. He hugged her back, happy to feel the warmth of her body.

"Let's do this right," he said. "We need the digital camera and recorder."

Brenda narrated their find with the recorder, while Harry used the camera. He had room for hundreds of high resolution pictures on his memory card and the attached flash was fully charged. He started clicking away, documenting the hoist, stone lid, and what he could see so far, then worked the hoist until there was a good twelve inches of clearance.

"That's far enough," Brenda said. "I want to get inside."

"Wait for me to brace it."

He found a floor jack in his truck and placed it on the edge of the stairs, pumping it up to push firmly against the lid. He hoped that it would hold if the hoist failed.

Brenda dropped to her stomach and wiggled inside, her feet churning for purchase in the sand. Her butt disappeared and then her legs.

"There's a room down here," she called out.

Harry knew that they should just stop right then, close the room up, and wait for Dr. Bancroft to return from Europe with the other students. She was in charge of this dig and it was her right to run this excavation. They needed to do this properly, patiently, documenting every step. Crawling in there after Brenda was just as bad as Indiana Jones, mucking up the site with their eagerness. It was just like investigators at a crime scene walking around and destroying evidence.

He knew all these things as intellectual certainties, but the urge to be the first to see, to crawl in that hole, was too strong. Patience had always been hard for him; that's why he had never been any good as a sniper. He just couldn't sit still that long.

He swore, figured that he was tossing away his budding career as an archaeologist, and dropped to his hands and knees. No one would ever hire him after this and he would have to go back to security work.

Harry crawled inside.

His flashlight revealed Brenda crouched at the foot of the stairs, just outside of the room beyond. The walls were made of basalt rock, carefully fitted together without mortar.

"Brenda, close your eyes and shield them with your hand," Harry said before taking several pictures. The powerful flash left stars in his eyes and he followed his own advice after that.

Moving down the stairs to Brenda's side, he joined her in playing their flashlight beams across the room. It was roughly ten feet wide by a dozen feet long, with walls made of the same closely packed basalt rocks, and a roof made of pine trunks. Pines grew dozens of miles away in the mountains and would have been a chore to bring there since the Chacoans possessed no beasts of burdens other than their own backs. Of course, the basalt had been brought to the canyon somehow, and that would have been another achievement of muscle and ingenuity over gravity. The room was deep enough, protected by the desert sand, that the trunks had not decayed. Or so Harry hoped.

Sand covered most of the floor, but when he looked closely, Harry saw seashells scattered all around. Seashells were occasionally traded inland by the Indians through intricate exchange networks, but he had never heard of such a large quantity found this far from the ocean.

An oblong box occupied the center of the room, laid atop a base made of basalt rocks. Harry felt a flash in his nervous system akin to an electric shock. The box was made of wood, ornately carved, and was obviously intended to hold a body.

Brenda talked rapidly into her recorder, describing everything, a flow of stream of consciousness that Harry suspected would embarrass her with its lack of scholarly detachment when they played it back later. He took more pictures, warning her to close her eyes.

"Do you think we will disturb anything if we go in?" Brenda asked.

Harry played his flashlight across the floor. "Looks like mostly just shells, but we really shouldn't go in. A statistical analysis of the shells in this room might show us something interesting—where they came from, which shells are considered more valuable, stuff like that. We don't want to break any of them by stepping on them."

"Screw that," Brenda said, taking two quick steps to reach the sarcophagus. He noticed that she stepped as lightly as possible, as if treading across fragile glass. Nevertheless, he heard the shifting and breaking of shells under her feet.

"Ohmigod!" Brenda exclaimed. "You've got to see this."

Harry joined her, kissing his career goodbye. The top of the sarcophagus had collapsed, leaving behind only small pieces of wood and splinters. The bones of a man lay inside, the skeletal hands folded on his chest. At least, Harry assumed that it was a man, since the length from skull to foot bones looked to be over six feet. Harry snapped pictures. What looked like glitter covered the body, like what Brenda sprinkled on her face when she was going into town to dance and tease the boys.

"Look at that. The skull is not attached." Brenda pointed with her flashlight.

"Yes, it looks disarticulated. Interesting to know if it was pre- or post-mortem."

"Quit talking like an archaeologist." Brenda scolded. "Look at that." She pointed her flashlight to a small box next to the skull, only about four inches long and two inches wide. Inlaid into its burnished surface was a symbol, three triangles within a circle.

"That's metal," Harry said, feeling giddy with stupidity. Only an idiot would state the obvious. "That doesn't belong here."

"What is it? Steel?" She touched it. "Odd, it's not cool. It sort of feels like ceramic."

"Don't touch anything. Let me take pictures."

The room flashed with the strobe-like effect of Harry's camera. He carefully took pictures of the box from all different angles, holding the camera out at awkwardly to avoid shifting his feet and disturbing the site any more than they already had.

"It's so strange," Harry said. "There are no funeral goods, just that box."

"Yeah. Where are the objects to accompany the deceased into the next life? No weapons, no goods. Nothing. Not even a pot or a bowl."

"Now who sounds like an archaeologist?"

She stuck her tongue out at him.

He ignored her. "I don't understand why the lid fell apart. The rest of the coffin is in such great shape."

"Maybe it was trying to escape," she intoned in a melodramatic stage voice.

"Perhaps they used a different type of wood, something that didn't preserve as well. Maybe it was too thin. I wonder what it looked like."

More pictures.

"That little box is the true find here," Brenda said. "We should take it out and see if it opens."

"What?" Harry was horrified. "We're not doing that! We've broken enough rules already. We need to back out of here and do this properly."

"I've already touched it," Brenda argued. "We might as well take it out and look at it a bit closer."

Harry reluctantly nodded. It annoyed him that he found it so hard to deny her any request. "Okay, but we don't try to open it. It's unique. We should wait until we have it in a lab so we can preserve whatever might be in it. If it is a box then whatever is in it would most certainly be extremely fragile."

Trying their best to step in their own footprints, they withdrew and crawled up the stairs. After the cool of the tomb, the sun-drenched desert felt like an oven. Harry lowered the lid back onto the tomb, ratcheting down the hoist. He didn't want any desert animals to get in and mess up the site—mess it up anymore than he and Brenda had already messed it up, he corrected himself.

"It's almost six o'clock and we skipped lunch."

They ate sandwiches, chewing quietly, shocked out of their normal verbosity. The box sat on the table between them, like a talisman of power. They shared a sense of mutual awe, as when faced with a technically perfect piece of art or a new technology with exciting possibilities. Harry remembered visiting the British Museum in London, a treasure trove containing the loot of an empire, and being amazed by objects that he had seen pictured in books as a child—the statues of winged bulls, fourteen feet high, that guarded the throne room of Sargon II of ancient Assyria; the crumpled remains of the Ludlow Man, tanned into leather by a peat bog; and the Rosetta Stone itself. Perhaps this find would someday rank with those icons of archaeology. But who was he fooling? He had completely ignored procedure. He was not angry at Brenda, just himself.

Brenda took the digital camera and recorder and copied the images and audio to her laptop. Harry took the camera and recorder over to his own laptop and did the same, finding data assurance by having many backups.

"I'll be back in an hour," he said.

"Where're you going?"

"Trying to salvage my career."

Harry drove over to the sole campground in Chaco Canyon, where tourists brought along all the conveniences of home in RVs, including satellite TV. This campground also had a wireless access point, provided for free by the Park Service. Harry sat in his truck, tapped out an e-mail to Dr. Bancroft about the find, attached a few pictures, and sent it off. He took ten minutes to surf the web, checking a few of his favorite news sites, then closed the laptop and drove back to camp.

CHAPTER THREE
FORT MEADE, MARYLAND

José Splith worshiped the Echelon system. Sipping at his coffee as he sat in the windowless basement of a National Security Agency building outside Baltimore, Splith watched the world. Three computer screens, filled with colorful graphics, kept him abreast of the millions of transmissions being captured every minute.

Using satellites, taps on undersea cables, and giant dish farms to capture radio waves out of the ether, Echelon captured every cell call, every satellite transmission, every e-mail, every web request; in short, every electronic communication sent anywhere outside the United States. Federal law prohibited listening to transmissions within the United States and curiously enough, despite the paranoia of the conspiracy-obsessed fringe, the NSA used to actually follow the law to the letter.

Nineteen hijackers on 9/11 changed everything. The legal barriers fell down and information flowed. A libertarian fringe of computer aficionados had always argued that information wanted to be free, that software should be free, and that there should no restrictions on who could know what; at the NSA, information was free.

A massive farm of computers culled through the transmissions, flagging messages of interest and sending them to other computers for automated translation. The results flowed automatically to the screens of intelligence analysts, where they decided if something was worthwhile or just chatter by normal people. Despite the best efforts of the computer programmers, the NSA functioned in a constant state of information overload.

Splith's job was to keep Echelon running, and that required spot checks—the best part of the job. He liked to listen, rather than read e-mail or instant messages, and so he preferred English. Earlier in the evening, a man and woman had argued on a transatlantic phone call about his affair with a waitress in Ireland. An hour later he found two lovers, parted by distance, having phone sex. He really liked that.

An alert window popped up on his computer screen, accompanied by a demanding beep. Splith sat down his coffee and peered closer. An e-mail sent from a computer in New Mexico to a computer in Scotland had been intercepted on a fiber optic cable stretched across the floor of the Atlantic Ocean. The analysis program had caught some keywords in the e-mail and prompted the alert.

Splith tapped a key and was surprised to see instructions scroll onto his screen. Normally an intercept was simply sent to the appropriate analyst, closeted in some other NSA building. These instructions told him to do three things: forward the e-mail to an outside e-mail account; print it out and fax it to a number in Indiana; and then make a phone call to another number and read the contents of the message into the answering machine at the other end.

He swallowed and blinked furiously. Those were phone numbers outside the NSA. He was being instructed to send top-secret data to outside numbers without a warrant or any form of oversight. He tried to wrap his brain around what this meant.

He did as he was told.

CHAPTER FOUR

Brenda lay on her sleeping bag, still in her clothes, her mind sparking with euphoria. She put her earplugs in and listened to her sat-radio for a while. She usually caught up on the world by listening to National Public Radio, but the world didn't interest her right then. Maybe Harry and she would be on NPR, interviewed by one of the anchors about their discovery.

"And tell me, Ms. Finnigan, where are you from?"

"I'm from Augusta, Maine."

"What made you want to become an archaeologist?"

"Oh, I guess I wanted to visit strange places, get my fingernails dirty, and get laid by exotic men, like that stud in *The Mummy*."

She imagined the interviewer blinking in surprise, but quickly recovering by looking at the next question on her notepad.

"How did you feel when you found the Chacoan tomb?"

"Better than sex."

Of course, she would never respond to the questions with such naughty answers. That was only to entertain herself when she couldn't sleep.

For all her romantic intentions, she remained a virgin.

CHAPTER FIVE

The morning air refreshed Harry as he went through his exercises. Thrust, kick, pause, deep breath through the nostrils, concentrating on finding his center. It was hard to keep his thoughts from intruding. He felt the heavy weight of acting like a fool and had slept poorly. Forty-four years old, a man of the world, his neurons laden with experience, and he had acted like a giddy teenager. How could he have agreed to go into the tomb with Brenda? What had possessed him?

If he was honest with himself, the kind of honesty that left a man bare before the bright glare of insight that came from not protecting the ego with platitudes or rationalization, he knew that sometimes he made self-destructive decisions. Drinking binges that left him puking blood, embarrassed by the flashes of memory of what he had done while his judgment was pickled by alcohol. Some people say that alcohol reveals your true nature. Harry was a happy drunk, always trying to have a good time, never violent, never hurting people.

His father had been a drinker too, an easygoing drunk, but able to support himself because he only drank on weekends, never on the job. Harry had not wanted to be like his father. He had wanted to find pride in being a responsible soldier, always reliable, who never let his superiors or his buddies down. Instead, he became a conscientious drunk, like his father; there had been mistakes, though he was never caught.

Like many of his Army buddies, on leave he had completely let himself go. It was really stupid. He had cheated on his wife while drunk—not often, but once too often. Sadly enough, he couldn't even remember the face of the woman who had given him the disease. There is no cure for genital herpes. He couldn't bring that home, not ever. That was how he had come to be divorced, the greatest failure of his life.

Maybe going into the tomb was like the drinking binges, a release from the restriction of always doing the right thing. Lord, he had been such a fool. He stopped, exhaling sharply, the meditative peace that came from his forms completely gone.

In the clear desert air, where sounds carry much farther than one might expect, he heard the sound of a car engine. That was curious. It came from the road that led down into the canyon— a restricted road, not to be used by anyone without a permit. A park ranger would not be coming up the road this early in the morning.

Must be an emergency of some sort.

Grateful for an excuse to quit exercising and flee the company of remembered failures, Harry made his way off the hill towards the road. Perhaps Dr. Bancroft had called the rangers and asked them to pass on an urgent message, since cell coverage did not reach Casa Ángeles. What kind of argument could Dr. Bancroft make that would compel a ranger to get up this early?

The sun still remained below the horizon, though the eastern sky glowed with promise and the stars had started to fade. A light breeze carried the scent of sagebrush and dust. Harry watched the ground carefully, wary of shadows that might hide rocks and tufts of grass.

The car engine noise died. Odd; he didn't hear the sound of a door being slammed shut.

Instinctively he crouched behind a large bush and strained to listen. Voices came to him. Two men, accents from the east coast, breathing heavily as they climbed the hill. He heard one of the men stumble.

"Damn, I hate the outdoors!" The voice had a Boston twang to it. "Always tripping you up."

"Shh, keep it down. And don't fall into the tomb. It's around here somewhere."

"We putting the bodies in the tomb?"

"That's the plan."

Again the Boston voice. "I get to rape her first?"

"Hell, no, we don't have time for that. Now do it right."

Vomit rose in Harry's throat, a bitter acidic taste mixed with cheese and lunch meat from last night's dinner. He swallowed furiously, his eyes watering as the acid hit his nose. An image of Brenda, broken and lifeless, innocence taken, no more future, seared his mind. He caught the image and held it, provoking a flood of cool, cleansing anger.

His fingers wanted to crawl across the ground, searching for a rock or a stout stick. He clenched his fingers into fists to restrain himself—he might make a sound, and surprise was his best weapon. The men were maybe forty feet away.

"I'm going around to come in from the back. Don't accidentally shoot me."

"Fine by me," the Boston voice agreed.

"Don't shoot me on purpose either."

The Boston man snorted.

Harry cursed silently. He wanted to take them together and keep the element of surprise, even if he was outnumbered. Closing his eyes, he concentrated on the sound of the other man moving away, a noisy clamor of stones. The tactic of coming into the camp from two sides was sound, perhaps even overcautious since they expected Harry and Brenda to be asleep.

The sounds of the other man grew more distant, but the Boston man sounded much closer now. Harry opened his eyes, straining to see in the darkness. Twenty-two years ago, when he had first gone into combat, he had pissed himself. With soggy pants he had rushed across the airfield runway in Panama, firing back at the gun flashes of National Guardsmen firing blindly at the American Rangers. It had been the dark before dawn then, just as now, and he had been glad that none of his squad mates could see his shame. Of course, perhaps they had done the same thing. He knew one tough sergeant in Delta, respected by everyone, who readily admitted that he stained his shorts during every firefight.

The Boston man walked noisily past, with no field craft, only about six feet away. Harry silently drew a deep breath and launched himself. He clamped his left hand over the man's mouth and drove his right fist into his kidney, knowing the explosion of pain that came from such a blow. They tumbled to the ground and he heard the sharp exhalation. The man would not be able to cry out until he sucked in more air, and Harry intended for that to never happen.

Scrambling in the dark, Harry kept his left hand on the man's mouth and searched with the fingers of his right hand. They found that man's eyes, wide open, then quickly clenched tightly shut at Harry's touch. The soldier-turned-archaeologist drove his middle finger past the eyeball and into the brain, pushing in as far as he could. He kept his hand there, growing sticky with blood.

The man thrashed wildly, banging Harry's outstretched left elbow against a small rock protruding from the ground. Pain shot up Harry's arm and down his side to his groin and he gasped. Why did they call that the funny bone? What a ridiculous name. Harry fell back, clenching his right fist as he did so, feeling the eye of the man come loose in his hand. His left arm was useless for the moment, and he heard the man inhale. Silence was absolutely necessary. Harry dropped the eye, grabbed a rock, no bigger than a small book, and brought it down.

He could not see well enough in the darkness to deliver more than a glancing blow and was not sure if he landed it on the man's head or neck. He struck again and heard the crunch of skull. Sure now of his aim, he struck again with all the force that he could muster and this time he was sure that the man with the Boston accent would move no more.

Harry held his breath, listening intently. He could not hear the other man returning. Running his hands over the dead man, he found a pistol jammed in the man's belt. The man from Boston had never gone for his weapon, instinctively protecting his eyes instead. Even though the sun had not yet peeked over the western ridge, the sky was getting lighter; only Venus, the morning star, was still visible.

Harry ran his hands over the gun. A small semi-automatic, with a silencer on the end. He rubbed his finger on the end of the silencer, gauging the opening to belong to a .22 or .25 caliber.

He hurried back to the camp, feeling more terrified than he ever had at any time in his life.

* * * * * *

Brenda came awake with a start. Wisps of a dream, of a desert tomb and a handsome stranger, jostled in her head. Why had she awakened?

She heard a rustling outside her tent.

"Harry, is that you?"

* * * * * *

Harry reached the camp, coming up the draw just in time to see the other man, standing only five or six feet from the front of Brenda's tent, point his pistol down. Harry didn't hear the shots, but saw the pistol jerk twice. Harry screamed, all his terror at the prospect of that young angel dying ripped from his throat. He dropped to one knee, braced his arm, aimed, and fired three quick shots, then burst to his feet and ran to his left, moving closer.

The assassin staggered back and dropped to the ground. Harry fired three more times as he rushed forward, cursing his unfamiliarity with the weapon, knowing that if somehow he had been given time to practice, he would have hit with every shot.

The assassin was twisting away, having lost his pistol, when Harry reached him. The archaeologist finished the bastard with a shot to the head, an unthinking act ingrained in him from hundreds of hours of hostage rescue drills. Always do the head in case the bad guy was a suicide bomber.

CHAPTER SIX

Harry ripped at the tent zipper, cursing his shaking fingers. Pulling the flap aside, he reached in to touch her. It was dark in the tent; all could see was a shape in a sleeping bag.

"Brenda?" he asked ever so tentatively.

His fingers touched wetness and she gasped, words quickly spilling from her. "Harry, is that you? What happened? It hurts so much...."

"One minute—I'll be right back."

He ran for a battery-powered lantern and the first-aid kit that they kept in the big canvas tent. His mind raced as if filled with amphetamines, random thoughts and memories flitting about the stage of his mind, at the same time that the task at hand received focused attention. He knew the effects of those drugs, having popped the pills the Army gave him on long missions and in surveillance jobs that required a soldier to stay awake and alert. Seedy drug pushers who pushed speed and uppers on the street went to prison, but not the Army.

As he grabbed the first-aid kit, he felt an awful sense of *déjà-vu* from a time over a decade past, though that other first-aid kit had been wrapped in brown, desert camouflage, with a red cross on it. One of the men of his team, a sergeant from Michigan, had sprayed too widely with his SAW and the bullets hit a little girl as well as a Taliban fighter. The fighter's AK-47 assault rifle had slipped from lifeless fingers as the girl dropped beside him, her long dark hair sweeping across her face.

Harry pounded back to Brenda's tent. Dawn was only

minutes away. Setting up the lantern, he pointed it inside. Blood stained her right forearm. The tissue around the wound looked torn and he was alarmed to see blood pumping out. An artery had been nicked. Harry popped the kit open. It was a complete kit, with bandages, scissors, two splints, a variety of small tubes of medicine, and a manual that he had no time to read.

He ripped open a bandage with his teeth, pressed it down on her wound, then wrapped the bandage around her arm and pushed the tape together. His hands were slippery with blood; it had already saturated the bandage. He needed to make a pressure bandage. Rooting through the kit, he found two more bandages. Leaving one bandage rolled up, he pressed it over the wound and wrapped it tightly in place with the second bandage. If the artery did not stop flowing, he would have to resort to a tourniquet, and Brenda would probably lose her forearm.

"Harry, what are you doing?"

For a moment he considered lying—for her own good, of course. But she was too smart; even in shock she would realize what had happened, so he went for honesty. Mostly. "You've been shot, honey. I just need to stop the bleeding. You'll be okay. It's only flesh wounds."

"Shot? Who would shoot me?" Her voice sounded distant to him, as if she was calling from another country.

The little girl, perhaps only ten or eleven years old, had blood on her lips and an ugly hole in her upper chest. The team's medic ripped open the medical kit and grabbed a bandage that he handed to Harry and ordered him to press down on the wound. Harry obeyed and watched the medic prepare an IV.

Harry searched Brenda for more wounds as he talked to her. "I don't know who they were, some guys from back east."

He tugged at the zipper of her sleeping bag. It was soggy with blood and he had to jerk at it to force the zipper to move. She moaned. "That hurt."

"Sorry, honey. I'll be more careful." He partially crawled into the small tent and unzipped the bag all the way to her feet, then withdrew so that he could see what he was doing.

"Where's the person who shot me?"

He pulled the sleeping bag open and found her wearing pajamas. Dancing bears and flying birds decorated them. He had seen them before, when she had gotten up early to relieve herself without bothering to change her clothes. He did not find the motif incongruous at all—a perfect match for her personality.

"I killed him. Killed both of them." Those words cut the chatter from her.

He found more blood under her left breast. He pulled up her top far enough to see the neat small hole from a .22 near the bottom of her ribs. Little blood was coming out. "I have to roll you over onto your side for a moment, honey. It may hurt, so I'm just warning you." He pulled her over and was gratified to find no exit wound. He didn't like the idea of a bullet inside her, near her lung or in her guts, but at least he didn't have the jagged hole made by a tumbling bullet leaving the body. There could be internal bleeding. Probably was, but he couldn't do anything about that.

Rolling Brenda back, he reached for another bandage.

The IV went into the little girl's small arm easily and the medic squeezed plasma into her. She tried to talk, but only bloody bubbles came out. Harry stepped back, reached for his mike and called for a medevac helicopter. Kneeling beside her, his eyes blurry with tears, he prayed to the God of his childhood that the girl would live.

Harry taped the bandage to Brenda and she bit her lower lip and shivered with pain.

"I have to get my truck," Harry said. "Don't go anywhere."

A faint smile creased her features. Harry dashed for his truck. Partway there, he remembered his keys. He found them in his tent and hurried to the truck. Sliding into the driver's seat, the keys slid from his fingers. He realized that his hands were slick with Brenda's blood. Maybe even blood from the man from Boston was mixed in. He hoped not; it seemed a desecration to have the blood of a murderer combined with that of an innocent.

He wiped his hands on his sweat pants and picked up the keys.

The engine turned over on the first try. Enough of the sun had risen to clearly light the camp, with crisp morning shadows, as if the day had not turned ugly. He drove into the camp and stopped near Brenda's tent, careful to not spray dust towards her.

He found her unconscious. While alarmed at this, he was also grateful. Talking to her was an awful strain. He thought about putting her in the back of his truck, laying her on the foam pads there, but he worried that she would roll off. He carefully picked her up, as tender as a father with a baby, and carried her to the passenger's seat. He sat her up, secured her seatbelt, and checked the bandages. Bloody, but not soaked through.

The girl's mother came running up, holding her dusty burqa up above her sandals so she could move more quickly. She was not screaming. Harry looked at her eyes, outlined by a rectangle of dark cloth. Her glistening eyes were resigned. How many children and relatives had she already seen die in three decades of war? Harry found that fatal acceptance unnerving and infinitely sad.

Harry drove quickly out of the camp, wincing at every bump. When he reached the car that the two would-be murderers had come in, he turned off the road and drove over brush to get around them. He glanced briefly at the car as he passed—a mid-sized sedan that screamed rental.

The medvac chopper landed a couple of hundred yards away, where the boulders dotting the hillside allowed merely a tricky landing, rather than an impossible landing. Harry shielded the medic and the girl from flying grit with a blanket, then they used the blanket to make a sling to carry her to the helicopter. The medic climbed in with her, but the mother hung back and shook her head when the medic motioned for her to come aboard.

Harry heard later that the girl lived. Not the outcome he expected, but he remembered the lessons from catechism from his childhood, and prayed again, thanking God for that child's life. He regained his faith that day; not a faith that took him to mass or to confession, but a faith that found comfort in reading the Psalms and the Proverbs and praying when in need. He knew little theology, though he recognized that this was because of laziness, not some ecumenical inclination.

That had been eleven years ago, and now he prayed for Brenda. No words, just a yearning for her to live, an incoherent beseeching of the universe. Let there be justice, let the innocent live. Let Brenda live just as the little girl in Afghanistan had lived.

CHAPTER SEVEN

Brenda had never imagined what it felt like to be shot. She had read about such accounts in books—history, journalism, and novels—but the actual experience was unexpected. It hurt, oh God, did it hurt, and she found it best to remain quiet, not move, and keep her eyes closed. She knew that at times she fell asleep, or perhaps fell unconscious. She could not tell the difference.

She felt them come down off the rough road onto the main paved road that ran through the park. The truck accelerated faster.

She didn't want to talk to anyone, not even Harry. Talking took too much energy. Her stomach roiled with nausea and she kept her eyes closed to help calm it. For some reason, probably discernable to a psychologist, she thought about her bedroom as a child. The house in Maine, the walls of her room covered with cedar slats that her father had built with meticulous care. She covered the walls with maps, since she loved maps, and her father gave up after a few attempts to stop her from sticking thumbtacks into his beautiful wood. She also had a mountain of stuffed animals in the corner and only a few dolls. She preferred animals.

The truck slowed, turned, came to a slow stop. She almost smiled. Harry was being so careful.

"Be back in a second," he said as he opened the door.

She heard him pounding on doors, shouting for help. She wondered where they had gotten to in such a short time. Had they reached town already? No, that didn't make sense. Oh, the ranger village. Every national park had one; some were just prefab houses, others had quite nice houses made of local rock, but there was always a place for the rangers and other employees to call home. The rangers at Chaco Canyon lived in a dozen dun-colored homes and duplexes located between the visitor center and campground.

Her door opened and she felt hands lifting her out and laying her on the ground. It felt like a blanket under her.

"She's been shot." Harry's voice quivered. "Two wounds. Her arm and her chest. The arm was squirting blood from an artery—I think that round passed through. There is no exit wound for the chest, so that bullet must be in there."

"Let's take a look." A woman's voice.

Brenda felt probing fingers and moaned at the sharp jabs of pain in her arm and chest. A needle pricked the back of her left hand and she felt it enter her vein.

Another voice. A man's, gravelly from sleep, and speaking with authority. He was used to being in charge. "LifeFlight is on the way. ETA is twenty-five minutes."

"Good, that's good. You got the right blood for her?"

The woman. "Yes, we'll get her volume back up. I've got to check her pressure."

Brenda felt the cuff go around her left arm and squeeze.

The male voice again. "So tell me from the beginning. What happened?"

"Two men drove up to the camp." Harry's voice was calmer, and she took comfort in that. He would not be calm if she wasn't going to be okay. "I was out exercising and found them before they reached the camp. From their conversation, I learned that they intended to murder us."

"Why?"

"I don't know. They mentioned the tomb that we found yesterday, but that doesn't make much sense. How would they have known about that?"

"You found a Chacoan tomb?"

"Yes."

"You didn't report it to us?"

"Good grief, we just found it yesterday afternoon. I just told Dr. Bancroft last night."

"No one else knew?"

Brenda listened for Harry's answer, but he was silent for a while. "No, no one else knew."

"Then what happened? You can make a formal statement later, when the FBI arrives, but I just need the gist now."

"The two men split up. They were both armed. I killed one of them."

"With your bare hands?" asked the woman holding Brenda's wrist.

"Yes, but the other one got to Brenda first. He fired shots into her tent before I killed him."

"Again with your hands?" The woman sounded dubious.

The authoritative voice cut in. "I've known Harry for years. He's an ex-operator. Master Sergeant. Army Special Forces."

"I was lucky and I had a gun by then," Harry said. "They didn't expect anyone to be awake."

"Cowards never do."

"I don't know that they were cowards," Harry said. "They just didn't want any complications."

"That makes sense," the authoritative voice said. "We'll need to go up there to do an investigation."

"Can't I go with Brenda?" Harry asked. "I'll be back."

"There won't be any room in the helicopter," said the woman.

"She'll be okay." Authoritative voice turned gentle. "You can go see her as soon as we get things squared away here."

Brenda could just imagine her mother's reaction. Oh, she was going to be mad. She had not wanted Brenda to come west to go to school and really didn't like it when Brenda announced her summer plans, thus missing the family's annual stay on the island. That's where they were right now, Flannery's Island, off the coast of Maine and a family possession since the Civil War. Her great-something-grandfather had made a fortune in the Clipper trade with China. The family didn't have much of the money left, but they had the island, shared with a couple of dozen other relatives.

She remembered summers on the island, digging holes with her older brother, Dirk, as they sought pirate treasure. Family stories about Drake the Blackhearted entranced Dirk and her. She now wondered if such a pirate had even existed. She really ought to run a web search and a bibliographical search on the name. Were the stories just fables made up to scare children? Walking the plank, shooting his own men in the back to provide ghosts to guard the treasure, murdering women and children. Who would shoot a woman or child?

Who? She pushed thoughts of the island abruptly aside. A man had tried to kill her. Two men, according to Harry. Whatever for? She took secret pride in being friendly to everyone, even if they didn't deserve it. Did they want to kill Harry and she was just in the way? He was the kindest man, but she knew that she saw only a part of him, that there was something else in him. She saw it when his eyes hardened in anger, a part without pity and forged in steel. Now she felt that she was glamorizing him as the hero of a romance novel.

The sound of Harry speaking brought her back to the present. "I should call Dr. Bancroft."

* * * * * * *

Harry remembered the hotel where Dr. Bancroft was staying in Scotland. He called information on his cell phone and a few minutes later had a connection.

"Hello, Royal Hotel. How may I help you?"

"Please connect me to the room of Dr. Bancroft."

Gone for a long moment. "Are you a relative?"

"No." Quickly, he thought the better of the honest answer. "I'm sorry, yes, I'm her cousin. From America."

"I'm sorry, sir, we can't release any information right now. Only to the immediate next of kin, and a cousin does not qualify."

Harry hung up. With a force of will, he pushed his feelings of dread away. Now was the time for clear thinking, unhampered by emotions, pure intellect in the service of survival.

He hit redial.

Same voice answered. Harry coughed and spoke in a more formal voice. "Yes, good sir, may I be connected to the room of Mordecai Herzog." Herzog was a graduate student from the University of New Mexico in the party with Dr. Bancroft, a husky Jewish boy from New Jersey, never to be found without his yarmulke firmly placed on his head.

"Are you a relative of Mr. Herzog."

"His brother."

"I'm sorry to inform you that he has been taken to the hospital."

Harry felt deflated. "Why?"

"He was attacked in his room. The police are investigating."

"Is he alive?"

"I don't have that information. He was taken to the hospital."

"What hospital?"

"Royal Victoria Hospital."

"Do you have a phone number for them?"

The clerk recited the number as Harry wrote furiously.

"Can I talk to someone else in Mordecai's party?" Harry asked.

"I'm sorry, you will have to take that up with the police. We can't release that information."

"What does that mean?"

"You are not their next of kin."

Harry swallowed the bile rising in his throat, too stunned to really think coherently, other than to dial the number to the hospital in Scotland and continue his charade. He found that Mordecai was still in surgery.

* * * * * * *

Brenda listened to Harry. Even in her muddled state, hearing only one side of the conversation, she felt chilled. Something bad had happened to Dr. Bancroft and Mordecai. She didn't care for Mordecai—he looked at her breasts too blatantly and she was not interested, but Dr. Bancroft's classes had inspired her to become an archaeologist. The archaeologist, in her mid-fifties, features wizened from the outdoors, eyes bright with curiosity and intellect, so enthusiastic in her lectures that she sometimes bumped into desks, always ready to encourage any student, and now something had happened to her. Brenda was sure that Dr. Bancroft had a first name, but she had no idea what it might be.

She heard the sound of a helicopter. Coming closer. First time flying in a helicopter and she couldn't enjoy it.

Gathering her wits and energy, she spoke. "Harry."

A hand touched her shoulder and Harry spoke near her ear. "Save your strength, honey."

"Harry, hide the box," she whispered. "Just hide the box."

CHAPTER EIGHT

Harry showed Chief Ranger Simon Ashbridge the first body. Already the blood had formed a crust and attracted flies. The ranger took pictures, moving around to cover different angles. Harry was struck by a sense of skewed *déjà-vu*: the ranger was acting as detective, just as yesterday he himself had been acting as an archaeologist. Hundreds of years, maybe over a thousand years, separated the dead.

Another ranger stepped closer, put on latex gloves, and went through the pockets of the deceased. He found a wallet, keys, a money clip holding seven hundred and twenty dollars, coins, and an extra magazine for the .22. Opening the wallet, he read the name on a New York driver's license aloud: Edward Ashur, thirty-six years old. Everything went into a plastic bag.

Ashbridge had brought four rangers with him. One stayed with Harry all the time—not a form of arrest, since Brenda and Harry were the victims, but just to be sure. Another ranger went over the car the bad men had arrived in. The last investigated the second body and the camp. Eventually, Harry sat down at the table and just watched and listened. The other would-be murderer also had a New York driver's license—Alfredo Travaglio, forty-one years old.

After posing for pictures, both men were rolled into body bags and taken away. The rangers carefully took apart Brenda's tent, taking more pictures, finding the bullets, and taking samples of her dried blood. Harry allowed himself a small amused smile. This was probably the most exciting event that had ever happened in their professional lives, and the rangers were going to do everything by the numbers, as befitted their federal training.

The rangers who took the bodies away to be stored in a freezer at the Visitor's Center returned with news of their computer searches. The car had been rented that morning at two A.M. in the Albuquerque airport—just enough time to drive to Chaco Canyon. A search of the car produced a map of the canyon, along with a map of the dig, apparently copied from Dr. Bancroft's request for a digging permit. A GPS receiver made it easy to drive right to Casa Ángeles. Simon told the archaeologist that the digging request was a public document and available on the web.

A search of the federal and New York law enforcement databases showed that Edward Ashur and Alfredo Travaglio were not model citizens. Ashur had arrests for loan sharking, financial fraud, and possession of an illegal firearm on his record, along with a three-year stretch in prison for armed robbery. Alfredo Travaglio had served six years for manslaughter and also had arrests, without any convictions, for loan sharking and procuring prostitution.

"These guys sound like soldiers for organized crime," the chief ranger said. "Especially the loan sharking." Ashbridge was a short, stout man, with muscles that demonstrated many hours lifting weights. Harry didn't know the chief ranger well, but had talked to him for a while once, and thought he was a pleasant enough fellow.

"You ever pissed anyone off in the mob, Harry?" one of the other rangers asked.

"Not that I know of. Any word on Brenda?"

"She's in the operating room. They think she'll be okay."

"I want to go to her. And I'd like to take some of her stuff—clothes, her cell phone, you know, so I can call her parents. Toothbrush and stuff like that, too."

The chief ranger scratched his head. His brown hair still stuck out in odd directions from being woken up, and he had not paid enough attention to himself to be embarrassed. "Everything here matches your story, Harry. We just have no motive or any reason for this. Why would mobsters come out here to kill you and that girl?"

"I don't know, but maybe it has something to do with Dr. Bancroft. Have you found out more about that?"

No new information from Scotland.

"Did you find any plane tickets?" Harry asked.

"No."

"What does that mean?"

"That they got to the airport by some other method?" Ashbridge said. "That they aren't going to fly back? That they came on a private plane? Take your pick."

"Are you going to find out?"

Ashbridge shook his head. "That's for the FBI to follow up. They are sending someone later today, I hope. The feds used to have an office in Farmington, but budget cuts closed that, so now they have to come from Albuquerque."

"None of this makes sense," one of the rangers said. "These guys didn't even try to hide their identity."

Harry laughed bitterly. "Of course not. They never expected anything to go wrong."

CHAPTER NINE
TASHKENT, UZBEKISTAN

A tall, blonde-haired women with strong features looked at the pictures with clinical detachment. Too many years of life had taught her to create a barrier in her mind, the kind that doctors and police officers and other people who become too intimate with death are forced to create. The photos were digital, of course, easily displayed on her computer screen, and the digital watermark on them gave her some confidence that they had not been faked. The two men in the photo lay in the grotesque way that bodies in rigor mortis often did, with their lips pulled back and limbs stiff. The men were naked, and if one looked closely, as she had to, the bruises around the wrists and legs showed that they had been shackled. The burns on their chests, working down their stomachs, and on their genitals, showed that the torturers had wanted them to talk. She typed notes of her analysis into her laptop, including vague details of the source who had smuggled the pictures out of the notorious Mustiu prison in a mountain valley outside of Tashkent.

She knew herself as Amanda, but everyone in Tashkent knew her as Anika Prokofiev, a human rights activist with a Russian passport that listed her city of birth as St. Petersburg. If asked, she described her grandparents as German communists who had fought the Nazis, then emigrated to the Soviet Union, which explained an accent that no one could place.

For a moment, anger surged inside her, bile rising in her throat. She wanted those men whom Uzbekistan employed to torture their fellow countrymen to feel the same pain that they caused others. She wanted to administer punishment. The moment passed quickly; she had found through bitter experience that she personally disliked killing or even hurting other people. But one had to act, and she had found her role: she believed in the power of speaking the truth, of bearing witness against those who did evil.

Her cell phone beeped and she glanced at the palm-sized screen. The message was short:

Need you in New Mexico now. Priority One—Franklin

Amanda blinked in surprise. She hadn't heard from Franklin for three years, and that time it was only to get a new infusion of funds for her human rights foundation. Switching to another computer in her small office, she brought up the web and checked for airline tickets. She knew that the Uzbek security services were monitoring every byte that flowed in and out of the office; that's why her laptop never touched a network and everything on it was encrypted. Strong encryption was a blessing for human rights crusaders everywhere, as well as other subversives of the established order, such as anarchists, hackers, criminals, and even terrorists.

There were only four international flights a day out of the country. She bought a ticket to San Francisco through Beijing. In a safe deposit box in San Francisco was stored her American identity, papers giving her name as Anna Mauss, as well as credit cards and tens of thousands of dollars in cash. She would buy a ticket for Albuquerque when she had changed names. No doubt Franklin would have further details for her when she got to the United States.

She tapped in a quick message to Franklin:

On my way—A

The flight left in five hours, just enough time to tidy up any loose ends and prepare for an extended absence. Putting away her laptop, Amanda went into the next room. Living space was at a premium in the capital of Uzbekistan, and she worked out of her apartment, as many people did. She lived in a simple room. The bed had a metal frame that she had spray-painted black, and the quilt on it was one of her treasured possessions, handmade many years ago by a good friend in Bangalore who had run an orphanage. The word for peace in thirty languages had been carefully stitched into white and blue panels. A bookcase made of stiffened cardboard sagged under books in five languages, an eclectic mix of history, novels, almanacs, and dictionaries. A hotplate shared her small table with stacks of newspapers, next to a small refrigerator that ran on either electricity or natural gas, whichever seemed to be flowing more reliably that day.

Even though she had lived in this room for five years, she had never bothered to buy a chest of drawers. Instead she lived out of two suitcases, which made packing very easy. She picked through her clothes, leaving most behind so that she would have room to pack the quilt and a couple of books. She looked forward to plane rides as an opportunity to read. Reaching under the table, she slid aside a board to reveal a concealed compartment. Three stacks of ten thousand American dollars each, all in twenties.

Amanda retrieved her laptop and stored it in the large purse that she favored. The laptop contained everything and was the heart of her operation. She looked over the apartment and office one last time, making sure that she hadn't left anything, and then locked the door behind her. The hall smelled of urine and decay. She knocked on the door of the apartment across from hers.

Suraiya opened the door. A tall Uzbek with weathered skin from a youth spent living in a yurt, she had the kind of eyes of someone who chose to roll with the vicissitudes of life and not let the cruelty of her fellow humans scar her. A lawyer by training, she diligently filed suits and requests with the Uzbek courts, requesting trials when none were offered, or asking exasperated bureaucrats for information about disappeared people. Most of the legal maneuvers came to naught, but she knew that the first step to a functioning judicial system was to act like it might someday exist.

"Anika, what's wrong?"

"I've received word that a relative in America is ill and I must go visit."

"How long will you be gone?"

"I don't know—perhaps a long time, but I will bring back some gifts." Amanda handed two bundles of the money to Suraiya. "Be safe while I am gone."

Their words were carefully selected, revealing nothing, because they knew that Uzbek internal security forces had bugged the apartment. The state-controlled bullies mostly just harassed them, stopping their car in the street to check for proper papers, demanding excessive bribes for bureaucratic services, and a rock through Amanda's bedroom window last month. Petty stuff, but petty minds dreamed up petty things. The reports that Amanda wrote to send to Amnesty International, Human Rights Watch, the European Community, and the United States State Department kept her work visible to the rest of the world, and that was what kept her safe.

Yurgi came over, his crutches scraping along the wood floor. A landmine in Afghanistan had changed his life; only his thick upper torso allowed him mobility on his stick-like legs. Suraiya and he had no children, though they were both fond of little ones, and Amanda suspected that he could not father children. He may not even have been able to function as a husband. Amanda had never pried and didn't want to know. The wife and husband were the only employees of Amanda's foundation, but she knew that they only took the money in order to live; they were true crusaders at heart, just as she was.

"I need you to drive me to the airport, but first I want to take you both to dinner."

As Suraiya drove to a restaurant that served the best Lebanese food in the city, Amanda looked out the window, wondering if she would be able to return. There were nicer neighborhoods, with nice homes and tree-lined streets, but the human rights workers chose to live as the masses lived. She had grown to love the Uzbeks and their city, even though too much of the city was dreary Soviet architecture, all crumbling concrete and barren lots. Very little was left to show that this sprawling city of two million was truly ancient, and had once been an important caravan center on the Silk Road from China to Europe.

She would miss Tashkent.

CHAPTER TEN

Simon Ashbridge couldn't get the stink of the dead men out of his nostrils. He rubbed at his nose, trying to be discreet, conscious that he had four other rangers with him. He knew that his obsession with looking competent in front of them was a bit silly, but being chief ranger meant a lot to him.

The second dead man had been taken away, like garbage in a bag, but the smell still lingered. Simon stood back away from the girl's tent as Harry rummaged through it, putting clothes, a brush, a cell phone, and other stuff into a backpack. It was a crime scene, but all the pictures had been taken, and Simon could think of no good reason to keep Harry from taking some of the girl's possessions to her.

Nothing in the archaeologist's story smelled suspicious, though the whole affair stank in more ways than he could name. National parks occasionally had problems with gun-toting idiots growing marijuana, but there was not enough water in Chaco Canyon to make that possible. Who were these men? His call to the FBI had not inspired him that *los federales* would come quickly.

"Uh, Harry, you might want to take some of your own clothes," Simon suggested. "Or even change clothes. Look at all that blood."

Simon followed the archaeologist to another tent and turned away as the man stripped and dressed himself. Despite an insistent urge, Simon did not sneak a peek. He had always dreamed of being a soldier; he loved reading books and watching movies about soldiers, the look of men in uniforms, and the idea being with other men in danger. The idea of war did not attract him so much as did the idea of living in barracks and the shared life of such a masculine world. After high school, Simon had joined the Army, and spent four years driving a tank. He enjoyed tearing up the countryside of Kentucky, feeling the power of sixty-three tons under his control, but was disappointed that barracks no longer existed except in boot camp. Dormitory rooms were the normal quarters now.

Being a private sucked, with long hours on guard duty, obeying the orders of petty tyrants, and feeling that his life was not his own, so he decided to use his G.I. Bill and get a college education, then rejoin as an officer. In college he came out of the closet and acknowledged that he was gay. He felt so relieved, but he couldn't put that part of him back into some secret place; he realized that rejoining the Army was a foolish dream. Don't ask, don't tell meant don't join.

He joined the National Park Service and dedicated himself to climbing the ranks. He didn't have a boyfriend. Three times a year he flew to San Francisco or New York or some other place with a vigorous gay scene. A bit of action and he was good until the next time.

Simon met Harry Deacon the first time that he drove out to check on the new archaeological permit for Casa Ángeles. He found Harry to be a real soldier, the kind of soft-spoken special operator that Simon idealized, with the subtle texture of muscles under his brown Puerto Rican skin and the confident way that he moved. Simon asked Harry about some of his experiences, not pumping for stories, just being friendly. Harry was a paragon of masculinity, and when Simon put out a few subtle signals, he found that Harry was also completely straight. Too bad.

* * * * * * *

Just outside the entrance to Chaco Canyon, on Bureau of

Land Management land, a poorly maintained gravel road stretched towards the south. Harry turned onto it and drove for three miles, keeping an eye out for anyone else, especially someone who might be watching him.

He recognized the paranoia gripping him and the hyper-alertness that kept his eyes constantly flitting about and his nerves quivering. He had slipped back into combat mode, where everything was a possible threat until proven safe. Long experience had shown him how exhausting such a state on perpetual awareness would be. He was not a young pup anymore, and the energy required daunted him, but he could not imagine any other proper response to the situation. The facts added up into a threat that he could not wrap his understanding around: strange men attacking Brenda and him, the apparent deaths or near-deaths of the rest of the digging team in Scotland, and the fact that an extraordinary find sat in a bag on the seat next to him. When gathering Brenda's gear, he found the box from the tomb, wrapped in plastic. He was not surprised that she had taken it to bed with her, like the treasure that it was. Fortunately one of the stray bullets had not hit it, though he would have quickly traded the box for her life, if the universe allowed such trades.

Like an island in the midst of alkaline soil and sagebrush, a rocky butte squatted against the pressures of geological time. Harry stopped in the middle of the road, not wanting to leave tire tracks to show that he had stopped there. Taking the box, he stepped from the truck, taking care to walk on rocks until he was far into the rabbit brush and sagebrush that lined the road.

The butte was only a couple of hundred yards away, and he scanned the horizon as he quickly worked his way past rocks and over a small wash to get to it. There were no helicopters around; the only indication of airplanes were the white trails following two airliners miles up in the sky. He knew that satellites could easily be watching him, but that was a bit too paranoid. There were no other people or cars that he could see.

Near the butte a clump of green stalks of greasewood grew as tall as Harry. The Chacoans had eaten the leaves of the plant and used its sturdy wood for lintels over doors and windows, and as firewood. Passing around the clump, he found a small overhang with a puddle of windblown dust nestled below it. Harry buried the box six inches below the surface and placed a rock on top as a marker. He figured that the plastic would protect it for a while, maybe even a few years.

Stepping out from the shade offered by the overhang, he wiped his brow. The heat seemed more oppressive today than yesterday. Probably not that different as measured by a thermometer, but the stress of his overwrought emotions made him more sensitive.

Once again he was committing a mortal sin for an archaeologist, hiding this precious discovery where no one could find it. What if he died on the road later that night? Then the box would be lost forever. No one would ever be able to open it and marvel at its manufacture, and its discovery would not rewrite the history of Chaco Canyon.

Breaking a branch off a rabbit brush, Harry swished it behind him as he followed his footsteps out. He felt like he was in a Western. It was obvious to anyone who looked what someone had tried to do, but he figured that the wind and any rain that might fall would more easily obscure the brushings rather than his footprints.

CHAPTER ELEVEN

Brenda lay on the hospital bed with an IV in her arm, an oxygen tube running under her nostrils, and a breathing tube coming out of her mouth. The room smelled of disinfectant and the low hum of machinery gnawed at the edge of Harry's hearing. The floor nurse was a large woman, with a face that had seen too much of life, yet a sunny disposition. She explained somberly but hopefully that the young woman had come out of surgery only an hour ago, her prognosis was positive, with good blood pressure, but that the surgeon had decided to keep her in a drug-induced coma so that she could heal better.

Harry had some medic training from the Special Forces and struggled to ferret out what the nurse's words really meant. The only person he had ever known who had been kept in an induced coma was a college friend who had hit a jackknifed semi-truck in her car. She had broken over a dozen bones; the coma had been induced to let her heal and to allow her brain recover. He swallowed and his vision turned blurry: that friend had died.

"Are they concerned about neurological damage?" he asked.

"I don't know." The nurse tugged at her sleeve as if to draw reassurance from the green cloth. "The doctor should be able to tell you more, but he's operating on another emergency case right now."

"When will they take her off the machine?" Harry asked.

"Couple of hours. The anesthesia has to completely wear off before she can breathe on her own."

"Can I stay with her?"

"Is there any family?"

"Not yet. I'm the only person who knows her."

"The rules say that a person can stay as long as the family agrees, so I guess it's okay."

"Thank you. Where can I put her things?" Harry held up the backpack.

"In the cupboard under the bed stand."

Harry slipped into the chair next to the bed, placing the backpack at his feet. He reached out and wrapped his fingers around Brenda's hand. She felt warm, for which he was grateful; he had anticipated her feeling cold.

He dug out her cell phone and turned it on. Good, no password. The screen was already open to some text and he started reading. After a few moments of scrolling he realized to his astonishment that it was a romance novel. Everyone has their secrets, both trivial and important. He certainly had his own secrets.

He found a phone database with Mom listed. No, he shouldn't phone in here, it might disturb her. A part of him knew that she was probably completely unconscious, but what if she wasn't and she heard him describe her wounds to her mother? That would be disturbing, wouldn't it?

Giving her hand one more squeeze, he crept from the room, trying to be as quiet as possible. The five-story hospital of white-painted concrete was the best medical facility short of Albuquerque and the intensive care unit occupied part of the fourth floor. The nurse sat at her station, tapping at the keyboard, and she barely glanced at Harry as he passed her. Her name tag said "Helen, R.N." and her brown skin and broad cheekbones indicated Indian heritage.

Harry went to the end of the hall near an outside window, where reception would be better. Taking a deep breath, he composed himself and thought about what to say before placing an earpiece in his ear and selecting Mom.

The phone rang four times before being picked up.

"Hello."

"Is this Mrs. Finnigan?"

"Yes." Her voice was wary and he recognized the familiar tones that made Brenda's voice interesting.

"My name is Harry Deacon. I'm working with your daughter Brenda in Chaco Canyon."

"You're the retired soldier."

That surprised Harry. He had never supposed that Brenda might have talked about him to her family. "Uh, yes."

"Is Brenda okay?"

"We've had an incident at the dig. For some unknown reason, men attacked us and Brenda was shot." He spoke more quickly to preempt her questions. "Brenda is okay and is recovering from surgery right now."

"Oh, my Lord," Mrs. Finnigan exclaimed. "Can I talk to her?"

"She is still recovering from the anesthesia and they want to keep her sedated."

"We need to come out." It was not a question, but rather an assertion of intent.

"That would be a good idea," Harry agreed.

"We're on the island right now and we might not be able to get a boat today." He had forgotten that Brenda's family left their Maine home every summer to live on an island off the coast in a home that the family had owned for generations.

Brenda's mother talked to herself, as if Harry was only a spectator. "Maybe Tony will take us. I'll have to call you back. What number can I reach you at?"

Harry gave her the number for his cell phone. After a few more words, the conversation ended and he thumbed an end to the connection. He wiped his damp palms on his jeans and struggled to control his trembling.

He needed to get outside, away from the bland beige paint of the corridors, the smell of disinfectants and other fleeting odors with no name, and the oppressive sense of sickness and demise.

Down three flights of stairs and out through the glass front doors, and he was outside.

* * * * * * *

Harry looked up at the sun. It was only midday but he felt punchy, that curious feeling that he remembered from many times in training or combat, when he hadn't slept for a couple of days.

Across the street from the San Juan Regional Medical Center was a strip mall containing a café, a Payless shoe store, a video store, and a place called L&J. Here in the high desert of the West—a place that the imagination wanted to be forlorn and dusty, full of ghost towns and characters exotic enough for a novel—was only suburbia. A Budweiser sign in the window, garish with neon colors, advertised what L&J offered.

He didn't care for Budweiser—too bland—but just looking at the sign brought the bitter taste of a dark brew to his tongue. Deep in his soul, he craved a beer, even a Budweiser, or something stronger. Just one, or maybe two, not enough to dull his senses, but enough to take off the edge.

Stepping from the curb, he glanced both ways down the street. No cars. He started across, but his steps grew shorter until he had drifted to a stop midway. What were the words? "My name is Harry and I am an alcoholic." He hadn't been to AA for three years, back when he had gone to a chapter that met every night in the multi-use room of a Presbyterian church in Salt Lake; he didn't need to go any more; he had whipped it.

Pride turned his feet around. A stone bench in the shade of a tree provided a place for him to slump, his face slack and his eyes focused in a thousand-yard stare.

Sometimes a man can force himself to forget, and other times he can never not remember, regardless of how hard he tries. Through an act of pure will, Harry had forgotten the name of the village in Afghanistan, but he remembered everything else. The village was near the Paki border, high in the mountains, and the Pashtuns in the village openly sympathized with the Taliban. Harry found it amusing, in a cynical and ironic way, that the villagers considered the Americans their mortal enemies, yet felt safe enough to not hide their Mullah Omar and Taliban posters.

Harry's team rode into the village on two Hummers and a six-ton truck, carrying twelve American special operators and six troops from the Afghan army. The team leader, a National Guard captain from Tennessee, found the tribal elders and went into the standard negotiating spiel, drinking sweet tea, offering money for information, and proposing to bring in heavy equipment to grade the road that snaked down from the village to the nearest large town. The captain also bluntly told the elders that they would search the mosque.

Harry took half of the guys to the mosque, where they removed their shoes as a sign of respect, and went through the building, arms at ready, covering each other. They were a scruffy-looking bunch, with unkempt beards, uniforms and combat webbing modified with personal touches, like the baseball cap that Harry wore and the Puerto Rican flag he had sewn onto his shoulder.

They found the weapons cache that intelligence had predicted: two 12.7mm antiaircraft guns with nine boxes of ammunition, and six hand-held rocket launchers with thirty projectiles. There were also seven boxes of dynamite and a box of detonators, just the recipe for making IEDs. The Americans and their allies hated IEDs, those improvised dealers of mayhem that blew off legs and arms if they didn't kill you. The real treasure, though, was a bottle of vodka with a Russian label. Did the liquor date back to the Russian occupation or had it been smuggled in more recently? Harry didn't care. Their base camp didn't even have beer and they hadn't been to Bagram Air Base for two months, where at least a man could sip some smuggled suds. During a moment when other eyes were distracted, the bottle went into his backpack.

The captain ordered the weapons cache carried outside the village and blown up. Everyone, even the women in their burqas, came out to watch. Harry wrapped blasting cord around the boxes of dynamite as the rest of the men stacked the other weapons nearby. They found cover behind a nearby rise and made sure the villagers were far enough away. When he twisted the igniter, Harry made a big enough boom to alert half the country that another weapons cache was no more. Because it was so late, the captain decided to bed down rather than risk a night ambush, and the tribal elders agreed that the mosque could be used.

The stars came out and Harry slipped out of the mosque to watch them. His fascination with the sky was a well-known quirk and no one questioned this. Of course he went fully armed: M4 assault rifle on a strap, 9mm Beretta in a holster, trench knife on belt, three fragmentation grenades, two flash-bang grenades, and a red smoke grenade. He found a small ridge near the village and hunkered down, pulling his jacket tight around him. Even in summer, the nights were cold. That was what made the stars so extraordinary, cold mountain air and no pollution. This was how people used to see the sky—as a great swath of white, the Milky Way, and thousands of distant stellar fires—before they learned to disturb the night sky with fires, lamps, and electricity.

Harry looked at the stars, but brought out of his pack the real reason that he wanted solitude. The vodka burned his throat and he felt the pleasant buzz that came over him like a familiar friend. After two drinks, it occurred to him that the Taliban could have filled the bottle with poison and left it for the next dumb American who came along. You could put a lot of different types of nasty stuff in vodka and no drinker would notice a difference in the taste. Harry felt a jolt at the thought, but already his mind was muddled and he consoled himself with the knowledge that liquor was not uncommon among the Arab fighters that flocked from the Gulf States to fight with the Taliban. It was as if being a warrior for God exempted them from the restrictions of the Koran.

He swallowed more vodka. Then came another boom, not as big as the one he had made earlier that day. So shit-faced that he could barely walk, Harry stumbled back down to the village, tripping over rocks and shrubs. The bottle slipped from his fumbling fingers and spilled its eighty proof alcohol into Afghan soil.

A bomb buried under the mosque had been set off by someone in the village. The villagers stood around, stony faced, not rushing to get their personal weapons, but not doing anything to put out the fire either. Harry found two other men of his team who had been on patrol and were still alive.

The three of them drove away in a Hummer, Harry's head pounding with a hangover, wondering why he was alive. He had been saved by his alcoholic addiction, but if he had not been so obsessed with getting a drink, would he have noticed something to tip him off that the mosque was a trap? Would he have overheard a villager say something? Or noticed some clue, like fresh mortar or a depression in the floor, where the bomb had been located?

A man can never know the answers to such questions.

Harry decided to not return to the village later that day, when the Rangers rolled in, recovered the bodies of the dead, drove the villagers from their homes, and used a pound of C4 on each house. They left only rubble behind. It wouldn't turn the villagers into allies, but it made the soldiers feel better.

With a loud sigh, almost melodramatic if anyone had been watching, Harry wiped at his eyes and looked out at Farmington, New Mexico. He had only bought one more bottle of liquor after that. A bottle of vodka in North Carolina. At Fort Bragg, there was a grove of trees east of the grassy parade ground where tradition demanded that each fallen Special Forces soldier have a tree planted in his honor, next to a plaque with the soldier's name and unit on it. The never-ending War on Terror was turning the grove into a forest.

Harry walked through the trees, leaves rustling in the breeze, and poured a bit of the vodka before each tree. Just a little, since he was not sure if too much alcohol would harm the saplings. Fallen friends, one last toast, never to drink again. He vowed to never let down a friend again.

CHAPTER TWELVE

Harry stood in a corner of the room, watching the surgeon and two nurses extract the breathing tube from Brenda's mouth. One smooth move and the plastic tube was out, dripping saliva. Brenda gagged, made a choking sound, then coughed. She was not awake yet; her brain kept her breathing on autopilot.

"Good air," Dr. Fulton pronounced. He had the stout shoulders of a weightlifter, but long, feminine fingers that carefully reexamined the stitches underneath the bandages of his patient.

"Good vitals," said the nurse, looking at the machines that monitored Brenda.

The surgeon looked over at Harry. "Everything is going to be fine, Mr. Deacon."

"When will she wake up?"

"I am keeping her sedated in order to maintain the coma. This will help her heal. If she were awake, she would be dealing with a lot of pain."

"Do you think that she might have had neurological damage?" Harry asked.

"I'll be frank, we just won't know until we wake her up and can run some tests while she is conscious. I want to be as cautious as possible and so I want to keep her under for a few days."

After the surgeon and nurses left, Harry pushed himself up from his chair and went over to Brenda. He stroked her arm and leaned close to whisper, "Everything is going to be okay. Your family will be here soon."

Holding her hand, feeling the difference between her soft skin and his rough palm, his eyes trawled over the machines next to her, red digits showing her heart rate and oxygen level, and a computer-controlled pump that dispensed micro-amounts of drugs along with saline into her IV. Harry recognized that medical science and technology had saved Brenda and he felt a deep sense of appreciation for all those thinkers, scientists, doctors, and engineers who made such miracles possible.

Harry had run into his share of social scientists who abhorred technology, were almost Luddite in allegiance to pencil and paper, but that was not a common attitude among archaeologists. Quite frankly, archaeologists worked with technology in every way, since most of the artifacts found in digs were things that people made, leading to a keen understanding of the uses and development of technology.

He squeezed Brenda's hand, hoped for an answering squeeze, but she remained limp. She had once confessed that other girls in junior high had called her a science nerd, and that she had been offended, but a talk with her mom convinced her to wear the insult as a badge of honor. Why wasn't everyone a science nerd? Had they no curiosity, no yearning to know?

Harry returned to his chair and pulled his laptop onto his lap. He had brought it in from the truck, knowing that he faced a long vigil with Brenda, but he didn't have the enthusiasm to turn it on. Instead he watched Brenda breathe, her chest rising and falling. She looked so peaceful.

Zipping the laptop back into its carrying case on the floor, Harry rubbed his eyes and leaned back in the chair. He still craved a drink and was so tired...so damned tired.

He slept.

CHAPTER THIRTEEN

"Special Agent Dwayne Brown, Albuquerque office. I'm investigating what happened in Chaco Canyon."

Harry rubbed his eyes and struggled out of the chair to shake the offered hand. Good grip, not too strong, but firm enough to not feel like a dead fish.

"I assume that you're Harry Deacon?"

Harry nodded, working his hands around his waist to make sure that his shirt was tucked in.

"I would like to interview you."

"Uh, let's step outside and not disturb Brenda."

Special Agent Brown led the archaeologist to a nearby unused room, where he set an audio recorder between them. Harry felt better as the interview proceeded. The agent asked the right questions, was thorough, and seemed enthusiastic to catch the bad guys. Describing them as bad guys sounded juvenile to some ears, but in Delta, oddly enough, where they trained to fight terrorists and to rescue hostages, they called them bad guys or hostiles, simple and to the point.

For the third time, Harry told his story in detail, including finding the tomb, but not the strange artifact. He briefly wondered why he was keeping the artifact a secret, other than pure contrariness and loyalty to Brenda. If he did give up the artifact, it would go into an evidence room somewhere and it could take years of legal proceedings to get it out and into a lab where it belonged. Harry's fingers itched to explore it once again, subject the box to x-rays, thermoluminescence, micro-radar, ultrasound, and anything else that he could think of in order to see what might be inside.

"So were the two men from the Mob?" Harry asked.

"Yes, they were. We have made positive IDs from the finger-prints. We are having them autopsied as we speak, at the coroner's in Albuquerque."

"Why would the Mob come out here?"

"It's probably not a Mob thing," said Brown. "They could've been hired by someone else, doing freelance work."

"Any more details about what happened in Scotland?"

"I just talked to the police in Scotland. They are befuddled right now. A whole party of Americans murdered, not as a group, but individually. Clearly this was not just a coincidence."

"Maybe Mordecai Herzog can tell us something?"

Special Agent Brown paused. "Herzog? Oh, yes. The survivor. Well, he died in the hospital. I'm sorry."

Harry stood up abruptly. "He was murdered in the hospital?" The archaeologist rushed from the room.

Brenda was still resting, her blankets pulled up snugly to her chin. Harry took the time to check the bathroom, the closet, and prowl around the room, as if he had the ability to scent danger if it existed.

"Please calm down, Dr. Deacon. Your friend in Scotland dicd during surgery, bleeding in the brain as a result of a severe beating."

"But what if whoever orchestrated this wants Brenda dead?"

"They would also want you dead, Dr. Deacon."

"That is not so important to me. Can you arrange for a twenty-four-hour guard for Brenda?"

The FBI agent sighed. "I will ask the local PD, but a twenty-four-hour guard detail can be hard for a small department to sustain. That sort of stuff is mostly for the movies."

"Please."

He nodded. "I'll try."

"In the meantime, I'm going to stay here," Harry said.

"Sounds good. I looked you up, Dr. Deacon, and saw your

background. Are you armed?"

"No, but I can be."

"I'll pretend I didn't hear that. You should know that while New Mexico does have a concealed weapons permit, you are not a citizen of the state and you would not be able to get such a permit in a timely manner."

* * * * * * *

Brenda's brother looked like her, freckles and red hair, but much larger, six feet tall and heavy about the shoulders and stomach. He wore a blazer, polo shirt, slacks, expensive leather shoes, and carried a briefcase. Harry was mildly amused to see a laptop and three buddies emerge from the briefcase. Brenda had told Harry about her brother Dirk, a high flyer in the financial district of New York, finger on the pulse of the flow of world capital, always ready with a tip on a new stock offering, eating at the best restaurants, a Internet-enabled cell phone never more than a few feet away, even in the shower, well on his way to a third marriage, and who regularly took antibiotics to kill the ulcer-causing bacteria that thrived in his gut.

Rusty Finnigan's hair was close-cropped, a heritage of thirty years in the Army, red hair turning an off-yellow with age. He still looked mostly trim, with only a slight paunch, and carried himself like the full colonel that he had once been. Liz Finnigan was redheaded and freckled, the laugh lines around her eyes now strained with worry. Only ten hours had passed since Harry had called her.

Introductions went around, with awkward handshakes. Harry repeated what the doctor had said about Brenda's condition and explained in detail what had happened at the dig site, rubbing his hands nervously. The story of the tomb and artifact seemed to be a distraction right then. He decided that if they wanted to hit him because he had failed to protect Brenda, he would let them do so. A few blows, at least. It would be a relief.

Brenda slept beside them, her chest rising regularly, and

Harry noticed that a healthy pink was returning to her cheeks. Liz stroked her daughter's arm, an urgent motion that included little squeezes, as she listened to the conversation.

"How are we going to catch whoever sent these assassins?" Dirk asked.

Harry told them what the FBI agent had said just a few hours earlier. No police guard had showed up and Harry doubted that one would be assigned. It took five men to provide around-the-clock coverage and that may have been as many men as the local police department had on patrol at any given time.

"So we really have no idea what is going on or what the continuing level of danger is?" the colonel asked.

"That's right, sir," Harry agreed.

"What were they looking for?" the colonel asked. His eyes bored into Harry, as if to accuse the archaeologist of withholding information.

Harry involuntarily straightened under the glare. Some habits never died, always waiting just under the surface for the proper trigger.

"Don't know, sir." He hated to lie, but his instincts demanded that the information was dangerous and should be restricted.

"Then we need to keep her alive on our own," Rusty said. "It's up to us."

Harry waited for the former colonel to elaborate.

"Can we buy guns?" Rusty asked.

"Yes," Harry replied. "But we can't carry them in a concealed fashion. I'm not sure that we can even have them in a car, and I'm sure there are hospital rules against them."

"Sometimes laws are inadequate to the circumstances," Dirk said.

"I agree," said the colonel.

Harry nodded and smiled faintly. He shuffled his feet for a moment and found his eyes riveted by the vinyl tiles on the floor. "Um, I just wanted to say that I'm so sorry that I wasn't able to protect Brenda better. I'm responsible for her being here."

"Oh, sweet Jesus," Liz exclaimed, grabbing Harry's wrist.

"You're why she's alive. If you hadn't been there, who knows what might have happened."

She began to cry softly. Her husband moved in to comfort her and Dirk drew Harry outside the room. The door closed on the scene.

"Let's go find a gun store," Dirk said.

* * * * * * *

The sign proclaimed *Protect Your Freedoms Guns and Ammo* and inside was an arsenal. Two walls were lined with shotguns and rifles, and a dozen glass-topped counters held pistols of every type, plus a wide assortment of knives. One counter contained throwing stars, a couple of swords, and a throwing ax. In the back was an assortment of hunting gear, sighting scopes, orange vests, and a nice collection of different types of targets. Harry noticed that the round bulls-eye targets had fallen out of style in favor of targets with outlines of men on them. A couple of targets had outlines of civilians on them, invariably women or children, with a menacing hostile holding a gun to their heads. Harry found it frightening to think that civilians were practicing with such targets, waiting for the day to make the clean shot and rescue innocents. Harry had trained to do just that, and had fired over ten thousand rounds of 9mm pistol ammunition to gain any confidence in the idea that he could make such a shot.

Dirk took out his American Express credit card and announced that he wanted four pistols. The owner frowned at the gold card and told him MasterCard or Visa only. Dirk dug out another card.

"I hope this one works," Dirk said. "I haven't used it for two years."

The two men found that New Mexico had lenient gun laws and required only a driver's license. Dirk decided to buy everyone weapons, and a short discussion between Dirk, Harry, and the store clerk, resulted in 9mm Beretta (92 series) semi-automatic pistols for Harry and himself, a .45 Colt for his father, and a smaller .32 Beretta Tomcat for his mother.

Harry ran his hand over his pistol, worked the slide, and detected the faint smell of metal and oil from the factory. The nine millimeter Beretta was the same weapon that he had trained with in the Army, and he still owned one, but it was in storage back in Utah, so he was grateful for Dirk buying him the loaner. He only really trusted a weapon that he had put at least a thousand rounds through and had stripped and cleaned at least a dozen times; then the gun became part of him. Until then a new pistol was still only metal and plastic, foreign to his fingers and palm.

Sitting in passenger seat of the car that Dirk had rented at the Albuquerque airport, Harry loaded the magazines with ammunition that they had bought. His fingers knew this operation so well that he could have slipped in each bullet with his eyes closed.

CHAPTER FOURTEEN

The colonel had gone downstairs to get some food at the cafeteria, leaving Liz sitting with their daughter, when a man dressed in work clothes came in and mumbled some words that she didn't catch. She wondered if the sounds had even been intended as words. The short man, with dusky skin and vague features that suggested a Hispanic or some blend, had dark curly hair and wore high-top running shoes. He had some sort of elaborate ring on his right ring finger, but she could not make out the design because he wore white medical gloves over both hands.

The orderly went into the bathroom, and Liz even heard the clang of porcelain hitting porcelain, like the lid of the toilet tank had been lifted and replaced. Coming out of the bathroom, again muttering words that she couldn't catch, he went through the closet. Not much there, since all of Brenda's clothes were back at Chaco Canyon. Then he looked in the medical cabinets and drawers, quickly sorting through the supplies; he even rummaged in the cabinets and drawers under the electronic monitoring equipment. Liz stood up to watch him, concerned that he might accidentally unplug something important.

The orderly crowded past Liz and bent down at the night stand with his back to her. She could smell his cologne.

"Excuse me," Liz said. "What are you doing?"

He didn't answer as he pulled open the drawer. Nothing there except a writing pad and phone book. He opened the phone book, riffled through the pages, and tossed it back into the drawer. Closing the drawer, he opened the cabinet where Harry had left Brenda's backpack. He pulled out the backpack, opened it briefly, and zipped it closed. The rest of the cabinet was empty.

"Excuse me," Liz said again, placing her hand on the man's shoulder. "I think that is my daughter's."

The orderly quickly stood and turned. He was the same height as Liz Finnigan. He placed his hand on her face and she smelled the latex of the glove just before he pushed hard. The fifty-one-year-old woman threw her arms out for support, found nothing to grab, and fell heavily to the ground. A small cry escaped her lips as the back of her head hit the vinyl floor.

Then the orderly was gone and so was Brenda's backpack.

* * * * * * *

"He said that he was a custodian and he acted really nice," Liz Finnigan said in a reedy voice. Her face was pale with shock and her husband gently caressed her shoulder. "He acted like he belonged here."

The nurse named Helen had insisted that Liz be taken down to the emergency room for an evaluation. The colonel went with his wife, pausing only to check on his daughter.

"We need to call that FBI guy," Dirk said. Harry looked at the young man and noticed that his fair face was flushed, his freckles becoming muted in a sea of red. Dirk opened his bag, took out his new pistol and slid it into the back of his waistband.

"I agree, but I think that the guns should remain in the bag for right now. You can keep the bag with you at all times," Harry said. "You can't really conceal that large of a pistol on your person."

"Maybe we should go back and buy smaller pistols."

"Maybe," Harry said as he prowled around the room. They had questioned the nurse and found that she had not seen a custodian on the floor and that none of the hospital personnel matched Liz's description. None of this made any sense. He found the nagging atmosphere of undefined danger so frustrating. How was he supposed to plan and fight when he didn't know who the enemy was? Was the box from the tomb the real object of desire here? Had the fake custodian been after the box? The backpack didn't contain anything important, just some clothes and toiletries, since Harry still had Brenda's cell phone in his pocket.

Harry took out his cell phone and called the number that the FBI special agent had left. No answer, which rolled over to voicemail. Harry left a message describing what had happened and asked the agent to call him as soon as he could.

CHAPTER FIFTEEN

The sun was setting, casting long shadows, coloring the western sky in the layered shades of orange so familiar to the people of New Mexico. The locals didn't even realize how spoiled they were by nature's beauty. Harry walked out to the parking lot of the hospital, feeling old, exhausted by the events of the day. He had waited for the FBI agent to show up and found the whole interview fruitless. The agent had no new information, or at least any that he was willing to share. The only compensation was getting to know the Finnigans better. They were a close family—good people—of course, he hadn't expected any less with a jewel like Brenda.

When he reached his truck, there was still enough light to see that the lock on his driver's side door was standing up like an accusing finger.

Curiosity wormed its way along his tired neurons. He never locked the truck at the dig, but always locked it back in civilization. Had he forgotten? He opened the truck door and looked inside. He instantly saw that the seat had been adjusted, as if someone had moved it to search behind it, and then set it back. Harry went to the back and found that the shell was also unlocked. His gear inside was not where he had left it.

He found a flashlight in the glove compartment and shone it around. Nothing was obviously missing, but it was obvious that everything had been thoroughly searched. Of course, whoever it was—that elusive force of hostiles that had both murdered people half a world away and tried to kill Brenda and himself—

had searched the truck after searching Brenda's room. Or maybe it had been before. Harry felt like he was not just two steps behind the bad guys, but not even thinking on the same level.

Should he call the cops? He doubted that they would find anything and he didn't want his truck impounded as a crime scene. He had a nagging feeling that this whole situation was beyond the capabilities of the local police.

Putting his laptop in the cab, he got in, adjusted the seat to how he liked it, and was about to start the truck when he stopped. What if it was booby-trapped with a bomb set to go off when electricity flowed to the starter? He had lived in several foreign cities where he had been required to check under cars every morning with an extended mirror to see if a bomb had been placed there overnight.

Was he just being too paranoid? Did he really need the habits of his old life? To hell with it. He turned the ignition.

* * * * * * *

The Red Rocks Inn catered to tourists, but it was the first motel that Harry found, so he checked in and carried his laptop and a backpack through the lobby. The room was clean and the bathroom had a jetted tub. Harry locked the door, securing the chain and the slide lock for good measure. He took out the pistol that Dirk had purchased for him and laid it on the tank on the back of the toilet. Stripping off his clothes, he was surprised to find a few specks of blood under his right arm, where he had failed to wipe it away earlier in the day. Was it Brenda's or one of the thugs'?

Sitting in the tub, he ran the hot water, turning the bathroom into a steamy sauna. He turned on the jets and lay back as the bubbles tickled his body. When was the last time that he had done something like this? Graduate school? No, earlier than that. In the Army? Not likely. What about with Marie, his wife? He had been home on leave and they spent three days alone in a Hilton hotel. That was the last time, in a hotel with her, fifteen years ago.

After dozing for a while and turning the skin his fingers and toes into wrinkles, Harry washed himself and got out of the tub. He padded into the motel room, naked except for the gun in his hand. Having a firearm made him feel in control, ready for anything, even more of a man. He knew that it was silly, so much macho posturing, but he couldn't deny the feeling.

The Inn offered free Internet and so he hooked up his laptop and signed on. He could easily get e-mail on his cell phone, but he refused to pay for the service. As usual, he had a dozen pieces of e-mail, most of them from archaeology lists that he belonged to, but one was from Dr. Bancroft. It was creepy to receive e-mail from the dead. He saw the time on it, early in the morning. He clicked on it:

Harry,

What an amazing find!! Great pictures. If I were here on my own I would drop everything and rush back, but the students want to see more of Scotland. Please keep the tomb closed and wait for me to return.

Did we break standard protocol? (I wanted to put a raised eyebrow here, but don't know if there is an emoticon for that.)

Lori

Harry read the e-mail twice before he began to shake—not dramatic tremors, just shivers of grief.

CHAPTER SIXTEEN

Chief Ranger Simon Ashbridge continued to ride the wave of excitement that had started the day for him. Woken at the crack of dawn, he had spent most of the day at the archaeological dig. At times he didn't even have another ranger to keep him company, since the rest of his staff had a national historical park to run, but Simon realized that he needed to maintain a guard on the scene, so he selected himself to stay.

At about two o'clock, Special Agent Dwayne Brown arrived. The two men knew each other casually, from law enforcement seminars in Albuquerque, usually on topics like how to combat pot-hunting. A premium ancient Pueblo pot could go for up to $25,000 on the collector's market; all the pot hunter had to do was lie and say that it was found on private land, not public land. Simon had noticed the agent's taste for cowboy boots and bolo ties with blue-green turquoise or red coral slides. The ranger took the agent on a tour of the site, showing him where the bodies had been, the ground stained with their blood.

The two men reached the piled dirt around the black stone, with the brace and hoist astride it like an oil derrick.

"This is a tomb, or so Harry says," Simon said.

"Why don't we open it up and take a look?" the agent suggested.

The ranger shook his head. "No, we shouldn't. This is a rare find and should only be opened under the right circumstances by archaeologists."

The agent crouched down. "Look at the marks on the rock

and how the soil is disturbed. Good grief, just look at the foot-prints. They already opened this place."

"Well, they are archeologists," the chief ranger said. "That's their job."

After the tour, conversation lagged, so the two men each took out their laptops, sat across from each other at the camp table, and tapped away. The nature of their jobs required far too many reports. The agent had brought a bag of corn chips with him, which he shared.

It was four in the afternoon before a CSI team arrived, borrowed from the Albuquerque police department, carefully driving up the rutted road in their van. The two investigators emerged, pulled on latex gloves, and recruited the ranger and FBI agent as labor.

Doing a crime scene investigation, especially outdoors, was not glamorous like on television. A grid was laid out using handheld GPS receivers and the men walked the scene, eyes wandering over the desert soil. Simon looked up at the others, at their intense concentration on the ground, and was reminded of arrowhead hunters. People liked to find Indian arrowheads. He had seen some impressive collections in private homes, hundreds of arrowheads, mostly black flint, but sometimes more exotic colors, all neatly glued into hanging display cases. Whenever he caught the arrowhead hunters on national park land, he had to chase them off. Twice he had been forced to arrest belligerent couples who thought that as taxpayers they had every right to take whatever they found on ground owned by the people and for the people.

By seven o'clock, the CSI team announced that they were finished. Nothing had been found that the rangers hadn't already collected earlier in the morning.

Simon bade the others farewell and drove home. His cat announced her displeasure over the issue of going the whole day without food with a few sharp meows. He had rushed out of the house so quickly that morning he had forgotten to take care of the calico. Instead of rubbing his legs while he opened the can of tuna-flavored food, she sat in the corner, waiting for service and an abject apology.

He was famished, having eaten only chips all day, and he found some leftover lasagna in the fridge. Eating alone was his habit and he usually read or worked during dinner. According to his calendar, today was supposed to have been devoted to the annual budget report, and he had gotten nothing done on it. He looked for his laptop, went out to his truck and realized that he had left it at the dig. The FBI agent had packed his up, but Simon had left it until he was done helping the CSI team. When everyone else left, he had followed, not even thinking that a couple of thousand dollars of government equipment was still on the table in the big canvas tent. It was not in his nature to forget things, but he had been out of sync all day.

The cat had still not forgiven him when he left for Casa Ángeles.

* * * * * * *

As Simon approached the top of the hill, he was surprised to see an SUV appear in his headlights, parked in the rutted road. Red paint job, a Toyota, with New Mexico license plates. He stopped his truck, turning off the engine and the lights. Who could this be? He had a bad feeling about this, so he reached for his radio and picked up the handset.

"Chaco Central, this is Ashbridge, over."

At this time of night, one of the other rangers would have the radio on in their bedroom, acting as dispatch for the night. Only one other ranger would be on patrol.

Simon turned up the volume and was surprised to hear static. He was used to a bit of a hum, but these new radios were supposed to filter out any static.

"Chaco Central, any ranger, this is Ashbridge, over."

Still just static. Simon bit his lip, a habit that he had deliberately left behind as a teenager because it looked too girlish. The smart course of action was to drive away, find backup, and return. What if it was just some other FBI people? What if it was not, but someone with bad intentions, and they escaped? What intentions could they have? There was no one at the archaeological dig now. Unbidden, the question popped in his mind. What would Harry do? Simon felt a surge of testosterone-laden adrenalin pulse through him.

In his heart, he knew that this whole line of reasoning was just macho bullshit, but it felt like great bullshit. He grabbed his flashlight, opened the door, and stepped from the truck. He rested his palm on his pistol and felt better.

Keeping the flashlight off, he walked past the SUV, and reached the rise where he could look down on Casa Ángeles. A set of work lights on a portable rack illuminated where the tomb had been found. Except now the tripod hoist had been used again and the black stone had been lifted up. There was a man down there, kneeling and peering under the stone.

It suddenly occurred to Simon that the radio problem was not failure on the part of his people to answer the call or odd atmospheric conditions. Those radios were completely reliable, as good as any the military had, and his people had never not acknowledged a call. It was jamming.

Ordinary people don't have jammers.

As his hand move to pull his pistol from its holster, a flashlight clicked on and caught Ashbridge in the face. Sparks danced before his eyes.

"Well, well, Ranger Rick," a voice said out of the darkness.

Two soft puffs and Simon fell to the ground. Had he ever given such a situation any thought, he would have expected being shot to be like in the movies, his body flung back as the bullets punched him, but it was not that way. He just crumpled. His shirt felt soggy against his chest. He desperately wanted to get his pistol out and at least take some revenge, but his cold fingers refused to move.

"Good shooting, Jeb," a voice said from above him. "Can I finish him?"

"Do it."

CHAPTER SEVENTEEN

Dwayne Brown stepped out of his government-issue Ford Explorer. An urgent call that morning to his office in the Federal Building in Albuquerque had prompted him to drive faster than was prudent to get to Chaco Canyon. Driving up the rutted road, he had been forced to stop at the end of what had become a single-file parking lot.

He walked past the cars, relishing the smell of morning in the desert. Being assigned to New Mexico was the dream of a lifetime. The only better assignment would be Flagstaff, Arizona, which included Monument Valley in its jurisdiction, where John Ford had shot so many of his greatest films. The special agent watched *Stagecoach*—the original one, of course, not any of the awful remakes, every year during Thanksgiving—and *The Searchers* every year at Christmas. Every other holiday had its special movie, sometimes picked for a reason, sometimes just because he needed to complete his traditions.

It was odd for a boy of his generation, especially one from in a suburb of Newark, New Jersey, where he grew up watching Western movies on cable television, dreaming of horses and wide open spaces. In his heroic dreams, he wore cowboy boots and carried a six-shooter. He loved the manly virtues that the Western implied: loyalty, courage, self-reliance, and patriotism—all found in the legendary rolling gait of John Wayne, striding across the cinemas and tubes of America.

A park ranger with a neatly trimmed beard caught sight of the FBI agent and hurried over. He gave Dwayne a quick tour:

Simon Ashbridge's abandoned truck, and the dark stain on the ground at the top of the rise, with a small trench through the center of the stain where a diligent ranger had scooped some of the red-encrusted sand into an evidence bag. Another plastic bag held two shells that had been found only fifteen feet away. Another shell had been found only a few feet away. There were so many footprints from the previous day that trying to track them was useless.

Every employee in the park had come, and they now swarmed over Casa Ángeles and the surrounding countryside like ants whose anthill had been disturbed. Dwayne sighed. Any evidence was being tramped all to hell; everyone was hoping that they could find the chief ranger before he died.

No chance of that. Dwayne had no idea what had happened at Casa Ángeles last night, but it had not been an accident that a person might survive.

Pulling out his cell phone, Dwayne made a call to his supervisor in Albuquerque, reported what was happening, and asked for another CSI team to be sent out. The ranger followed him like a familiar spirit as he walked around the site. The tents had literally been torn apart and all the gear inside was scattered around on the ground, with coolers tipped over, clothes strewn about, and in some cases cut up. Papers drifted across the ground like tumbleweeds in the breeze, though the heat of the midday was coming on, which would quell most of the air movement.

"Did your people do this?" Dwayne asked.

"No, of course not. It was this way when we arrived this morning."

Dwayne put his cell phone in record mode. "Now, let's go through it one more time, just for the record."

The ranger looked exasperated. "Okay, for the third time. This morning the chief ranger failed to show up for our staff meeting."

"What time was that?"

"8:30."

"Then what did you do?"

"We went to his home and he was not there. We tried the radio and he didn't respond, so we used the GPS tracker to find his truck."

"Do all the park vehicles have GPS transponders in them?"

"Yeah. We installed them last year."

"And you found Simon Ashbridge's truck here?"

"Yes."

"Anything else?"

"You saw the blood in the sand. We took a sample. You also saw how the camp has been ransacked. It wasn't that way yesterday."

"How did all these people get here?"

"We put out a general call for assistance. What if Simon's hurt somewhere? He can't last long in this heat." The ranger paused. "We all liked...I mean like...him."

Acting on a vague hunch, perhaps because tombs hold a visceral attraction for many people, Dwayne walked over to the black rock. The tripod still stood above the rock, but it was immediately obvious that someone had been there. The sand and soil was even more disturbed than the day before. A small stain of darker sand prompted Dwayne to crouch down. He knew what it must be and touched the crusty sand reverently.

"Let's get this rock moved," he ordered.

* * * * * * *

Three hours later, the press presented itself in the form of a television crew from Albuquerque, two newspaper reporters, and a blogger. They arrived in time to see Dwayne, a CSI technician, and two rangers struggle out of the Chacoan tomb, each holding the corner of a sagging body bag. The FBI agent allowed himself to be interviewed on camera, but refused their request to film inside the tomb. It was a crime scene, still being worked by the CSI team, and he was embarrassed by the obvious destruction.

The floor was covered with crushed seashells; pieces of wood scarred with fresh marks from a hatchet and claw hammer were piled atop a raised stone; and the mummy was literally torn apart, bones scattered everywhere. The walls showed gouges and scrapes from where the vandals had violently examined every cranny.

Finding that the agent had no more information, the reporters moved on to get the human interest angle from the clumps of park employees standing around, their haggard faces showing shock. Many of the women had been crying, encouraged by a sense of group catharsis, while most of the men refused to join in.

With the reporters leaving him alone, Dwayne walked back towards his Ford Explorer, dictating a few notes to himself in his cell phone.

"Special Agent Brown."

Dwayne looked up. The speaker looked like he had just walked out of central casting at an old-time Hollywood studio. About thirty years old, sandy hair with a standing wave in front and not a strand out of place, chiseled features to distract young girls and their mothers, and a grey suit that could only be tailor-made. Wrong face for a Western, but it would work for most other movies. He carried a burnished metal briefcase.

"I'm Special Agent Marshall Stone. I've been instructed to take over this investigation." He held out his ID, the initials F.B.I. prominently emblazed in blue on it next to his picture.

"Was I doing a bad job?" Dwayne asked. He felt somewhat bewildered. Shouldn't the special agent in charge in Albuquerque have called him and told him about this?

"Not that I'm aware of." The newcomer looked around, his eyes hidden by sunglasses. "I was just told to get out here as quickly as possible and take over."

"What office are you from?"

"My current assignment is in New York. Foreign Intelligence Division. I am here only temporarily, until we get this mess cleaned up."

CHAPTER EIGHTEEN

Brenda still lay in a coma, the rise and fall of her chest regular, her cheeks pallid, rather than rosy with life. The four people who loved her maintained their vigil. Harry had been there all morning, trying his best to be sociable, and failing by any measure. He just wanted Brenda to get better. Motes floated in the beam of sunshine that streamed in from a window. He hadn't really looked at motes since he was a small child, back when the world held more fascination for him; now he watched the motes, but did not see them.

Sometime during the morning, Liz Finnigan stood up and turned on the television, leaving the volume low, before returning to the bedside and taking up her daughter's hand again. At least it filled the room with some sound.

The mention of Casa Ángeles brought Harry out of his thinking fugue and he looked over at the television. A reporter was standing in front of the pueblo ruin at his archaeological dig, interviewing Dwayne Brown. Harry listened with growing alarm and felt a pang of sadness that the chief ranger had been killed. After the news report ended, going onto golf scores, Harry stood abruptly and walked out into the hospital hall. He fished around for the card the FBI agent had given him and pulled out his cell phone.

"Agent Brown?"

"Yes."

Harry heard the sound of a car in the background. "This is Harry Deacon. I just saw on the news that Simon Ashbridge has been killed. Could you tell me more?"

"That's all part of an ongoing investigation, Harry, which means that I really shouldn't go into it."

"I understand that you're constrained by rules, but I am worried about whether Brenda is at risk or not. Is there still a threat to her?"

The FBI agent's sigh was audible. "Yes, there probably is still a threat."

"Can we get police protection?"

"I don't know. I'm not longer officially on the case. They brought in someone new."

"Why?"

"I don't know."

"Can I talk to him?"

"I'm in my car right now and I don't have his contact info. I'll find it and e-mail it to you."

"Thanks."

The agent paused. "I do have a question for you, Dr. Deacon."

"Yes."

"The tomb that you found at Casa Ángeles. Was there anything special about it?"

"Other than it's a rare find, since the Chacoans didn't build tombs. It was also in pristine shape. The sarcophagus was mostly intact, except for the lid. The body was in good shape considering that it must be seven or eight hundred years old."

"Really?" The agent sounded surprised.

"Absolutely, the kind of find to make a career. It would take months to properly investigate such a jewel."

"It's not a jewel anymore."

Harry felt a shudder go through him, icy fingers playing on his spine. "What do you mean?"

"Vandals destroyed the tomb and left the body of the chief ranger inside. A real mess. Completely trashed."

"That's awful." Harry stumbled on his words, seeking a way to express his horrified outrage. "That's a crime against knowledge and science."

Harry ended the call. The conclusion could no longer be denied—all this killing was over the tomb.

"So what's happening?" Dirk asked.

Harry looked up in surprise. The young man had followed Harry out into the hall, and while Harry didn't mind Dirk listening to his end of the telephone conversation, he was rattled that he hadn't noticed Dirk. Was he so rattled that he had dropped basic awareness? That didn't bode well for the task ahead of him.

"I think that this nightmare has just started," Harry said.

CHAPTER NINETEEN

"You know what's going on?" Dirk asked. His nerves felt jittery, confused, ready for fight or flight.

"No, but I'm getting some ideas," Harry said. "We should talk. Tell your parents that we're going out for a bit."

"They would want to be included."

"They won't want to leave Brenda's side, and we have to assume that the room is bugged."

Dirk looked bewildered. "Bugged?"

"That's what I would do if I wanted to keep tabs on us."

Dirk slipped back into the room and whispered briefly in his mother's ear. He would have talked to his father too, but his father's hearing of low tones was completely shot, and he didn't want to talk too loudly. The room suddenly felt like a trap, a stage where the audience wore menacing sunglasses and carried weapons.

Dirk's first words on returning to the hall came out in an accusing tone, though he had not fully intended that they sound that way. "You know more than you are telling."

Harry looked at him briefly, appraising him with somber eyes. "Maybe. Let's walk the halls."

Dirk was so successful in his Wall Street career not because he matched the stereotype—aggressive and brash, a master of the universe—but because he practiced another skill. He was a keen listener in a world where everyone wanted to talk about themselves and thus appreciated, on a gut level, anyone who listened sincerely. Listening had not saved his marriages—he understood why his wives were frustrated with his obsessive approach to work, but he just couldn't stop himself.

So now he listened.

"I guess that I thought that ignoring it would make it go away," Harry said. "I really didn't think that the two were related. How could they be? It just doesn't make any sense."

"What doesn't make sense?" Dirk had internalized the primary rule of listening from a university communications course, to repeat back to the other person what they had said in the form of a question.

"The tomb. The damned tomb." The whole story spilled out, leaving out no details.

They took the stairs down to the first floor, passed the pediatrics ward, hearing a small child whimpering behind a closed door. Dirk noticed a cute nurse leaning over a counter, talking to another nurse, her buns and thighs tight under her green hospital scrubs. He wanted to find an excuse to loiter, to see how pretty she was, the personality behind her eyes, and if there was a ring on her finger.

Harry led him out the side entrance and through the parking lot. Dirk noticed that the older man was carefully scrutinizing everything that they passed, even as he talked. They had circled the building twice by the time that the full story had been told and Harry fell silent.

"So this tomb is pretty special?" Dirk asked. His interest in archeology was minimal; he preferred history, where the books and documents spoke the thoughts of their writers, not the suppositions that archaeologists wove as they looked at inert artifacts.

"Yes...no...I don't know," Harry said in exasperation.

"You're the archaeologist, Harry. This is your field. Is this worth killing people over? I mean, by my count, we have what, five dead people, plus the two that you killed. That's a lot of death for a tomb."

"It's an unusual tomb, but the true gem is a box that we found. Very interesting, very unique."

"Where's this box?"

"I hid it," Harry admitted. "Brenda thought that I should."

"Is it really that unique? Enough to kill over?"

"The people of Chaco Canyon liked exotic goods. They had shells from the ocean, and even freshwater shells from as far away as Arkansas. They imported turquoise from deep in Mexico and even imported macaw birds from southern Mexico. We assume that they liked the feathers, since there's a room in Casa Bonito that had twelve macaw skeletons in it. Maybe one of the clans had the macaw as its totem. There are even copper bells in Chaco, though no one knows where they came from. They are crudely cast and we haven't found a copper-working workshop. The Chaco Canyon people never really left the stone age."

"You are sounding like a professor," Dirk said, keeping his tone dry. "What makes *this* box so unique?

Harry looked a bit annoyed to have his info-dump cut off. "Well, for starters, it's made of some material that is not immediately obvious, but it's obvious that the people of Chaco Canyon could not have made it."

"Who made it then?"

"No idea."

"That's not helpful."

"I know. I would really like to get the box into a proper lab, where we could x-ray it, look over the surface with a microscope, subject it to more tests that I can't think of right now."

"Are you sweet on my sister?" Dirk asked, the question coming out of left field.

Harry looked embarrassed. "I'm an old man compared to your sister."

"Biology doesn't pay attention to age," Dirk said. "Are you sleeping with her?"

Harry's jaw actually dropped open. "Of course not."

"I know you archaeologist types are a randy bunch, always scoring on each other. My sister would fall hard for a guy like you."

"That may be true for some of us, but your sister and I did not relate that way."

Dirk shrugged. "I just wanted to know. Sorry to pry."

Harry waved his hand dismissively. "I'm glad you got it off your chest and out of the way."

They walked along in silence for several minutes, circling the building once more. Other than the strip mall, the hospital had been built in an industrial section of the town, near metal shops and construction equipment storage yards.

"Do you know what woods shock is?" Harry asked.

Dirk looked at the older man oddly. "Not even a clue."

"You learn about it in survival school. You see, we all have a mental map of where we are. When someone gets lost in the woods, they are confused because their mental map isn't working anymore. It is very stressful and most lost people make awful decisions because of woods shock. They don't take care of their basic needs, they wander around too aggressively, they don't sit down and think."

"So?"

"I have a mental map of how the world works. You have a mental map, too. But now we have no idea what is going on—it's just like woods shock. We are lost...."

"...And now am found," Dirk sang, a low lilt that showed only mediocre musical talent.

Now it was Harry's turn to give the younger man a strange look. "What?"

"*Amazing Grace*, one of my favorite songs. You know," he sang, "I once was lost but now am found...."

"Let's be a little more serious about this," Harry said with a frown.

"Sorry. I get silly sometimes."

"My point is that we need to avoid woods shock and think through this."

"Okay, what are some other survival rules?" Dirk asked.

"To be in the now. That means that you are focused on your environment as it really exists, not as you wish it existed. Don't be thinking about how you would like to be somewhere else or doing something else. Be in the moment and pay attention. Another rule is that only you can solve your problem. Waiting for someone else to help is sometimes useful, but it can too easily be an excuse to avoid solving your own problem. We have a problem and we have to solve it. The FBI seems lost, almost clueless."

"So what does all that mean?" Dirk asked.

"I need to think about the now."

* * * * * * *

Harry prowled the halls of the hospital, telling himself that he was looking for possible dangers, people who didn't belong there, anyone carrying a concealed weapon, but mostly he walked because that was the best way to get his thinking juices flowing. How was he going to protect Brenda? The obvious way was to find whoever wanted to hurt her and take care of them. He realized that he was a target also, and while he feared dying, he feared Brenda dying much more.

Why had they been attacked? Because they were in the wrong place at the wrong time? Because of something that they knew? Because both the Casa Ángeles site and the rest of the team in Scotland had both been attacked, they must have something in common. Only the archaeological site was in common. Were the attacks associated with the tomb? That didn't make any sense. Was it about the small box with the strange symbol? How could that be, when the box had been found after the rest of the team had left for Scotland? And how would have anyone have known about the box, which had been buried for hundreds of years? Too many questions.

He agreed with Brenda that the box was important. What could possibly be in it? What if the hostiles thought that there was something in the box that wasn't really there? He decided that really didn't matter, since the box was what they really wanted right now. Should he just give it to them? How would he tell them he wanted to give up the box? Should he give it to the FBI? He bristled at the thought of turning an archaeological find over to the government. Look at what had happened to the Kennewick Man—years of litigation before archaeologists could properly examine a nine-thousand-year-old skeleton found on the banks of the Columbia River. Besides, he told himself, the box really couldn't be the reason for this. How could anyone have known it?

He stopped and sat down in a waiting room. A television blared too loudly in the corner. Asking himself all these questions wasn't getting him anywhere. Every explanation he came up with, no matter how vaguely defined, was rejected as the chain of logic broke down, foundering on the shoals of too little information.

The key had to be the most unlikely coincidence, which was that Dr. Bancroft and the other students had been attacked at almost the same time as Brenda and he. If the bad guys had wanted to kill the whole archaeological team, the sensible and easy way to have done it was before the others left for Scotland or after they came back. That meant that the timing of the attacks couldn't be changed. What if Dr. Bancroft or one of the others in Scotland had stumbled onto something or done something that set all these events in motion? It was a tempting thought, but frustrating because it meant that he had no idea about how to find out anything more.

If he couldn't figure out why the bad guys were after them, he needed to tackle the problem from a different angle. He needed to gain the initiative. How to flush them out into the open? He had to go with the box, since that was the only thing that had a chance of being important. How might someone have out found about the box?

Ah, of course. E-mail. He had e-mailed photographs and a description of the box to Dr. Bancroft just two nights ago. He wished that he knew more about computers and networks, but it made sense that somehow, someone had listened. He had been on plenty of missions where the intel came from a cell call intercept, or something else that the electronic wizards at the NSA had snatched from the cyber-ether.

Of course, that was pretty fast reaction, to intercept the e-mail and send out a couple of thugs from the East Coast in a matter of what, six or seven hours?

CHAPTER TWENTY

Harry asked the intensive care nurse for some paper and a pen. She handed him a pad with the name of a pharmaceutical corporation emblazoned across the top. Harry sat down and wrote quickly.

Dirk,

I have a plan to figure out whoever is doing this. I don't want to talk about it in case we are being listened to. Maybe I'm being too paranoid, but it's better to be safe. I want you to find an Internet café or a public library and create a free e-mail account in the name of Dr. Joséph Poe. He doesn't really exist, but we want it to look like he does. After that, I want you to go buy some tools for me:

- full-sized shovel
- small pick
- a pulaski if you find one (firefighting tool that is a combined ax & hoe)
- 8 large burlap bags
- AR-15 rifle (no scope) - this will cost you a bit and I will pay you back later
- 5 extra magazines and 200 rounds of ammo for AR-15
- side holster (9mm handgun)

- survival knife with serrated blade on reverse
- 4 water bottles (each 2 liters in size)
- 2 boxes of protein bars
- package of cardstock paper
- brown duct tape (1 roll)
- baby monitor with earplug on receiver and two sets of long-life batteries
- notebook and two pens

Other instructions:

ONLY USE CASH!!!
　　Remove the battery from your cell phone, so that no one can track you.
　　Destroy this paper afterwards.

Harry returned the pen and rest of the paper to the nurse and went back to Brenda's room, where he found her family talking quietly among themselves. Harry motioned for Dirk to come out into the hall.

Dirk did so and took the proffered paper. He read it and looked up, his face a little puzzled, but mostly thoughtful.

"I'll pay for all this later," Harry said in a low voice.

Dirk raised his hand. "Not an issue. My pleasure." He kept his voice low. "Let me tell my parents that I'm going out for a while."

* * * * * * *

Harry watched Dirk drive away from the hospital parking lot before heading for his own truck. As he walked, Harry slipped the battery out of his own cell phone, because he knew that the cell network kept track of where he was. Otherwise how would the cell network know where to send incoming calls? Harry followed the younger man, keeping far enough away that he chanced losing the rental car among the Farmington traffic. The car was easy to keep track of, a late-model four-door Lexus. Dirk stopped at the first bank and went in. Harry stopped two blocks away and waited. He constantly twisted around, looking every direction, memorizing the cars, trying to see if anyone was following Dirk or himself.

A woman passed in a green minivan, two children in the back seat, and Harry wondered where she got two kids to provide a plausible cover. The minivan passed the bank and kept going. An older man, white muttonchops compensating for wispy hair on top, walked his two dogs along the sidewalk, approaching the bank from the opposite direction. The light changed at the intersection two blocks away and a herd of cars approached. Which ones carried surveillance?

Harry closed his eyes to calm his jittery nerves. Excessive paranoia just paralyzed you. Fifteen years ago he had been trained as a bodyguard, since it was not uncommon for Delta to provide protection for generals in war zones and foreign officials at high risk for assassination. He had even been detailed to guard the president of Afghanistan for six months. It was the most boring duty he had ever pulled, but in its own unique way, the most nerve-wracking duty he had ever pulled, as he felt constantly drained by the perpetual vigilance.

He knew that it was practically impossible to detect surveillance in an urban area if you had enough skilled teams working on the trail, switching in and out of the chase randomly, keeping the net tight through radio contact. If the bad guys were any good, he would never see them coming.

For the next hour Harry followed Dirk around town. Mulling it over, Harry realized that the enemy was probably making it up as they went along. Whoever they were, they had not yet brought enough assets to provide complete surveillance coverage.

At least he saw no hint of surveillance.

* * * * * * *

An hour later Harry was driving back towards Chaco Canyon

in Dirk's rental car, the trunk filled with the items on his list. He had left everything else behind in his truck except for his laptop, some clothes, and a paperback. His favorite old camo hat was pulled down to his ears. He was comfortable in the gritty interior of his own pickup truck; the leather seats of the Lexus, its smooth ride, and electronic dashboard felt wrong. The car also talked to him, asking him where he wanted to go so that it could display the route on the navigation screen. He didn't like cars that talked to him and felt a moment of relief and triumph when he told the car to shut up and it actually did.

He scrutinized the side of the road as the desert flashed by, looking for wires on the ground, freshly dug earth, a pile of trash, or even a bush that looked disturbed. The enemy liked to place their little devil bombs on the side of the road, just waiting for American soldiers to come by. Improvised explosive devices were often just an artillery shell with a cell phone attached to the bottom. The bad guy made a call and the bomb blew up at just the right time.

Harry slowed the car, blinking his eyes furiously, and drifted to a stop by the side of the road. There was little other traffic.

What a weird flashback. Not remembering some specific event in the past, but bringing the past to the present, melding them together. He had spent seen too many buddies die, too many mangled civilian bodies, even come too close to his own death at the hands of IEDs in too many countries in the Middle East and Central Asia. He told himself that there were no IEDs out there; no Taliban or insurgents or terrorists, or any other of his old enemies; only the New Mexico desert that he had grown to love.

As he got out of the car, he sniffed the air, smelling the desert air, the heat of the midday sun, and the faint scent of asphalt. A semi truck appeared in the distance, coming from the south. Harry watched as it grew larger, and as it passed, his eyes locked briefly with the eyes of the trucker, an older woman with a face lined with cracks of experience. The wind of the passing truck ruffled his hair and blasted his face with hot air.

The world felt real again. He turned to look out over the desert. Somewhere near here was the Great Northern Road, one of the odder constructions that the ancient Pueblo people had created. The roads stretched out from Chaco in all directions, running straight, regardless of the obstacles in way, crossing hills, and going across canyons. They weren't real roads, apparently not intended for travel, but symbolic roads with some religious significance. He smiled. Archaeologists so often resorted to religious explanations when they couldn't understand the purpose of an artifact, and people often mocked them for it, but religion was a powerful motivator and organizer of human behavior; to believe otherwise was foolishness.

The Great Northern Road ran directly north and south, some fifty miles, from Chaco Canyon up to Aztec Ruins, a Chacoan outlier community with its own great houses, including the West Ruin with four hundred rooms. Oddly enough, if one followed the north-south meridian indicated by the Great Northern Road all the way down into northern Mexico, one ran into Casas Grandes, where there were more great houses. An archeologist from Colorado argued that after the Chaco Canyon great houses succumbed to climate change, refugees had moved up to Aztec Ruins, where two rivers provided more water, and after a century there, moved down to Casas Grandes.

Grateful at how quickly he had returned to the present, Harry got back into the car, ready to take the fight to the enemy.

CHAPTER TWENTY-ONE

The mouth of the canyon was perfect for his needs. A huge gnarled oak, three feet wide at its base, grew out of the sand near the wash that ran down the center of the canyon. The tree was so old that rot had hollowed out the center, forming a small cave of wood. Branches stuck out of the top of the tree like the arms of an angry witch. Though most of the tree was quite dead, enough life flowed so that two of the branches still sprouted leaves. A third branch had a few dried leaves stubbornly clinging to it, showing that it had sustained life until last winter, but could no longer grow buds when spring came.

The Chacoan people lived in a world where water gave life and this small canyon had been used to control the water. Nature had created this canyon through occasional runoff from rain showers. A dry streambed ran down the center. Mixed in among the pebbles and stones of the streambed, rubbed shiny by sporadic floods, were sandstone slabs, now flat and worn. The slabs had once lined the banks, turning the stream into an irrigation canal.

Harry remembered the place from an archeological survey he had participated in three years earlier, walking across the land and recording any artifacts that lay on the surface. The tree had remained in his memory. He admired the majesty of a tree that had survived so long, sustained by the occasional runoff that brought not only water, but violent pressure that had toppled lesser trees.

Scouting around some more, he found a sandy bluff across

the canyon from the oak. Harry carefully examined his chosen terrain. Two large rabbit brush shrubs grew close together, with clumps of cheat grass and some sagebrush behind them. He had dug in enough places to realize that the bluff was probably not just a thin veneer of dirt on rock, but really a large pile of dirt, mostly clay and hard-packed sand.

Harry dropped the pile of gear that he had carried two miles from the parking lot for the tourists who wanted to visit Pueblo Bonito. After taking a long drink of water, he went to work with the shovel, digging a hole just behind the two rabbit brush. He carried every shovelful of dirt away from the hole, scattering it about so that he wouldn't have a mound of dirt next to his hide.

He hit hard clay a foot below the surface, which he broke up with the pick. The sun baked his back, turning his shirt soggy. He knew that he should pace himself, work slowly, conserve energy, but attacking the clay felt too damned good, a cathartic release of frustrated aggression.

After twenty minutes his left leg began to ache, where he had taken shrapnel once. The surgeon had removed the big pieces, but had left behind the tiny pieces of metal that were too small for her to find. They migrated to the surface over the next several years, expelled by his body; Harry remembered squeezing them out through his skin like wood slivers. At least those fragments had come out. The small of his back still had small gray bumps all over it, where fragments from a grenade in Afghanistan remained.

He slowed his pace and an hour later he had a hole two feet deep, seven feet long, and two feet wide—just like he had taught scouts in the Afghan army to dig in their Long-Range Reconnaissance Patrol training. After becoming proficient, the scouts made their hides and watched for Taliban infiltrators and supply trains of mules crossing the border from Pakistan. Sometimes they found something and sometimes they spent a week, crouched in an awkward position and shivering from the cold, collecting their own feces in a plastic bag. When they succeeded and radioed for American support, bombs fell from the night skies to decimate Taliban and mules. A hard business.

Harry cut the burlap bags so that they were no longer bags, but shaped like blankets, and lined the hole with the burlap. That would help keep the dirt out of his equipment. The rifle, water, and other gear went in. He walked farther up the canyon to find some large sagebrush, which he cut down and dragged back, artfully piling it over his hole. A proper hide was good enough to withstand close scrutiny, but he didn't have time to make that; this hide was good enough unless someone walked up onto the bluff and came within five or ten feet.

He paused to drink more water, grimacing at the gritty taste, then cupped some in his hand to rub over his face. It felt good, but now the dust had turned into smears of mud on his cheeks and chin.

Now for the second phase of the plan. He went down to the big oak and took a reading with his GPS, writing down the coordinates. Removing his boots and socks, he climbed up the oak from the back side, being careful to not leave any marks. He placed the baby monitor between the trunk and a branch, using duct tape to hold it down firmly. Turning the monitor on, he jumped down, put his boots and socks back on, and walked about twenty feet away. Holding the receiver to his ear, he shouted and pleased to hear his voice. Then he talked in a more normal tone and was again pleased to hear his voice coming through the baby monitor. Paranoid parents demanded good equipment.

He wished he had a parabolic microphone to pick up the conversations he expected to take place near the tree, but he had no idea where to rent or buy such specialized equipment, especially in rural New Mexico.

Harry took a branch and obscured his footprints at the rear of the tree. In front of the tree, he attacked the ground with his shovel so that it was obvious that someone had been digging there. He also stomped about, creating lots of footprints, then walked out of the canyon, leaving an obvious trail. After several hundred feet, he came across some exposed shale. The shale wouldn't leave footprints, so he used that to walk by a circuitous route back up to his hide.

There were about three hours of daylight left. Harry wondered if Brenda had improved. He wanted to call and find out, but his survival paranoia wouldn't let him. If he was right and the bad guys had sophisticated technical capabilities, then they would be able to trace his phone call. He had seen it happen before. Back in 2001, he had led a team that waited in ambush to kill a Taliban leader, located because he regularly called his wife back in Pakistan. Harry had let him finish his last call before he signaled the sniper to shoot the man with a .50 caliber bullet from six hundred meters away.

Harry distracted himself from his worries by double checking every detail of his hide, then finally admitted that he was just restless.

Time to go set the bait.

CHAPTER TWENTY-TWO

Harry had considered using a real person, sending the e-mail to someone he knew, but he suspected that whomever he chose would be drawn into the web of murder. He hoped that the very act of sending the e-mail would trigger his plan, since the enemy must be intercepting and reading it.

He sent the e-mail to the account that Dirk had set up.

Joe,

I need to tell someone in case something happens to me. Brenda Finnigan and I found a curious box in a Chacoan tomb. I have included some pictures. Because we were attacked by unknown gunmen, I decided to bury the box at the base of a tree at GPS coordinates 36° 4' 34.62" North, 107° 58' 1.22" West. Brenda is in the hospital and does not know where it is located.

Live long and prosper,
Harry

The bait had been cast out.

Sitting in the rental car in the campground, Harry continued to tap on his laptop. A search for any new information on the crimes in Chaco Canyon found a news video from an Albuquerque television station that gave the grim details on the death of the park's chief ranger. The reporter, a young fresh-faced man with an earnest expression, also interviewed the FBI agent in charge of the investigation. Harry was surprised to see that it was not Dwayne Brown. Someone new, with a handsome face that stuck in his memory.

He also looked up the weather report and found that a storm front was coming in. He looked at the predictions. Cloud cover coming in first, then a change of precipitation. Rain would ruin the show, turning his hide into a deep mud puddle, and a flash flood down the canyon would destroy his bait site.

Of course, any other time he would have loved to have rain. A desert storm turned the sky a dark grey, bringing pelting drops, floodwaters, gusts of wind, and then suddenly stopped, leaving the desert to look like it had been washed by God, raindrops glistening on leaves and grass, rocks shimmering in the sun. A person felt clean after a desert rain.

Harry copied all his e-mails, personal information, and the pictures of the tomb to his cell phone. Always a good habit to make backups.

Fortunately, there was an extra campsite. He left the car parked there, paid his fee by leaving the money in an envelope in the drop box, and set out across the desert. It was only three miles, but with no trail. He used his GPS to keep track of himself. Those twenty-four satellites had made everything so much easier—perhaps too easy. He had learned with compass and a topographical terrain map, with lines showing elevation changes. A man could not get into Delta without proving to himself and the examiners that he wouldn't get lost.

Walking across the desert in the evening coolness was much different that his first Delta qualifying run. That had been twenty miles, carrying a full kit of forty pounds, running from point to point with only a compass and a map to guide him. That spring day fifteen years ago had been misty, with occasional rain to chill him, as he gasped his way up and down the lush green hills of North Carolina. He had trained as a Ranger jumping out of planes and fast-roping down from Blackhawk helicopters, gone on numerous hikes and done calisthenics every morning, and thought that he was in top condition. That run for Delta taught him that conditioning only went so far—after that it was his mind driving forward, refusing to quit. As he pushed himself, with legs that seemed like mush and lungs that labored for more air, he kept the image of a good friend in his mind. He did not want to disappoint Master Sergeant Rodríguez.

Rodríguez was a soldier's soldier, moving with presence, always informed, not in a gossipy way, but with useful information. He could quickly strip and clean any weapon offered to him, even something obscure like a Finnish Lahti L-35. He walked with a limp that was so severe that he had to swing his entire body, like a man walking a large piece of furniture across the floor—the result of some incident that remained classified. That forced him out of Delta, but the Army, in one of its wiser moves, had not forced medical retirement on Rodríguez, but allowed him to remain in the Rangers as an armorer. He was the kind of man that every soldier who truly respected his profession wanted to be, or least see if they had the stuff inside themselves to be like him. Rodríguez had told Harry that he had the right stuff and recommended that he try out for Delta.

And he failed.

He came in two minutes late at the second-to-last waypoint, pushed himself to go faster, and still came in two minutes late at the last waypoint. The qualifying officer had shrugged and invited him to try again if he wanted. Harry tried to avoid Rodríguez when he got back to his barracks, but the sergeant was not to be denied.

"Since you didn't come find me, I assume that you didn't make it."

Harry shook his head, staring at the floor and wishing that he had never joined the Army.

"You only missed by two minutes."

Harry looked up sharply. The sergeant must have kept tabs on him through his old buddies in Delta.

"You passed everything else: all the psych exams, the interview. They were interested. They are still interested."

"I have to wait six months."

"Harry, I know that you can do it."

He joined the Special Forces instead. Two years of intense training, costing over a million dollars, left him with a passable knowledge of Arabic and considerable skills in small-unit tactics. After another three years, he considered trying for Delta again. He had thought a lot about why he wanted to be in Delta. He didn't seek glory, though living up to the master sergeant's expectations was important. In the end, he decided that his career was soldiering, and he just wanted to be the best of the best in his chosen profession. On his repeat of the qualifying run, he passed by ten seconds.

Harry slowed his pace as he reached the mouth of the canyon, making sure not to leave tracks. A jackrabbit bolted from behind some greasewood and bounded up the canyon. The Chacoans must have liked the stringy meat, because piles of jackrabbit bones had been found in their middens. Deer tasted better, but was harder to find. The Chacoans would have used a small canyon like this, spreading a net from wall to wall and driving the terrified jackrabbits down the canyon, beating the entangled animals to death with sticks or impaling them with spears. Just like the ancient Pueblo peoples, he was setting a trap in this canyon.

When he reached the hide, a glorious sunset was being painted by God. The clouds of the storm front glowed pink on the western horizon and pillars of sunlight cut through them, forming a starburst effect. He rechecked the baby monitor— still working—and canvassed the bluff one more time to see if he had left any traces, then climbed down into the hide. He arranged a gunny sack roof over himself, pulled the branches over to camouflage himself, and settled down for a long wait.

Like a monk going into cloister, upon entering a hide, a scout remained there until the mission was completed.

CHAPTER TWENTY-THREE

The first call had come a day ago, when he was relaxing on the beach outside his apartment. He loved sitting on the beach, watching the teenyboppers in their bikinis. He had known his entire life that he was not a good-looking guy, but the Army had showed him a different way to get girls. He still worked out every day to make the muscles on his torso bulge in perfect proportion. Tattoos covered his body: a dragon on his thigh, a skull and crossbones on his left bicep, an American flag on his right bicep, and an eagle across his chest, with turbaned rag-heads in its talons. The tattoos scared some of the girls, and he found a secret delight in that; besides, those skittish girls weren't the type to easily put out. He didn't want dates, with dinners and movies, he wanted them coming back to his beach bungalow and taking off those thin strips of cloth.

When his cell phone rang, he instantly picked it up, even though a bleached blonde bimbo was talking to him. Only Mom and his agent had that number. A short exchange later and he agreed to take the contract—open-ended services for forty thousand in Euros upfront, three thousand a day, and bonuses based on a sliding scale for actual deeds.

"Sorry, honey, I have to run. Be back in a week if you're still around."

He left the puzzled girl behind, grabbed his ready bag and full surveillance kit, and was at the Miami airport in an hour. A privately-charted jet was already waiting for him and he was bound for New Mexico.

The second call came in the evening, as he waited in the motel room on the road outside of the Albuquerque airport. He dropped the porn magazine on the bed and answered. The instructions were longer this time and included GPS coordinates and a map as attachments in his e-mail. Everything was encrypted, of course.

It was dark by the time that he arrived at the Chaco Canyon National Historical Park. The map on his cell phone showed him to the parking lot next to something called Pueblo del Arroyo. He didn't like leaving the car where the park rangers could find it, but he didn't have much choice. Besides, the car had been rented by a shell company that couldn't be traced back to him, and there just weren't a lot of places to leave a car, so he took the risk. He pulled a large athletic bag out of the trunk and took the trail towards the Indian ruins. When he was far enough from the road that headlights would not illuminate him he set the bag down and started to rummage through it. Five minutes later he moved out, his face blackened with camo grease, a pistol on his hip, various goodies attached to the webbing across his chest, an M4 assault rifle with a short stock hung from a strap over his shoulder, and night-vision goggles jutted out from his eyes like some alien insect. He converted the bag into a backpack as he walked.

The nighttime landscape glowed green in his eyepieces. Tapping the side of the goggles brought up GPS numbers and an overlay of the map that he had been sent.

Three miles of hiking ahead.

CHAPTER TWENTY-FOUR

One of the hazards of hides was bugs. In the desert, scorpions, tarantulas, and other spiders crawled around at night and liked the warmth of a human body. Harry really hated bugs. The feeling was completely visceral. The sight of a large spider made his skin crawl and provoked that odd feeling in the testicles that is impossible to describe unless one has felt it. In Iraq they had sand spiders as big as dinner plates. They completely freaked Harry out. He shot every one that he saw, even if his fellow soldiers laughed at him.

He didn't expect any of the bad guys to arrive until morning. The terrain was pretty rough to be walking around at night, but he planned to stay awake until at least midnight, doze for a while, and wake before dawn.

* * * * * * *

Red numbers from the GPS built into his goggles showed the mercenary that he had about arrived at his assignment. He paused, taking off the goggles to get a better feel for the land. The night-vision electronics made the world seem flat, two-dimensional, rather than the three dimensions that we all live in. There was a half moon that night, but the clouds kept it covered, making the night darker than usual. There was a canyon in front of him, maybe twenty meters away. According to his GPS, the destination was about forty meters ahead, off to the left.

The aerial photo that came with his maps showed him that

the canyon was only about thirty meters wide at that point, though he couldn't see the far side in the dark. He could see that the next five meters was clear. He put the goggles back on, blinked his eyes to readjust and slowly walked forward.

There is always a margin of error with GPS receivers, of anywhere from one meter to thirty meters—and it varied from moment to moment, depending on where the satellites were overhead. The mercenary paused, then put on gloves to protect his hands, positioned the assault rifle on his back so that it wouldn't drop down and make an unwelcome noise by clattering against a rock, and got down on his hands and knees. He crawled forward, always checking with his hands to make sure that there was ground in front of him before moving. The canyon wall made him cautious.

He stopped when his hand felt only air. The GPS showed that he still had another ten meters to go. He lay on his belly, reached as far as he could, and touched rock. Taking off the goggles, he could see rock below him. It was just a small drop-off. Goggles back on face, he crawled over, swung around, and reached down with his leg before going over the shelf like a spider. More crawling on his hands and knees, and then he saw the lip of the canyon.

Wiggling on his belly, he reached the edge and peeked over. According to the numbers, ten feet below him was the assignment. He scanned the greenish-tinged world of the canyon floor. Rocks glowed a bit more strongly as the heat from the day bled off. A few flashes of green puzzled him for a moment until he realized that they were was just small rodents dashing about. A larger green flash bounded down the center of the canyon. Rabbit. He removed the goggles and waited until his eyes adjusted. He could see a large tree just below him, on the other side of the canyon.

He settled down, rifle next to his right hand, goggles resting on his left fist, chin on the rock.

He watched.

* * * * * * *

Harry dozed, waking when his bladder told him that he had forgotten to take care of business earlier. Awkward with drowsiness, Harry's hands felt along his body and legs down to his legs to where the four jugs lay. One was half full, the others still full of water. Normally he would have an empty jug around, but he hadn't drunk that much yet.

Best to stay hydrated. He hoped to spend only a day or two in the hide, but he was prepared to spend a week, if necessary. He had done so in Afghanistan, in a hide nine thousand feet high in a pass in the Kandahar province on the Pakistan border. Actually, not a complete week, only six days and eleven hours. The target he was waiting for had taken another route and his watching had been for naught.

He sipped the rest of the water in the jug until his bladder could stand no more of this contrary behavior. The organ wanted to void, not get fuller. Shuffling around, Harry worked his trousers open and peed into the jug. It was all part of the discipline. Don't break hide discipline for anything, even calls of nature. He had some plastic baggies for when he had to defecate. Feeling much better, he screwed the lid back on the jug and placed it at his feet.

In training there were always lots of jokes about mixing up the two containers. A man just had to be careful and sniff before drinking, and hope that he wasn't too congested to tell the difference, because his taste buds certainly would.

* * * * * * *

The mercenary thought he saw something. A part of the rock that seemed brighter than it should be, maybe even moving. He watched intently, but the glow didn't move any more, so he put it down to eye fatigue or a glitch in the night-vision electronics. Such things happened when you concentrated too much.

Besides, the glow didn't look like a man at all. People showed up in the goggles really well, with their constant body temperature, though cover could distort the image or even block it.

He had been told to watch for anyone approaching the target site. So far, no one had come.

CHAPTER TWENTY-FIVE

An hour after sunrise, Harry heard a vehicle drive up. He put away the protein bar he had been nibbling on and rubbed his finger across furry teeth, trying to clean them a bit.

A door slammed, then another. Sounds carried well in the still morning air. People in the city who are used to constant background noise—which they obscure by listening to music or learning to tune out—don't realize how quiet the countryside can be. Yet even out here, civilization could intrude. A faint, far-off roaring sound came indicated a passenger jet passing overhead, seven miles up.

He heard two men approaching. He could only hear their voices, not the words, until they got closer.

"The GPS says it's twenty meters that way," the first voice said.

"Meters," the second voice scoffed. "What the hell are those? Turn it over to feet."

"You need some education, you moron," said the first voice. "A meter is about a yard."

"Moron, huh? A meter is more like forty inches, not a yard— that's thirty-six inches."

"What? Where did you go and get some learnin'?"

"Your momma."

"Your sister."

The two men came into view. They both wore suits and sunglasses, with ties in place and dress shoes completely unsuited to the terrain. Each carried a shovel, the kind with a handle half the length of a regular shovel and ending with a grip. The first man had his blonde hair shaved down to bristles, as if that would disguise his receding hairline. The second man had brown hair and broad shoulders, and a weak chin that did not match in his physique.

"There's the tree," bristle-head said.

"And look at all these footprints," weak-chin said. He stopped and carefully looked around, like a prairie dog checking to see if any predators or their shadows were about.

Harry didn't move, other than shifting his head to get a better view through the small opening above the lip of the hole and below the rabbit brush. The opening was in shadow and he was certain that no one would see him even if they looked directly at him.

Bristle-head stepped up to his tree and looked down at the GPS in his hand, holding still while the small computer used the satellite signals to refine their location down to ever smaller increments. Harry placed the earpiece in his left ear, which was more sensitive than his other ear, and turned on the baby monitor receiver.

Some static, but he could hear well enough.

"This is it," bristle-head man said. "Let's dig."

The men removed their suit jackets, showing that each carried a pistol in a belt holster. Big grip, probably a .40 caliber Glock, favored by law enforcement types all over the country. The magazine carried fifteen or seventeen rounds.

The two men attacked the ground, digging quickly, flinging the dirt aside every which way. Their lack of care offended Harry's archeological sensibilities. What if the object was really there? They could damage it with a shovel blade or even toss it aside in one of the shovelfuls of dirt.

Amazing how much dirt that two men could move in such a short time. Wet stains appeared under their armpits. They hit the clay layer about two feet down and that slowed them down, but they still pounded at it, digging deeper. Harry smiled to himself: if they stopped to think for a moment, they would realize that he hadn't buried the artifact deeper than the clay because the hard clay would have been disturbed by his digging. Furthermore, if they had been archaeologists, they would have noticed that they were digging in hard ground above the clay that had not been disturbed. The two men split up their work, one jabbing at the clay, while the other widened the hole.

The sound of two boots landing on the ground, not more than twenty feet away from his hide, startled Harry. He froze and felt warm urine, startled out of his bladder, wet his thigh.

CHAPTER TWENTY-SIX

"Yo, guys, call me John, from Miami," the new man called out. "I was told that you were expecting me."

He walked right past the hide and scrambled down to the floor of the wash. Harry fingered his AR-15, relieved that his field craft had kept him concealed, embarrassed at peeing on himself. It had happened once before, outside of Basra, when an ambush had surprised him. Taking shallow breaths to calm himself, he watched the back of the new man, taking care to observe the assault rifle slung over his back, and the night goggles sticking out of a pouch on his hip.

The men apparently were not surprised by his appearance, since they didn't reach for their sidearms. They stopped working, leaning on their shovels.

"You see anything up there?" bristle-head asked.

"Not a thing," the newcomer said.

"What time did you start your surveillance?" weak-chin asked.

"As fast as I could," John said. "About oh-one-hundred. I would have liked to come in earlier, but the plane only flies so fast."

"We have a fast-moving situation here," bristle-head said. "We are playing catch-up and having to cut corners."

"Ready to do some digging, John from Miami?" weak-chin asked, offering his shovel.

John laughed. "Not in my contract. I'm a watcher, not a bull-dozer." The man sat down on a nearby rock, setting down his pack and peeling off his webbing and jacket. Tattoos covered his arms and shoulders. He pulled out an energy bar and munched on it while the other two went back to their digging.

Harry fingered his rifle, examining the plans emerging in his mind from every angle, like a man looking at an auto part, and then rejecting them. Having soggy pants didn't help his concentration. These three men were not talkative enough and Harry was not getting the insights he needed. He considered launching an ambush by getting the drop on them with his AR-15, forcing them to disarm, and interrogating them for information. That idea had been quite reasonable when there were two of them. Now the third man, with his assault rifle leaning against the rock next to him, made an ambush much more risky.

The only choice was to shoot the third man, taking him out of the situation, and then getting the drop on the other two men. Harry ran the scenario through his mind: the moment of mental preparation, stepping from the hide, the sticks and brush and dust cascading down his back, aiming at the third man. Two shots to the chest, another to the head. Turning to cover the other two, swearing at them and telling them that the first to move would die. Quick check with the eyes to see if the third man was really down. Back to the first two. Hands to the back of their heads. No, even better, hands in the air still holding the shovels. Harry was too far away to be threatened by the shovels; they couldn't move quickly without discarding the shovel, which took too much time. Then instructing them, one at a time, to remove their sidearms, keeping them in the holster, and throwing them far away. Final move was to have both men strip naked, making them psychologically vulnerable to the interrogation to follow. It would get ugly if they didn't cooperate.

As a plan, it seemed to be workable, but Harry just couldn't bring himself to effectively execute another man before finding out if that man deserved to die. John from Miami had just flown in, so he hadn't been around to have killed the park ranger. Maybe he had been in Scotland and had killed Dr. Bancroft and the students? A possibility, though no evidence of that. John was obviously ex-military, perhaps a private contractor brought in to only do surveillance.

Then he must have been up on the bluff overhead, watching for most of the night. Harry had been lucky to not be detected. Wait, he didn't believe in luck. Life was full of random chances, and a man who prepared himself, was cautious, and ready to take advantage of opportunities, was considered lucky. The only thing that had saved Harry was maintaining hide discipline even when he thought no one was around.

The hole grew bigger, almost ten feet across, exposing more of the clay surface. Bristle-head must have realized that the clay meant something, so he stopped digging deeper and joined his partner in making the hole bigger.

The sound of another vehicle driving up. More doors slamming. The third man picked up his rifle and stood on the rock, looking to the mouth of the gully. Satisfied with what he saw, he sat back down, holding the rifle across his knees.

Two more men appeared, wearing suits. Harry recognized one as the handsome FBI special agent on television. Harry cursed silently. This was all much worse than he had suspected, an awful conspiracy that involved at least one government employee. The other man also looked like a government employee—clean shaven, with trimmed hair and sunglasses.

"What've you found?" the FBI agent asked.

"Nothing," bristle-head reported. "There were footprints and the ground was all torn up, but we haven't found anything."

"Keep digging."

"What if Deacon came and dug it up already and took it somewhere else?" weak-chin asked.

The handsome agent spat out the words. "If you hadn't lost track of him, we would know if that had happened, wouldn't we?"

"At least we still have close surveillance on the girl," blonde man said. "She may lead to something."

"I think that she's a dead end," the agent said. "She certainly doesn't know where the box is. The fact that Deacon has gone to ground means that he suspects something."

Harry smiled to himself; he had truly gone to ground.

"Can we use metal detectors or something?" blonde man asked. "Just digging doesn't make a lot of sense."

"The box is not metal and won't show up on anything like that."

The digging continued as the agent turned to the third man. "You're John from Miami?"

The man with the assault rifle nodded.

"We may require your services further," the agent said. "Standard contract rates?"

"Sounds good to me."

Like the proverbial fly on the wall, Harry listened intently, picking up words from the baby monitor and with his other ear when one of the five men spoke loudly enough. So it was all about the artifact. It was satisfying that his instincts had proved correct, but as the men continued to make small talk, they didn't say anything that even hinted at why the artifact was valuable or how they had known about it. Harry was certain that nothing like it had been found at any digs in North America. Being one of a kind made it valuable as an art object, but not something that someone would kill over.

The hole grew larger. The FBI agent and the man that had come with him removed their jackets, showing that they also carried handguns, and took over the shovels. This surprised Harry; he expected the head honcho to not get his hands dirty. The agent proved to be quite the gopher, slinging dirt as fast as he could and not stopping for a rest. Not only was the man blessed with good looks, he had the stamina of a hardy peasant. The other man couldn't keep up and handed his shovel off to John from Miami. Apparently his standard contract rates now included digging.

The digging men reached where they had been flinging the dirt, forcing them to do twice the work to get any further. The day grew hot and plastic bottles of water were brought from their cars. Harry wanted to see what they were driving, expecting to see government license plates, but the angle was wrong from his hide. Harry took a sip himself, making sure to sniff beforehand.

By lunchtime, the bottom of the wash had been excavated, all the way from side to side. The men had found only clay.

"To hell with this," the FBI agent said. "We aren't going to find anything."

"What now?" bristle-head asked.

"We regroup. John, you come with me."

Harry reached for his assault rifle. Now was the time to act, before the man from Miami got to his weapon. The other men were standing around, widely spaced, not in a clump like he would have liked.

The whole tactical setup felt wrong; Harry forced himself to calm down and wait. An attack now would force him to kill at least two or three in order to bring the total number of men down to a manageable group. They were so far apart that even with some accurate shooting, Harry might easily find himself receiving return fire. And, in the end, he had to admit to himself that it had been five years since he had fired an AR-15 and this copy was not a weapon that he had become intimate with, firing thousands of rounds from it, stripping it down, cleaning it, putting it back together, and learning its quirks.

John from Miami reached his pile of stuff and picked up his pack, his webbing, and his weapon. Too late now.

Harry watched the five men walk away, frustrated that his plan had worked exactly as he intended, and he now knew how important the artifact was, but he didn't know any of the details.

Two cars growled to life. Harry considered leaving his hide to see what they were driving, but the lesson taught him by John of Miami still applied. Hide discipline above all else.

He heard them drive away.

Harry removed the earplug from his ear, sipped some water and chewed on an energy bar, and settled down to consider what to do. He needed to track the FBI agent down and get more information out of him. When should he leave the hide? If Harry had been the agent, he would have left John of Miami behind to maintain surveillance on this site, but the agent had told John to go with him in the car. Maybe it was a trick to draw Harry out of his hide. That didn't make sense; if they had suspected that Harry was nearby they would have beaten the bushes to flush him out. Still, keeping the site under surveillance seemed to be a good idea. But the artifact obviously wasn't here, so wouldn't keeping watch here be a waste of resources?

His thoughts ran in circles, going over the same ground again and again.

Eventually he decided that there was no way to draw any firm conclusions. The only question that really mattered was when should he break cover and return to the rental car. It made sense to leave now if he wasn't under surveillance. He could wait and move under cover of darkness, but nowadays darkness was more of an enemy than an ally. He remembered the night goggles that John of Miami had.

Just sitting there kept him from being in a position to protect Brenda, but dying prematurely would do her no good, either.

CHAPTER TWENTY-SEVEN

Her body was her tool.

The green hospital scrubs, rented from a costume shop, did not flatter her figure. Amanda tugged at the top of the blouse, frustrated that she could not show more of her breasts. She knew that her looks and a touch of cleavage addled the brains of most men; even women were nonplussed in her presence. By attracting attention to her physical attributes, she made it easy for people to underestimate her and be too distracted to notice what she might be doing. The bellhop at the hotel when she checked in last night couldn't keep his eyes off her—she had pretended not to notice.

Amanda had arrived in Farmington late yesterday afternoon, after driving up from the Albuquerque airport. A bottle of whiskey from a liquor store on the highway had provided the necessary boost to her energy level to keep her alert and help shrug off the jet lag. She scouted out the city, imprinting the layout of the streets in her mind, where the hospital, police station, and other important locations were.

That morning Franklin had sent her an update on the local situation. Two days ago, an archeological dig had been attacked, and a victim by the name of Brenda Finnigan, twenty-one years old, had been severely wounded and hospitalized. More information followed on the male archaeologist who had defended her. All the information had come from open news sources, not from other sources that Franklin cultivated and kept only to himself for reasons of operational security.

Franklin had also shipped a large box to her overnight, which had been waiting for her at the airport. She viewed those tools with distaste: a pistol, a sniper's rifle, and a variety of field gear.

Satisfied with her disguise, she left the hotel room and went down to her rented Jeep Wrangler. The rifle and other gear were in the back seat, underneath a blanket. She checked the magazine of the pistol, a small .38 caliber semi-automatic, just the right size for her smaller hand, then slid it under the front seat. Fortunately, she hadn't had to shoot anyone for many years, and she wanted to keep it that way.

A five-minute drive brought her to the hospital. The only problem with her disguise was the lack of a hospital ID, but she was not going to be there long, and if she acted like she belonged there she didn't expect to be challenged. She also had three different excuses ready in case someone asked her where her ID was. The rest of her disguise was a clipboard with a piece of paper on it. The scribbling on the paper was illegible, except for the name: Brenda Finnigan. She hoped it looked liked doctor's orders.

Through the front door, to the stairs, then she quickly made her way to the fourth floor. She paused outside the grey metal door and removed a mouth swab from her side pocket. Removing the plastic cover, she swirled it around in her own mouth, drowning it in her saliva. Pursing her lips to clean it, to make sure that it was not too soggy, she slid the plastic cover back over the swab and put it back in her pocket.

She opened the door and walked down the hall, not looking at anyone deliberately, but noticing out of the corner of her eyes that there were two orderlies on the floor moving a patient in a gurney. A nurse sat at the nurse's station, where a male doctor was talking to her. He looked up as Amanda passed and she felt his eyes dragged along with her as she went to the room at the end of the hall.

* * * * * * *

Dirk Finnigan sat across the room from his sister, reading a paperback mystery that he had purchased in the hospital gift shop. So far, so good—three murders, a femme fatale, a detective tenacious as a bloodhound, and five million dollars in missing diamonds. He looked up as a woman in scrubs entered the room.

He felt his jaw drop open. The blonde woman moved with such grace. Dirk knew many beautiful women—one of the reasons that he had chosen to pursue a career on Wall Street—and considered himself to be a connoisseur of their physical form. He had read enough psychology to know that symmetry was a sign of health, of genetic fitness, and the key to great beauty. Most women had faces or figures that were slightly off. This woman was perfect, everything matched.

"Hello. Is this the room of Brenda Finnigan?" she asked. Dirk was a little disappointed that her voice was not more enchanting, like a song of perfect tone.

Liz Finnigan put down the magazine she was reading. "Yes, this is it. That's her."

"I'm from the medical lab and I need to take a swab of her mouth. You know, to run tests and make sure that the antibiotics are working correctly."

"Okay."

"I need to see her wrist band and make sure that she really is Brenda."

The woman picked up his sister's hand and scrutinized the blue wristband with her name and medical identification imprinted on it. She looked at her clipboard.

"It matches. I'm going to swab her mouth for a sample. It doesn't hurt."

Dirk barely noticed as she took the swab out of her side pocket, removed the plastic cover, inserted into his sister's mouth, and rubbed against the inside of Brenda's cheek. The she replaced the cover and stowed it back into her pocket.

"That's all. I hope she gets better soon."

"Thanks," his mother said.

The blonde woman left the room, the door closing behind her, cutting off her presence, and he blinked as if surprised.

"You're going to catch a bug if you don't close your mouth," Liz Finnigan told her son.

CHAPTER TWENTY-EIGHT

Sometimes a woman gets a job that exactly fits her temperament. Stephanie lived in the cage sixteen hours a day, inside walls impervious to electromagnetic signals, protecting the information that came from America's eyes in the sky to the National Reconnaissance Office. No spy, no matter what his equipment, was going to watch what she did in that room. Computer screens surrounded her, as did the soft hum of computer fans. She kept the lights down low and most of the room was in shadows.

Her skin was pasty from a lack of vitamin D, her hair cut short so that she didn't have to maintain it, and she wore sweats and a t-shirt, though the military people wore their uniforms and the civilians wore at least business casual. She had a small apartment in the building—just a bed, closet-sized bathroom with a shower, and a hot plate. No one else had their own quarters. She cleaned it herself and no one bothered her.

The shrinks called it autism or Asperger's syndrome. Stephanie just thought of it as the ability to concentrate, though she did admit that other people and their noises, their coughs, farts, music, and chatter, annoyed her, sometimes so much that she just had to scream.

A yellow light flashed, demanding her attention. Someone wanted to come into the cage. Stephanie flipped the switch.

A man wearing a dark suit entered. A faint scent of aftershave came with him, and that irritated her. Why couldn't people just wash themselves and leave it at that? Why did they insist on adding smells to their bodies? No one in the department wore colognes or perfumes. She had made sure of that by throwing a fit.

He handed her a piece of paper. "This authorizes me to request the services of the NORAM-SAT."

Stephanie looked at the paper and saw that it was signed by the Secretary of Defense. She fed the paper into a scanner to pick up the watermark and a long sequence of letters and numbers across the bottom of the paper. They seemed random but were really a digital signature. A message automatically went out over the National Security Secure Network, and the authorization server at the SecDef's office looked at the words on the letter, the watermark, and the digital signature. A message popped up on her screen verifying that the contents of the letter had not been altered and that everything was authentic.

"What can I do for you, Mr....uh, I don't know your name."

"You will call me Mr. X." He sat down and opened a brief-case. "Please reorient NORAM-SAT to survey these coordinates. All sensors."

Stephanie turned to her keyboard. NORAM-SAT was really six satellites in polar orbit, positioned to pass over North America in sequence, only two hundred miles up, so that at least one satellite was always over the continent, its cameras pointed down, always watching. Right now the satellite was running broad sweeps, alert for incoming aircraft or missiles. There were hundreds of such contacts, all of which were checked with air traffic control computers. Those that didn't match were automatically forwarded to NORAD under Cheyenne Mountain. Most of them were just drug smugglers or pilots who had failed to file a flight plan, but someday one might be a terrorist.

She checked the coordinates as she entered them. "You want to look at New Mexico? Chaco Canyon? Why?"

"You don't need to know why, just do your job."

Stephanie decided that she hated Mr. X, a feeling so visceral that it caused her guts to churn. Her fingers slipped into a drawer to find an antacid tablet. She hated everyone who refused to answer her questions. She had the highest of security clearances and there was no reason to keep any secrets from her.

The string of six satellites turned their cameras, focusing their attention on one small spot of desert.

CHAPTER TWENTY-NINE

After a nap in the shade of his hide, Harry decided to break cover at five in the afternoon. Staying there served no purpose. He burst from the hide and ran to some cover near the canyon wall. Crouching to make himself a smaller target, he scanned the opposite wall of the canyon over the sights of his assault rifle. So far, so good. No incoming fire.

He suddenly realized why there would be no incoming fire. The bad guys wanted to capture him, in order to find the artifact. He was useless to them dead, at least until he led them to the artifact. Then he would certainly end up dead. Everyone who had anything to do with the artifact, even if they lacked direct knowledge, had been murdered. That meant that Brenda was still in danger.

Harry walked back to his hide, filled his pack and left the rest. It felt wrong to leave a mess behind—a hole with gunny sacks, plastic bottles, and protein bar wrappers in it, and the baby monitor still in the tree. The ethic of leaving nothing behind, no littering, as little impact on the land as possible was ingrained deeply into him. No time to tidy up.

He climbed out of the canyon, keeping out a wary eye. A short walk brought him to where the canyon overlooked his hide and the old oak tree and the ridiculous wide hole that the bad guys had dug. He found where John from Miami had lain on the ground, leaving crushed grass, pebbles disturbed, with crusted dirt crumbled into fragments. The mercenary had left no litter.

Harry saw that John had chosen a spot directly above his

hide. Nervousness turned to pride at how well his hide had worked. Still, he had been damned lucky.

The dust and sweat caked on his skin chafed against his clothes like used sandpaper as he walked back towards his car. Evening was coming, with the heat of the day radiating from the rocks and sand. High clouds of streaked grey, the remains of the storm that had threatened but not delivered, muted the shadows formed by the western sun. Where others saw a desolate waste-land, Harry saw solitude and quiet.

Just before the slope down to the campground, he came to a small bluff with several large rocks below it. Harry worked his way around the sandstone boulders, weathered by millennia of wind and rain and snow since they had broken away from the bluff.

The handsome FBI special agent stood before him, Glock in his hand, sunglasses turning his eyes into mirrored voids. Harry stopped, his heart pounding faster, ready to move as soon as his startled brain figured out what to do. Three other men also stood there, two on the left side of their leader, the other on the right side, guns pointed at the archeologist.

"Good evening, Dr. Deacon," the FBI agent said. "Place your rifle on the ground very gently. No sudden moves."

Harry moved slowly, slipping both his rifle and small back-pack to the ground. His eyes methodically moved back and forth, sucking in information. John from Miami was there was the guy on the right of the special agent. One of the other men was the same man that had arrived with the agent that morning. Harry noticed with a wry sense of amusement that the new man, the second man to the left of the agent, wore silver earrings in both ears, just like a pirate.

Having a droll sense of humor when facing death helped make the fear a tool, not a quick ticket into panic. That's what the best of his trainers had taught him, though he was too keyed up for the memory to be any more than a passing thought, a ghost among a herd of stampeding thoughts.

Details. John from Miami had his assault rifle with him,

finger indexing alongside the trigger guard, not on the trigger. Proper military procedure, though a bit odd if they wanted to cut him down. The other men all had handguns, and the only one with his finger on the trigger was the main FBI man. Everyone else was practicing proper safety. They wanted him alive.

The soldier-turned-archeologist had only his Beretta on his hip.

Of course, the FBI agent had noticed this, part of the procedure of methodically dressing down a prisoner. "Now take out your pistol and put in on the ground. Move very slowly or I will have to ventilate you."

Harry reached for the handgun. It was his favorite weapon, an extension of his hand. He had practiced with it for endless hours during Delta hostage rescue training, learning to burst into a room after throwing a flash-bang grenade and quickly dispatching terrorists with measured shots. Delta believed in realistic training, always using real bullets and even real people as hostages.

The FBI agent's chest spouted blood as his eyes widened in surprise. His hand went limp and the Glock tumbled to the ground.

Harry was moving even as the echo of the rifle shot rolled across the desert like a clap of thunder. He dropped to his knee, in Delta mode, flashing back to training. He made the decision and released his body to rely on muscle memory, ingrained so deep that his actions required no conscious thought.

He drew his Beretta, his thumb sliding off the safety as his arm came up. At the same time he stepped to the side and lowered himself into a crouch to make himself a small target. Both hands on the pistol, he aimed not so much with his eye as with muscle memory honed by firing the Beretta thousands of times in quick-moving simulations.

Because of the assault rifle, John from Miami got it first. Two rounds into the center mass of his body. No need for head shots since no one was wearing body armor. Sweep left, two more rounds in the man with earrings. Sweep right. This man had started to move, leaping to his left, finger on trigger, squeezing it.

Harry heard the bullet pass by him, a snapping sound that sounded familiar. He squeezed the trigger of his Beretta four times in rapid succession.

The man tumbled to the ground.

Harry tracked his pistol across the prone bodies, checking for any movement. John from Miami twitched, as if the life flowing out of him into a pool of blood around his chest needed to make one last effort. Harry looked around. Where had the rifle shot come from? From the small entry hole on the back of the facedown FBI agent, the shot must have come from in front of Harry. There were no bushes of sufficient size nearby, but a small rise in the land about a quarter of a mile away provided the right vantage point. He saw no movement there; he had no idea who the sniper might be, but obviously if he had wanted the archaeologist dead, the deed would have been done by now.

Returning his Beretta to its holster, Harry started with the FBI agent, checking for breathing while going through the pockets of his jacket, shirt, and pants. The man still lived, shallow breaths struggling get enough oxygen. He found the man's cell phone, turned it on, and found that it was encrypted. Not much of a surprise. It would take the skills of the NSA to break through that barrier. Even so, Harry put the cell phone in his pocket. The wallet revealed what he expected. One side of the inside was completely occupied by an ID card, with a picture of the handsome man, not smiling, looking directly into the camera. The soon-to-be-deceased Marshall Stone really was a special agent of the FBI. The wallet also held credit cards and over two hundred dollars in cash.

Oddly enough, Harry also found a silver flask in the inside of the suit jacket. Who would wear a suit jacket in this heat? Harry twisted open the cask and sniffed. Tears of yearning came to his eyes at the smell of whiskey.

John from Miami had a Georgia driver's license in the name of John Darby. Probably an alias, though the US Army Reserve

ID card in the same name, made Harry wonder. The pockets of the other two men had FBI IDs inside.

Maybe all the ID cards were just fakes, even the FBI ones. No, that made no sense. He had seen the FBI agent on TV. It would take *cojones* of steel and the brain of a marshmallow to impersonate a federal agent on a live broadcast. At the very least another agent would see the broadcast and realize that no agent by that name existed. The man must be genuine, even though his henchmen might be fake.

Only the handsome FBI agent was still alive. He was not bleeding as much as Harry would have expected; any vital internals like the liver or an artery must have been missed. Harry knew that he should call for help. Part of him wanted the bastard to just lie there and die, but another part wanted the man to live so that he could interrogate him. Of course, with three dead men and one barely alive man, Harry was not going to be interrogating anyone; he was going to be answering questions that he had no answers to.

In fact, from any perspective that came to mind, he was screwed.

"Hi there."

Harry jerked his head up, going for his Beretta, stumbling as he came up to his feet. The pistol was in his hands, wrists locked, pointed at the newcomer.

"Please, I'm no threat to you."

A tall woman with long blonde hair stood before him, a sniper rifle with a scope cradled in her arms. She wore hiking boots, khaki pants, and one of those camouflage shirts that had become fashionable. He didn't recognize the model of the rifle, but the stock looked Russian. She looked like she had walked out of a Hollywood action movie, all beauty and guns, but she was the real thing. Oddly enough, her perfect symmetry reminded him of the FBI agent that she had shot who now lay at their feet. By any measure, she was a striking woman, with high cheekbones and the body of an athlete, having slim hips and firm breasts.

Harry lowered his pistol and put it back in his holster. That was hard, an act of faith, since he felt more in control with the pistol in his hands. "I assume that you are to thank for my rescue?"

"I am."

He noticed that she seemed to be avoiding looking at the bodies.

"Who are you?"

"A friend," she said with a smile.

"Most friends don't carry sniper rifles."

"But they come in handy sometimes," she said. "Like this time."

"You have a name?" Harry asked.

"Call me Amanda." She offered her hand.

Harry stepped forward, looked at his hand and saw that he had some blood on it from going through the clothes of the bad guys. He wiped his palm across his pants leg and took her hand. She didn't flinch.

In spite of his suspicions, he decided to trust her.

"We need to get moving," she said. "My car is about a mile away."

CHAPTER THIRTY

Stephanie stared at the computer monitor. Clouds from an incoming storm front over New Mexico ruled out using the visible light camera on the NORAM-SATs, so she had switched to infrared. The humans walking about showed up as splotches of red. Cars were also red, with the engine showing up as a bright spot. At first there was nothing at the site. Then a car drove up and two people got out, walked about two hundred meters, then stayed near the same spot for an hour or so. Near them was another hot spot—perhaps a person, but it seemed a bit cooler. and never moved. Perhaps it was a small pool of sun-warmed water. Occasionally the image flickered as one of the satellites automatically handed over surveillance to the next satellite as they orbited the Earth every ninety minutes. Then two more people arrived in another car. The other spot also started to move, making a total of five people. Everyone milled around for hours, then went back to their cars.

The stranger with the authorization papers kept hovering over her shoulder, leaving the room, then coming back to hover some more. She noticed the cell phone in his hand and assumed that he was calling someone. He couldn't make calls from inside the cage.

This is too boring, she said to herself. She distracted herself by thinking about the program that she needed to write by next week and made notes of the necessary database calls and matrix transforms that she wanted to devise. She really wanted to work on the program, but she had to take care of this first. To her surprise, after the five people had left, another spot grew hotter and a person emerged. She was suddenly intrigued. He had been hiding. She assumed that it was a man, since she just couldn't imagine the stranger with the authorization papers wanting to watch some women go out into the desert for a chat.

"Follow that target," he ordered.

She sent commands to the satellites and they watched the man walk east. This seemed to really animate the stranger, who rushed out and was gone for five minutes before he returned. He hovered even closer and she could feel his creepy breath against her hair. She wanted to say something to him, but he intimidated her too much.

After about thirty minutes, the walking person came upon four other people. They stood around. Another person showed up, there was some milling about, and then the new person and the original person walked off, leaving the group of four behind.

The stranger raced off again.

As the minutes went by, the stranger did not return, and Stephanie noticed that three of the remaining people were growing fainter. What could be causing that?

Then the answer struck her. Their body temperatures were falling because they were dead.

CHAPTER THIRTY-ONE

"We need to move faster," she said, picking up her pace, slinging the rifle over her shoulder in a nonchalant way. "We are under surveillance."

"What? How?" Harry asked.

She pointed up.

Harry scanned the sky. The clouds were still there, threatening moisture but not delivering. No aircraft were visible, though a small unmanned aerial vehicle would be next to impossible to see. Back in his earlier career, he had often used an UAV that measured only eleven inches across, though it couldn't handle any sort of winds aloft. That the clouds were moving showed that there were winds up there even if the ground air was still. That left only one answer.

"Satellite?"

"Yes."

"Are you sure?" Harry asked.

"Mostly sure."

"That means that we are running from the United States government?"

She looked over at him. "Only certain elements of the government. I'm a government agent who's trying to ferret them out, expose them for prosecution."

"Shouldn't you have tried to arrest those men back there?"

"In the normal course of events, that's what I would have done," she said. "But they were about to kill you."

"They wouldn't have killed me," he said. After the words left his mouth, he desperately wanted to get them back. How could he be so loose with his secrets?

"What do you mean, they wouldn't have killed you?" she asked sharply, leaping at the opportunity that he had opened. "They have been killing everyone else with carefree abandon."

Before he could stop the words, they spilled straight from his brain and out his mouth, as if his editing function had been turned off. "I have something that they want and only I know where it is. They need me alive." He sought for some way to stop her from asking the next obvious question. "If you were trying to save me, why did you only shoot one of them?"

"I figured that you needed to do some of the work yourself," she said, smiling at him.

He stared back at her, then stumbled over a rock. He quickly righted himself. They were almost running across the desert, skirting bushes and clumps of rock as she led him north, away from Chaco Canyon.

"Seriously," she said. "I would have fired on the others, but you had them down so quickly that I didn't need to. I got the most dangerous of them."

"Are you sure there are others?" Harry asked. He already knew that there must be at least two more—the other two who had originally come to his trap.

"I have positively identified four others, and a probable fifth," she said. "There are more that they can call on."

"What resources do they have?"

"The conspiracy can draw upon almost any of the resources of the US government."

"Then what can we do?"

"We must get away and get to my people," she said. "Hiding is the best option right now."

"What about Brenda?" he asked. Amanda kept up such a quick pace that his breath came in ragged bursts, encouraging him to speak in short sentences. She didn't seem winded at all by her pace.

"The girl in the hospital?" she asked.

"Yes. She is my friend and I will do anything to protect her," Harry said. "I can't just leave her in danger."

"I think that she's in more danger if you are near her than if you are far away," Amanda said. "After all, you say that you are the only one that the Cabal wants."

"The Cabal?"

"What we call them, the bad guys, the ones that killed your friends."

"Were those guys we killed really FBI agents?"

"Probably."

Her answer sent a jolt of sober reality through him. "The government is not going to forgive the killing of federal agents."

She looked at him. "You're right, so we had better not catch the blame."

"How are we going to do that?"

"We really don't have to do anything. The Cabal doesn't want to draw attention to itself, so they will obstruct and confuse the investigation, and make sure that it doesn't go anywhere that they don't want it to go."

"They have that much power?"

"They do. You have stumbled onto something that is so big and powerful that you are only a bug on a windshield. Their windshield, that is."

"Which agency do you work for?" Harry asked.

"I know that it sounds like a bad movie or something from *The X-Files*, but my agency is not one you would recognize."

"I worked with black ops for years," Harry said. "Perhaps I've heard of you, or at least rumors."

"We don't have a real name; our people are spread among legitimate agencies. For instance, I have an ID card that says that I'm with the National Weather Service."

Harry worked over all this information in his mind. Hard to swallow stuff. "How did you come to be out here with a sniper rifle?"

"We have been monitoring their comms—not all of them, but enough to figure out what's happening. That's how we learned about you, and then we found that they had a satellite available. Just a couple of hours ago we discovered that they were laying an ambush for you, so I hurried to get here. Just in time, too."

"Thanks for that."

Amanda had left her car on a dirt road, one of the many that crisscrossed the BLM land north of the national historical park. Other than a layer of dust covering its blue paint, the Jeep Wrangler looked new. Probably a rental.

Her rifle went onto the back seat. Harry added his backpack and his own rifle. "What about my car?" he asked.

"Where is it?"

"Parked in the campground."

"We can't go back into the park. There's only one main road out of there and a few smaller roads. We'll just have to leave it."

"It's a rental. I'm sure that it'll be impounded and towed," Harry said. "Will that be a problem?"

"Anything in there that you don't want to lose?"

"My laptop. My life is on it," he said. "But I can't think of anything that I can't replace."

"You got your data?"

"Copied over to my cell phone."

"Smart."

A large cloud of dust trailed behind them as Amanda drove too fast for the road, as if a banshee from hell was nipping at their rear bumper. Harry didn't dare engage her in conversation, since he wanted all her attention concentrated on her aggressive driving. They passed a few Navaho homesteads, some with a house, others only a trailer, but all of them with a traditional round-shaped hogan and a sweat lodge, which looked like a stack of logs stacked vertically.

The sky grew dark as the storm finally gathered its resources and started to spot the windshield with drops. Harry would have turned on the headlights, but Amanda did not do so. He hunkered down in his seat, checking that his seatbelt was secured.

"Where are we going?" Harry asked.

"North."

CHAPTER THIRTY-TWO

Dusk found them in the Colorado Rockies, driving in and out of shadows cast by the mountains. They stopped at the Green Motel, where the steep mountains parted to allow enough space for the buildings. Harry took off his pistol holster and pushed the pistol into his pants, behind his belt, just to the right of his zipper. With his shirt out, the bulge of the weapon disappeared. Amanda reached into the back seat and retrieved a large leather purse, with swirls and leaping deer imprinted on the surface. Harry could not imagine her as the kind of woman who carried a purse, but as they left the Jeep behind, he saw that the purse fit her shoulder as if it belonged there.

The man at the desk had dreadlocks down to his shoulders, framing a face grown rugged from years spent in the sun, and earrings in each ear. His faded t-shirt proclaimed "Save the Whales and the other Wee Fish." Amanda asked for a room with two beds. When she found that the motel had individual cabins out back, she changed her request and got a pair of keys.

The motel also sold t-shirts. Harry bought a green one with "Rocky Mountain High" emblazoned across a background of white peaks. He briefly wondered if the John Denver estate got a cut from the sale.

Amanda drove around the main building to the cabins while Harry walked around the building. Evergreen trees came all the way down the mountain to the fifteen cabins, clustering up next to them like an enthusiastic mob of townspeople eager to overwhelm intruders. Most of the other cabins already had cars packed in front of them, with license plates from all over the country, and two from Canada as well.

The cabin contained two beds, their frames made of carved wood with hand-carved eagles perched on top of the bedposts. A large flat-screen TV on the log wall was attached to a surround-sound system with disc player. In back was a door to a spacious bathroom.

"Curious combination of rustic and modern," Amanda said, putting her suitcase on the floor of polished planks.

"No wonder the cabin cost so much," Harry said, setting down his own backpack. He pulled the bedspread off one of the beds and went back out to the Jeep to wrap up the rifles and carry them in.

Oddly enough, the cabin required that a large rectangular metal key attached to the smaller room key be placed in a wall slot next to the front door in order to activate the room's electricity. Harry had seen such arrangements overseas, but never in the United States. Electricity was normally too cheap here to worry about such strict conservation measures.

"I get the shower first," he declared.

"That's fine," she said, pulling out her cell phone. "I've got to check in."

The bathroom had a separate shower from the tub, a luxury usually reserved for more upscale lodgings. Baths held no attraction for him, like sitting in a puddle, and moments later he was in the shower, enjoying the feeling of water wetting his skin. He scrubbed the soap into his hands and under his fingernails, trying to get the dried blood out of his pores. The idea of having the remains someone else's living fluids on him seemed obscene. The blood of a friend was only sad; the blood of an enemy was disgusting.

Even after he was clean, he stayed in the shower. Having warm water running over his skin normally soothed him as effectively as a deep massage from expert hands, calming his emotions, clearing his mind, releasing his creative juices. It wasn't working this time. He was used to finding women attractive, but the woman in the next room created an ache in his heart that made it hard for him to act normal around her. It was rare for him to be drawn to a woman so instantly, a connection much deeper than physical attraction. The last time it had happened, he had married her. It took a long time and many mistakes to erode that feeling and finally vanquish it.

He finally turned off the water and dressed. He had a change of underwear in his backpack and the new t-shirt was clean, even it had a stale factory smell; he had only his old pants to wear, filthy and reeking of urine when he put his nose too close. He would wash them in the sink before going to bed and let them dry overnight.

Amanda sat on the edge of the bed nearest the front door, flipping through the channels on the television. She looked so relaxed and confident. "There's no news about Chaco Canyon," she said.

"Did you expect any?"

"No," she said. "Only if someone else stumbled onto the bodies first and alerted authorities, and the press got wind of it. I suspect that the Cabal has already cleaned up everything and is hunting us."

"Are we safe here?" he asked.

"I think so. We could keep running, but I am arranging for us to be met, so we have to wait awhile. We probably won't spend the whole night here." She turned off the television and stood. "My turn in the shower."

"I'm going for a walk." He certainly wasn't going to stay around while she got naked in the other room.

"Don't forget your gun."

"Never."

CHAPTER THIRTY-THREE

The sun had disappeared behind the mountains that stretched steep into the sky across the road from the motel. The evening twilight that remained was still good enough for Harry to find a well-worn dirt trail behind the cabins that led further up the draw. He followed the trail far enough up among the trees that he could no longer see the cabins. The smell of evergreens filled the air. He stopped near a rockslide and sat down on a convenient rock.

He watched the twilight fade and a single star appear. Venus? No, the evening star was blocked by the mountains. It was a strong star though—maybe even a planet, like Jupiter or Saturn. More stars appeared. As a child he had enjoyed sleeping outside during the summers, looking up at the stars, even though they were a pale imitation of what he saw now. Light pollution from his neighborhood had drowned out so much.

Having watched enough documentaries on television and at school, he knew that there were other planets circling those stars. Astronomers had started to find them in the mid-1990s. No real details or pictures, but enough to show that perhaps humans weren't unique in the universe. Such ideas found expression in his fondness for science fiction: tales of other worlds, aliens, time travel, and the other familiar tropes.

A satellite moved across his vision. Was it watching him? He felt the urge to hide, but told himself that he would only be an infrared blob, not someone identifiable as Harry Deacon.

The clarity of thinking that had animated him before the

ambush today was gone, replaced by thoughts that came and went with bewildering frequency. He couldn't grab hold of a notion long enough to thoroughly examine it before some new idea intruded in its place. Most of the ideas were just useless, like whether the Canadian rock group Rush was going to release a new album. He had all their previous music. What made the artifact so important?

Was this how a person with attention deficit disorder thought? Now that was an interesting notion. So many ideas were coming at him that he found it difficult to concentrate. Like a man walking through a garden of flowers, finding each new one entrancing, but never lingering long because there was always a new flower to catch his interest.

He was used to being in charge of his own life, making the decisions that mattered, but now he had placed his life in the hands of Amanda. He didn't even know her last name. Was Amanda her real name? She had plans for him that remained vague, yet he trusted her. Why?

Pressing the small light on his watch showed that it had been forty minutes since he left her. Long enough for her to shower and get dressed. He followed the trail back, not able to see the ground, even though his eyes had adjusted to the night, feeling his way by the way that his boots found the trough of the trail. When he strayed his boots brushed against grass.

His mind still raced, though one thought surfaced repeatedly, demanding his attention. Sleeping in the same room with her, even in separate beds, was going to drive him nuts.

He came upon the cabins. From the flickering lights behind so many of the curtained windows, it seemed that many of the cabin tourists needed their nightly fix of television. There were lots of cars—it seemed that some of the cabins even had two cars.

He paused to knock before pushing the key into the door-knob. There was no answer. Could she still be in the shower? It must have been almost an hour. He pushed open the door and the light from the interior spilled out, silhouetting him and making him blink as his eyes adjusted.

Amanda sat on the edge of the far bed, wearing fresh clothes, with her wet hair uncombed, darkening her shirt where it lay on her shoulders. A strip of grey duct tape obscured the lower part of her face, tightly binding her mouth. She sat at an angle, with her torso turned, that allowed Harry to see that her hands were confined behind her by the burnished steel of handcuffs.

In the middle of the room, near the television, stood the handsome FBI agent, alive and healthy, wearing a neat suit and holding a pistol. To Harry's left and to his right were two other men, also dressed in suits and holding pistols. One of them he recognized from his surveillance at the hide. The other was a stranger. At least those two hadn't come back from the dead.

Each pistol was a standard law enforcement issue Glock, maiming machines with their .40 caliber bullets. Harry felt the burning pressure of his own pistol at his waist, casually stuck in his belt.

"Come in, Dr. Deacon, and close the door," the agent said. "We need to talk."

Clint Eastwood could have taken care of this situation, but three pistols aimed at the archaeologist indicated that not much realistic hope remained. The fog that had affected Harry's mind for the past several hours dissipated in the face of surging adrenalin and single-minded focus. He pushed aside his astonishment at seeing the agent alive. If they threatened Amanda's life to force him to talk, Harry knew that he would spill the location of the artifact. If they got the artifact, then his life was forfeit, and they would then clean up after themselves, as they had shown a penchant for doing, by killing everyone. Brenda would die.

Harry pushed the door shut behind him with his left hand. As the door clicked closed, his hand came back up and snagged the metal key in the slot that allowed electricity to be supplied to the cabin. He yanked it out, plunging the cabin into darkness, going for his pistol at the same time, dropping to the floor on his butt to make himself a smaller target. Safety off. He fired to the right, three quick shots, where the man to his right had been standing.

The shots went off like a strobe light, briefly illuminating the room. Sweep to the left, four shots widely spaced in an attempt to hit the agent and other man, trying his best to make sure that he wasn't firing in Amanda's direction. Hopefully she had dived to the floor. One of the men fired back and Harry's stomach exploded with pain.

"Don't kill him!" a male voice roared.

Harry fired back at the flashes. Three more rounds. A well-trained part of his brain kept track of the total shots—only seven left. He wanted to scoot along the wall, confuse the enemy, but he found he couldn't move. His legs felt wrong.

A mass collided with Harry, knocking his pistol out of his hand. He gasped at the wave of agony from his stomach that threatened to black him out. Scratching and clawing, wishing his nails were longer, he fought back with desperate abandon, expecting to die, his only thoughts to save Amanda and Brenda before he went away.

Well-aimed blows from a fist hit Harry's face. His nose, a bundle of nerves, sent shards of pain directly into his brain. He heard bones crack and felt his face turn mushy.

The blows stopped and, as if from a distance, he heard a woman cursing in a foreign language. Curse words are readily identifiable whatever the source. The man on top of him cursed back in the same language and Harry felt the weight of the man shift.

Harry reached out, trying to find a weapon, anything to fight back with. His fingers came across a pistol. Not his, the handle felt wrong. One of the Glocks. His finger checking to see that the safety was off, he brought it around, using his other hand to find the man's head. He grabbed an ear as tightly as a drowning man clings to a rope.

He brought the pistol up to the head and fired point-blank into the man's skull. The room flashed. Since his eyes were inches away, Harry only saw streaks of color in the afterimage that his retinas and brain struggled to interpret.

The ear that he clung to was slippery with blood and bits of stuff. He felt the body on top of him go limp.

A shudder went through Harry as he slumped back, letting the pistol slip from his fingers. He felt spent, so exhausted that nothing existed except the throbbing in his stomach. He smelled shit and wondered if it was his own or someone else's.

A soft hand touched his face. "Harry, are you still alive?"

She lived.

He went blank.

CHAPTER THIRTY-FOUR

Her pupils abnormally large to let her see in the dark as well as a cougar, Amanda had dived to the floor, twisted her arms around her feet and legs to get her handcuffed hands out in front, and joined the fray. She was so pissed that she was shouting vile curses in her native tongue, kicking Marshall Stone in the back as she grabbed his arm and tried to twist him off the archaeologist. Then Harry had solved everything for them by shooting the FBI agent in the head.

The other two men were out of the game, either dead or dying, thanks to Harry's bullets.

Grabbing a small flashlight from her purse, Amanda examined the unconscious Harry quickly. He had been shot once in the stomach. She felt gently under him for the exit wound and found exposed vertebrae that moved at her touch. His spine had been shattered and the spinal cord inside was certainly damaged.

The pillowcases from the bed made ready bandages. She spat into the open wound, jammed a wadded-up pillowcase over the back wound, and then used another pillow case to cover the front wound. She needed to bind it somehow. She found the duct tape that the FBI agent and his hirelings had brought on the end table between the two beds and used long strips of it to bind the covers over the wounds. At least that slowed the bleeding.

He was breathing in short and shallow gasps, but already the helpers she had given him were doing their work. She opened his mouth with her fingers and swirled her tongue around inside, giving him more helpers. The microscopic machines knew their jobs.

Turning off her flashlight, she peeked out the window. Several people were milling around with flashlights, and some of the cabins had their doors open, spilling light out onto the parked cars. Amanda moved quickly, pulling Harry away from the door. She pulled the FBI agent aside too. His body was still warm.

Stripping off her clothes, she washed her hands and arms quickly in the sink, hoping that the towel would catch any blood that she had missed. Putting on a bathrobe, she went to the cabin door and opened it.

The man with dreadlocks who ran the hotel was only a dozen feet away, coming toward her.

"Did you hear gunshots?" he asked.

"I thought so," she said. "I was asleep and thought it was a dream."

"No dream, everyone else heard them too," he said, sweeping his flashlight around as if he expected to find the gunshots lying about.

"Where did the sounds come from?" she asked, stepping outside in her bare feet and pulling the door most of the way closed behind her. Her hand brushed against the key that Harry had left in the door as he entered. She moved to block the view with her body and pulled the key free, its large metal electricity key attached to it like a handle, and placed it into her robe pocket.

"People think it was over here," he said. She stepped forward, off of the small porch of wooden planks and onto the ground, placing her hand on his forearm. Oxytocin and other trust hormones chemicals flowed from her touch directly into him; she knew that he felt only the warmth of her hand, perhaps a bit more, and this he would attribute to having such a beautiful woman actually touch him.

"I think that it must have been further up the canyon," she said. "Perhaps it was a rock slide. That would make some awful noises, wouldn't it?"

"Oh, yes, ma'am," he said quickly. "That makes sense."

Even in the darkness, she could see that his face had grown flushed.

"Are we in any danger?" she asked. "From further slides?"

"No, not at all. We're far enough away from the mountainsides, I'm sure." He looked up in the dark.

"So the sounds were a slide, not gunshots?" she asked.

"I'm sure you're right." He moved away, passing on this new information to his customers.

Amanda went back into the cabin, made sure that the blinds were all tight and turned on the lights. What a mess. Pools of blood on the floor and splatters of blood on the wall from the spray of bullets going through people demonstrated that human bodies are no more than bags of water, salt, and chemicals.

There would be more people from the Cabal here soon, both exiles and mercenaries. She changed back into the dusty clothes she had worn in the desert, still in the bathroom where she had been surprised by Marshall Stone and his men. No time for regrets or wondering how she had been careless enough to assume that he would take longer to find her. She quickly repacked her suitcase.

Amanda turned off the light and drew her pistol before opening the door peering out. Her eyes adjusted quickly and she scanned for any movement outside the cabins. Everyone had returned to their televisions or sleeping or whatever else they had been doing. Ideally she would have waited for a better vehicle to be brought to her. One was due at about four in the morning, being driven from Denver even now. One of the frustrations of being part of the Humanists was that the Cabal had a lot more resources.

She decided to take her own vehicle. She loaded the rifles, then the suitcase and Harry's backpack, and finally picked up Harry to carry him outside. He didn't even moan, too deep in a helper-induced coma to be aware of anything. It was petty, but she couldn't resist giving the FBI agent a kick in the ribs on her way out of the room.

Placing Harry gently in the back seat, she arranged a blanket around him and a pillow taken from the motel under his head. His skin was burning, as if a fever raged inside him: excess heat from the work of the helpers.

One last look in the cabin. She saw the FBI agent stir, just a twitch of his legs. His brains had been sprayed all over the room by Harry's bullet. She closed the door; the maid or the nice man at the front office would get a shock when they opened it, though she suspected that the Cabal would get there first and do a clean-up.

Once she was on the road and headed north, she pulled out her cell phone. This model was technically illegal; she could switch identities so that the device looked like a different phone to the cell network, stopping whoever was trying to trace its use. She called a special number in Alaska, which was routed back to British Columbia.

Franklin answered and she explained her problems. The rendezvous with the other car was changed and new plans made.

A few minutes after finishing the call, Amanda came upon a small town, pulled into a convenience store and gassed up. If anyone looked in the car, they would only see a man sleeping in the back. The blanket covered all the caked blood. Inside the store she found that they sold multivitamins, so she bought their entire supply of four bottles.

A few miles farther down the road she pulled over, opened a book to act as a tray and broke up the vitamins with her fingers. The butt of her pistol served as a hammer to crush the pieces into vitamin dust. She pulled her suitcase over and opened it, extracting a bottle of vodka. She took a long drink, then poured the dust into the bottle, shaking it to mix it well, turning the clear liquid murky.

Getting out of the car and opening the back door, she tilted Harry's head up and poured some of the vodka in. Her own throat ignored the burning of the alcohol, which was pure energy to the helpers in her own bloodstream, but Harry coughed and spit up some of the vodka. She would give him more later. The helpers inside him needed the raw fuel and the materials provided by the vitamins: iron, zinc, calcium, potassium, chloride, copper, phosphorous, iodine, molybdenum, manganese, and vitamins A, B6, C, D, E, and K. Even the traces of boron, nickel, silicon, and lycopene were useful. Everything a body needed to repair cells and make new ones.

Back on the road again, putting more miles between her and the Green Motel.

Now that she had some time to think about it, how had the Cabal found Harry and her so quickly? Satellite tracking was a possibility, but it would require a satellite dedicated to following her as she went north. That was a stretch. The United States only had a handful of satellites with strong optics in orbit and most of those were tasked with watching foreign countries, not the homeland. Had they tracked her cell phone? Unlikely. Had someone followed them? She had been watching for that and had not spotted a tail. How about betrayal by another Humanist? Unthinkable.

She yawned and drank a little from the vodka bottle, then pulled over again. Harry looked asleep, but she forced more of the vitamin-enhanced drink down him. She had found her first sight of Harry—unshaven, dirty, with his floppy camo hat down over his eyes   charming in a fundamental way. She had used her trust hormones on him, which normally made a man as cooperative as an eager puppy, but everyone had their limits. His limit was keeping the location of the artifact to himself. She had been content with that, but if her helpers failed and he died, the secret went with him. Even if he lived, he might have forgotten where the artifact was.

The FBI agent Marshall Stone certainly had forgotten a lot.

CHAPTER THIRTY-FIVE

Marshall Stone lay in his sticky blood, a glimmer of consciousness shining through half-closed eyelids. As minutes leaked by, the flow of blood slowed to a trickle. A medical doctor would have been astonished. Beneath the shattered bones at the back of the skull a thin new layer of pink was forming, catching the blood and holding it in. The new skull sparkled and radiated heat from microscopic industrial operations.

The hole in the forehead closed. The fat and muscles in other parts of his body deflated and turned into blood and basic proteins to be raced along his veins to the brain to preserve those neurons not shattered by the chaotic passage of the bullet.

Occasionally he twitched, muscles responding to random firings along his nerves, messages coming from nowhere and going nowhere. His body had never been this close to final termination; his helpers struggled, an army of tens of millions, individually useless, finding a rudimentary intelligence and power as a mass.

Images and short snippets, like scenes from a movie, flittered through his mind, like the spasms of his muscles. A mountain overlooking a small valley, green grass everywhere and trees with branches that arched down to the ground, each tree forming its own thicket, two suns in the sky. A city spread along a river, its roads made of grass that never grew more than an inch or two high, no building more than two stories high, merged into the landscape like the homes of hobbits. Walking through another city, its silver spires reaching into the sky in ways that defied gravity, passing through zones of different music, performances of new pieces from composers who had lived for thousands of years.

The games. Running as fast as he could, gasping for breath, not being able to catch the two men in front of him. Bounce-ball with teams made up of both men and women, their sleeves rippling as they moved, striving to put that small ball through a hole that seemed much smaller. Struggles of mock combat where the victor received the cheers of people really there and people visiting in the form of holograms.

So many fragments of memory of the place with two suns, so much activity, yet so boring.

Pain stabbed through his body, making his arms and legs rigid as he trembled, smearing blood across the floor. He made no sound. The helpers had made a mistake, crossing nerves, and his body went limp as they found the error and cut the nerves. Programming routines were consulted, a workaround created, and the nerves reconnected in a different way.

Another memory, loaded with high emotion and satisfaction, crushing the skull of a man who had bested him in mock combat one too many times. Pouring acid into the skull, watching the grey matter bubble, creating the long death. No attempt to hide his crime. Welcoming the inevitable sentence from a tribunal of his peers.

Exile.

The long trip in sleep, a new world with one sun, people with short lives, and freedom from laws. He ranged across the landscape, finding past mock combat exercises useful in real combat. He thrilled in domination and having no rules. All conceivable experiences were now possible.

He loved all the women who readily went to his bed, or to the ground, or against a tree, because he was their lord and master. One woman was different. Gretel had loved him on the old world, and he had ignored her for it. She had followed him into exile and become his mate. Sometimes they loved each other, other times they hated each other, times of living together, longer times living apart in their own private exiles.

They were back together now, working as a team. Where was she?

And then Gretel was there, touching his face with soft hands, whispering his name in his ear, urging him to drink a foul liquid that burned. He was still blind, but his nostrils picked up that tangy scent that he knew was pure Gretel.

CHAPTER THIRTY-SIX

Brenda came awake, a slow process, like coming out of a dream. She felt awful and her throat hurt, but she was aware that someone was holding her hand. Opening her eyes, she found her mother sitting next to her, sleeping with her head on the bed, fingers intertwined with Brenda's.

Her father slept in a chair against the far wall. Her brother stood at the window, looking out at the dawn, sipping from a cup that obviously contained something hot. She noticed a pistol protruding from a holster in the small of his back.

It all came back with a rush—the terror of the attack, the pain of being shot, Harry's worried words, spoken with forced calm, and the rough ride to safety—and she moaned at the horror of it all.

Her brother turned instantly. Their eyes locked and he smiled with such profound relief that she felt better; to be loved cures many ills.

"You're awake," Dirk said, moving to her side.

Her mother and father woke as if they had been waiting for any sound. Everyone clustered around her, full of words, touching her on the hands, arms, and face. So overwhelming.

"How do you feel?" her mother asked, speaking softly near her ear.

"Like I was run over by a truck, which then backed up and did it again." Her voice felt scratchy. She learned later about the breathing tube in her throat that had kept her alive.

Everyone laughed with relief.

"Water," she said.

Her mother poured a small cup and helped Brenda drink it. That simple act exhausted the young woman and she drifted away for a while.

When she came back, two women were standing over her, one in a white coat and the other in green scrubs. Both had stethoscopes around their necks. Brenda assumed that the one in the coat was a doctor. "Welcome back, Brenda," the doctor told her. "Your recovery is simply amazing."

"What happened?" Brenda asked. The words didn't exhaust her as much as she expected.

"You were shot, honey," her mother said from behind the doctor, fluttering around like a moth, peeking over one and then the other shoulder of the tall woman.

"One moment, if you please," the doctor said. "I need to ask you some questions."

"Okay."

"What is the last thing that you remember?"

Brenda tried to sort through images that ran together like watercolors on a frantic painting. She remembered getting shot, Harry shooting back, him there helping her, driving her, waiting for the helicopter. He had called for Dr. Bancroft and something bad had happened to her. What?

"I remember the helicopter," Brenda said.

"That's good," the doctor said. "You were shot twice, in your left arm and in your chest. The bullet that entered your arm cut an artery, but you got good first aid and we were able to repair that. The wound in the chest didn't hit anything vital, thank goodness, but any kind of trauma like that is hard on a person, so we kept you in a light drug-induced coma. You've come out of that."

"Will I have scars?" Brenda asked.

"Some small scars, probably," the doctor said. "Nothing disfiguring. One on your arm and the other under your left breast, on your ribs."

"I guess no more bikinis for me," Brenda said. "Granny one-pieces from now on."

The doctor laughed. Brenda wanted to laugh too, but restricted herself to a wan smile. Laughter shook everything inside her around and she didn't want to that happen.

"I want to go through some neurological tests with you," the doctor said.

Brenda told her what she felt when the doctor touched her in various places, blinked at the blinding afterimage of having a flashlight shined into each of her eyes, and felt a sense of elation as she was poked and prodded. It felt good to be alive.

"You are running a bit of a fever," the doctor said. "Other than that, you are recovering remarkably quickly."

"So I can leave tomorrow?" Brenda asked.

The doctor smiled and patted her shoulder. "That would be a miracle recovery. Let's give it a few more days. I'll come back this afternoon." She turned to Brenda's parents. "Please let her rest and don't exhaust her with too many questions."

Her brother came to her side as the doctor and nurse left and squeezed her hand. "Welcome back, sis," he said.

Her father kissed her on the forehead. He smelled just as she remembered, a hint of pipe smoke and an unidentifiable mix that spoke of Ireland, the Army, and salt air.

"Where's Harry?" she asked.

"We don't know," her father said with a sharp tone in his voice. "Your brother knows, but won't tell us."

"Dad," Dirk said, his own tone matching the colonel's. "I've told you that we are being listened to."

"Who's listening?" Brenda asked.

"We don't know," Dirk said, kneeling down next to her. "Harry had to leave. He didn't want to, but he had to."

"He saved your life, honey," her mother said, taking hold of her other hand. "We will always be grateful."

"How do we know that he wasn't the one who brought the danger to her?" the colonel barked. "We don't know a damned thing."

"That's not what happened, Dad," Brenda said, intending to

add more, but her brother's finger pressed on her lips, startling her into looking up into his eyes.

He shook his head, then leaned close to her ear. "We are being bugged. I know this for certain. Say nothing. Dad is having a spell."

Brenda blinked.

The nightmare was not over; it had followed her into this hospital room. Rolling her head to her side, she looked at the window, seeing only sky through the partially open blinds. She hoped that Harry was okay.

CHAPTER THIRTY-SEVEN

The impound lot for the New Mexico State Police was on the outskirts of Albuquerque. Dirk estimated that there must have been close to sixty cars there, some of them for long enough to have layers of dust turn into dirt on them. He asked the woman leading him across the asphalt why some of the cars had been there so long.

"Those are evidence," she said. She had the brown skin of a Native American, with a wide face and dark eyes, her hair wrapped up in a bun. Her name tag said Sarah Cleghorn. "It takes years to get rid of them."

She stopped before a Lexus. "Is this yours?"

Dirk looked at the car. The middle-aged man who ran a local rental service had called three hours ago in an irate mood. Dirk didn't blame him, since the car that Dirk had rented two days ago had been impounded by national park rangers at Chaco Canyon and turned over to the state police.

"I guess so," he said. "Do you have any keys?"

She looked at him like he was an idiot, and he felt like one.

"You lost your car and your keys?" she asked.

"It's a rental," he said. "I lent it to a friend—made a mistake."

"I guess he had the keys?" she asked.

"Yes." He tried to recall some details from his Criminal Procedures class in law school. Since he had had no intention of practicing criminal law, he had memorized and dumped, reserving his enthusiasm for his corporate financial law courses. "Ah, you did an inventory of the contents?"

"Of course," she said, flipping the papers on her clipboard. "There was nothing."

"What do you mean, nothing?"

"There was nothing in the car except your signed rental agreement."

"No clothes, no...." He almost said "guns," but caught himself. He had left his newly purchased pistol back in his other rental car. No reason to make unnecessary trouble for himself.

"Nothing."

She finished filling out a release form and asked him to sign it. He had already paid the $300 impound fee and $280 tow truck bill.

"It's a Lexus," she said. "This year's model. They come standard with a satellite remote control. Contact your rental agency and they can unlock the car and start it for you."

Dirk got on his cell phone and a few minutes later, thanks to an encrypted transmission from a satellite, he was driving away. After getting out of sight from the impound yard, he stopped and searched the car. She had been right. Nothing.

Where was Harry?

Dirk had no idea what Harry had intended to do, and the list of equipment that he had purchased for the archaeologist did not bode well for peaceful pursuits. Was Harry dead? Had Harry sanitized this car? That seemed unlikely. Dirk just didn't see the older man as that fastidious. Someone else had cleaned it up, before it had been turned over to the state police. Dirk did not like that idea.

He dropped off the car at the rental company, finding out that the fee for not returning the keys with it was another $300. Dirk appreciated the fact that his Platinum American Express had no limit.

Waiting for a taxi cab to show up to take him back to his other rental car parked outside the impound lot, he took out his cell phone and dialed Harry's. Voice mail.

New Mexico did not feel safe. It hadn't felt safe ever since he heard about his sister's shooting. Perhaps her quick recovery provided an opportunity, a way to get a step ahead of the bad guys, and a plan formed in his mind. The day was about to get even more expensive.

He would have liked to talk over the idea with his father, a man who had always given him sage advice, but that no longer seemed possible. The colonel had been diagnosed with early-onset Alzheimer's just five months ago. The proud man had told only his wife and Dirk. Brenda was so happy and full of life that their father had decided to not tell her. Dirk didn't agree with the secrecy, but respected his father's desires.

Up until yesterday the symptoms had mostly been limited to minor lapses in memory. Dirk was a keen observer of other people and he had concluded that the stress of Brenda's shooting and hospitalization had aggravated the disease. The colonel's demeanor was more sour than normal and he could not be trusted with any secret.

Giving his father a gun had probably been a mistake.

As Dirk drove the rental back to Farmington, he worked his cell phone. Amazing what a credit card could quickly obtain. A private two-engine plane would be at the Farmington airport at eleven that night, with an experienced flight nurse to tend Brenda. The nurse was based in Phoenix; a separate charter was flying him in from Arizona.

Dirk passed the turnoff to Chaco Canyon National Historical Park, marked by only a small sign, considering the wonders of the site. Should he go looking for Harry? Where would he start?

As much as he wanted to be proactive, the best tactic was to hunker down.

When he entered the hospital room, Dirk found his sister walking around the room, holding her white gown closed with a hand clasped behind her. The colonel and his mother sat in chairs, beaming with smiles and jokes. Dirk gaped in astonishment.

"Give me a hug, big brother," she said.

He put his arms around her. She felt so warm as she pulled his head down to her lips. "What's going on?" she whispered in his ear.

"We're going home," Dirk whispered back. "To the island."

CHAPTER THIRTY-EIGHT

His mouth yearned for water and his body felt like it was on fire. Even his brain burned, sending fevered images through his consciousness like mirages in an infernal desert. He remembered meeting his wife for the first time. Maria was eighteen years old, dark-haired and pretty, with a mole under her left earlobe that she picked at when she was nervous. He had just returned from basic and advanced infantry training, sixteen weeks of hard physical exertion that gave him a pleasant masculine glow of health and confidence. A frantic romance, fueled by him only having two weeks home in Minneapolis, holding hands, pawing at each other, spending so much time together that his mother got irritated that she wasn't getting any time with her son.

Getting married the next time that he came home to the neighborhood on leave, Maria in her white dress and Harry in his dress uniform, in Our Sacred Mother cathedral. Her family was also Puerto Rican, but her parents were still together, and he felt like he had married an entire clan, not just a girl. He found to his pleasant surprise that Maria was not just a bundle of attractive hormones, but bright. She went to college as she followed him from posting to posting, getting a degree in business, then a master's in accounting. She never matched his image of an accountant, but there she was, always sitting at her computer, moving numbers around.

Plenty of images in bed with Maria. Those were the good years. Then James came along, making their family into three.

Still a good time, when he was home. The War on Terror meant long tours away from them. They drifted apart, he did stupid things, they fought, he did more stupid things, she called it quits. At least one of them was smart.

When he was fifteen he had seen the movie *The Wild Bunch*. He liked Westerns and this one looked gritty. After the opening sequence, the gang of ruffians shoot their way out of a bank robbery gone bad, killing civilian bystanders at the same time. He hated that. He wanted them to be heroes. With perverse determination he watched the whole movie, including the well-choreographed bloodbath at the end. Everyone died. He liked heroes that died in service to a noble cause, but these were not heroes and their cause was not noble. He was depressed for two weeks, moping around, just like after reading the novel that the movie *Blade Runner* was based on. Great title, *Do Androids Dream of Electric Sheep?*, but Philip K. Dick painted such a bleak picture of the future that Harry went back to reading more optimistic sorts, like the masters, Heinlein, Clarke, Asimov, and Burroughs.

Just quick flashes. More images from movies he had seen, books that he had read, daydreams that had passed the time.

One memory kept demanding attention. Lying on the ground in a litter of brittle pine needles after having slipped and fallen against a jagged rock, a gash on his left arm so deep that he might bleed out, trying not to sob because he hurt so much, searching for something inside himself. His twenty-third birthday had been only three days earlier, celebrated by eating four worms. The "Q" course in the North Carolina pine forest was designed to test a Special Forces soldier, to force him to find the core of his personality, to acquire a determination to succeed no matter what the toll.

Everyone was afraid of dying. No, not true—suicides obviously weren't afraid of dying, or at least not so afraid that they didn't commit the final act. He wrapped his shirt around the wound, tying it tightly enough to hopefully staunch the flow but not so tight that he would lose his hand. Five miles to the west was a small town. The locals were used to the soldiers training in their woods. Some of them even regularly acted as prisoners of war or rebels in need of instruction in the training scenarios.

Bailing from the course would mean that he failed, but because of the injury he would be allowed a second chance after he healed. On that five-mile walk, shivering from the cold, woozy from blood loss, Harry found a new part of himself. Pure determination, willpower as a force stronger than any obstacle.

A week later, half buzzed on beer, he realized that the moment on the forest floor had been the defining moment of his life. There was before the forest, and after the forest; getting married, becoming a father, earning a doctorate, were all simply part of the process of life; that moment in the forest made him a new person.

His fever spiked. It burned. Harry had once taken a round in his leg that tore up his thigh muscles. Someplace in southern Iraq, fire from a Shiite ambush, on a winter morning, with cold like only the desert could make that seeped into your bones. The medic had used a new treatment, sprinkling QuikClot on the wound. The chemical agent looked like sand and caused the blood to clot up, closing the wound, but it reacted strongly enough to burn.

Better to sizzle than bleed out.

He abruptly came awake, his eyes seeking the real world, a blurry mess of colors. He blinked and tried to speak.

"Are you back?" The voice sounded warm and caring. Something blonde came into his view.

"Burning up," he croaked.

"It's just the increased metabolism of the cure," she said.

"Amanda?"

He felt her touch on his arm. "It's me," she said.

"Where are we?" he asked.

"Canada."

CHAPTER THIRTY-NINE

Either the man watching them was the world's most incompetent tail, didn't care, or was being deliberately provocative. He wore a red blazer more suitable for a pimp than anyone with any fashion sense. Dark glasses, hair shaved to a military cut, and jeans that bulged around thighs built by weight lifting completed the image. He held a pornographic magazine rolled up in his hand; no doubt for the articles.

The man was waiting for them at the private air terminal, leaning against the side of a hangar as the Finnigan family disembarked from their flight. Brenda moved like she had never been hurt, a development that gnawed at Dirk, but the need to keep her safe kept his mind preoccupied with other matters. What else was there to do? Brenda was better; she had remarkable recuperative powers, a blessing.

While his family waited, Dirk walked through the main terminal to take a shuttle bus to long-term parking. When he pulled up in his father's SUV back at the terminal to pick up the family, the man in the red blazer was still there, watching them. Dirk loaded his family into the car and drove away, seeing in his rearview mirror that the man was now moving to a nearby four-door black sedan.

The sedan followed them all the way from Bangor to Jonesport, occasionally dropping back a car or two when someone eased in front of it, but always returning, keeping a proper following distance. Just to verify to himself the completely obvious, Dirk drove around a few blocks when they passed through Midbridge.

The car dutifully followed them.

At Jonesport, Dirk drove down to the harbor. The ferryman stood on the stern of his ferry, an open barge able to carry no more a dozen cars, waiting for his ten A.M. run. He visited five islands and only made another run at six P.M. Dirk drove onto the ferry and parked. He was surprised that the tail didn't follow them right onto the boat. Instead, the man parked his car, got out with his magazine and stood there looking at pictures, not unless reading a page took five or ten minutes before turning the page. Dirk had not pointed out their tail to his family. Exiting the vehicle, he greeted Frank, the ferryman he had known all his life, and walked up the slope to the tail.

The man looked up at Dirk, his expression bland.

"Why are you following us?" Dirk demanded.

The man looked back down at his magazine, seeming to ignore the young man, though from the way his shoulders tensed, he obviously was not as nonchalant as he wanted to appear.

"Who do you work for?"

Still no answer.

Dirk bit his lip in irritation. He had never been so completely ignored in his life and he felt his face flush with anger. He was reminded of a phrase that his sister had used when she was in her early teens, "so rude." Such a perfect description. Dirk still had his pistol, concealed under his jacket. Of course, the conspicuous man undoubtedly also had a pistol under that red blazer. Escalating the confrontation seemed foolhardy.

"Stay away from my family." Dirk spit out the words and stalked back to the ferry. He refused to glance back and see what the man was doing. Probably still looking at the pictures.

CHAPTER FORTY

Harry Deacon awoke, feeling completely refreshed, and lay in the comfortable bed. His eyes wandered around the room. Wood panels with pine knots all over them like spots on a dog covered the walls. Sunlight poured in through white lace curtains to illuminate two oil paintings, each large enough to dominate opposite walls. The first was of a forest glade overlooking an idyllic river, a waterfall and the rising sun in the background, lots of yellow and softer colors, with the sunlight reflecting off the water. Perhaps from the Hudson River school of the mid-nineteenth century. The other painting was of a young woman, wearing the thick dress of an earlier time, having just risen from her seat at a table, stretching her back, with stained glass windows before her. A truly striking painting. To get that arched back so flawlessly accurate showed great skill. It looked Pre-Raphaelite, a mid-nineteenth-century British school. That art history class, taken two decades years earlier, had nibbled its way into the corners of his brain more effectively than he thought.

The furniture in the room seemed to be all antiques, made of sturdy materials, crafted by men and their hand tools, not factory machines: a wardrobe on the opposite wall, a chest of drawers, a small vanity with a mirror, and two chairs, carved arms and trim and upholstery in the older style, not overstuffed. Two low bookshelves, stuffed with books, encouraged him to move. Never could resist books.

Sweeping back the covers, he found that he was nude. There

was a small pink spot of new skin on his stomach, where he had been shot. He ran his hand across his back, finding the tautness of new skin covering a much larger spot about six inches across. When he stood, he expected to feel dizzy or ill, but he felt as fit as when he was a younger man. In the wardrobe he found a pair of new jeans, a short-sleeved flannel shirt, hiking boots, underwear, and socks. His wallet, car keys, pistol and other gear sat on the bottom of the wardrobe.

It meant something that they had left him his weapon. After he dressed, he checked the Beretta. It had been cleaned and was loaded—no bullet in the chamber though. Just good safety practice. If they trusted him enough to leave his weapon with him, he trusted them enough to feel that carrying it was unnecessary.

Of course, the key question, who were they?

He went to the bookshelf. All of the books had the leather binding so common a century ago for books that were meant to last. Mostly history, some on science and technology. A whole row of blue books, not bound in leather, was an encyclopedia set from 1917. The last volume was just entitled "The Great War." Harry looked through it. World War I had lasted from 1914 to 1918. For the publishers it was an ongoing event, the most important happening in the world, and of course, it was not yet the first of two world wars. How depressed they would have been to know that all the carnage was for naught, and that it would take a sequel to clean up the European mess.

The door opened and Amanda walked in.

She looked as beautiful as he remembered, dressed in jeans and a flannel shirt like his own, her blonde hair tied back in a ponytail. She moved with confidence and smiled at him.

"Welcome to Raven's Nest," Amanda said.

"Thank you." He pointed to the woman stretching her back. "Tell me about that painting."

Amanda glanced at it. "It's called Mariana, painted by John Everett Millais."

"Pre-Raphaelite?"

She nodded. "I believe so. I'm impressed by your knowledge."

"Don't be. A little knowledge goes a long way, sort of like knowing all the answers in a Trivial Pursuit game." He put the book away and stood up, still amazed at how good he felt. "How is it that I was healed? I was shot, wasn't I?"

"Yes, you were." She took one of the seats and gestured for him to take the other. "Very badly. We have some new medical technology that is very effective."

He sat. "My thanks for saving my life."

"You saved my life. Things would not have gone well for either of us if you hadn't started shooting."

"Just an act of desperation. I'm just glad you weren't hit."

"So am I." She shifted in her chair, leaning closer. "You are our guest here and have full run of estate. Just don't use your cell phone, that might be traced. We have other computers if you need Internet access."

"And where is here?"

"An undisclosed location in British Columbia. That's all I want to say."

"What day is it?"

"Saturday."

The answer staggered him. "It's been ten days since I was shot?"

"No, only three days."

He stared at her. "What kind of technology did you use?"

"We call them helpers. They are microscopic robots, based on nanotechnology, that can repair damage to your body. Think of them as the world's tiniest surgeons."

"How's Brenda doing?" Harry felt negligent that the young woman had not been his first thought.

"Her family took her to an island off Maine where they have a summer home. We are watching her. So is the Cabal. They haven't made a move yet."

"How are her wounds?"

Amanda smiled. "Oh, I also put helpers in her. She is completely better."

"That's wonderful. Am I also completely better?"

"Better than better. You're the twelve-million-dollar man now."

"So what happens now?" he asked. "What's our plan of action?"

"Patience, for the moment."

"I like patience to be combined with a plan."

"We are working on that." She paused, biting her lower lip. "I don't mean to pry, but is Brenda your girlfriend?"

Harry looked exasperated. "Why is it that people make that assumption? We are good friends, nothing more. I'm old enough to be her father."

"I'm sorry, it was wrong to pry."

He waved his hand. "It's okay. Her brother asked the same thing. I guess I should get used to it."

A thought suddenly occurred to him. "How did that FBI agent recover so quickly from that wound you gave him? I couldn't believe my eyes when he showed up at that motel."

"He also has access to healing helpers," Amanda said.

"That fast? He was up and around in a matter of hours. I took three days to heal. What am I saying? This is all crazy."

"Stone already had helpers inside him, so they worked much more quickly. You had to have helpers put in you and they needed to organize themselves as they helped you."

"What about the other three guys back in Chaco?" Harry asked. "The ones I shot. Are they also alive?"

"No, they didn't have helpers in them."

"So they are really dead?"

She looked away and he saw her swallow hard. "Yes, they are really dead," she said.

"You don't like killing, so you?" Harry said.

She glanced back at him, her eyes shiny. "Does anyone?"

"Unfortunately, yes, there are people who like to kill. I have met plenty of them, but I'm not one of them. I don't lose sleep over it though, if it was justified. I will not lose sleep over those men."

"I will," she said.

"You knew when you shot Stone that he wouldn't be killed?"

"Yes."

"You are fighting a strange war here," Harry said. "Where people don't die, or at least not all the people die."

"You see that quilt on your bed?"

Harry had not noticed the quilt. He saw a different word in different languages stitched into each of the blue and white panels. He saw "Peace" in English, the same word in Spanish, "Paz."

"I assume that all of those words are the same word?" he asked.

"Yes, a friend of mine made that quilt for me. That word describes me. I'm really quite a pacifist."

"Yet you're a secret agent."

"Not by choice," she said. "I do what I have to do." She abruptly stood up. "Let me take you on a tour of the estate."

CHAPTER FORTY-ONE

The mansion was built of wood; no drywall, no wallpaper, just the polished texture of nature. The house had been built on a slope, so that the front faced inland, and the rear faced the ocean. The front was two stories high, while the rear had a basement that opened out onto a patio. An outdoor pool and indoor pool met via a narrow neck of water, like the shape of the symbol for infinity laid on the ground. A covered deck formed a veranda that ran around the entire house, forming a porch in the front, and a deck overlooking the patio and outdoor pool in the back.

Harry and Amanda stood on the deck, looking out towards the ocean, perhaps five hundred yards away, down the hill. A path led down to a boathouse and dock. On the horizon were several islands, a few among the thousands protecting the Inland Passage that ran along the coast of British Columbia. A white cruise ship a couple of miles away sailed south.

Majestic spruce trees covered the hillside around the mansion, some over a hundred feet tall. Amanda led Harry down among the trees. A trail led to a stable, where three horses neighed a greeting from a corral designed to hold many more horses than that. Another trail led to tennis courts, made of concrete that had been patched many times as the harsh winters cracked the surface. A nearby wind sock showed that the courts were probably more often used for helicopter landings.

"What did this place used to be?" Harry asked. "A resort?"

"Yes, built back in the 1950s," she said. "Franklin bought it when they went bankrupt."

"Franklin?"

"The owner and my boss."

"The government seems to be funding your group really well," Harry said. "This place must have cost millions to build."

"This is privately funded, no government funds here."

"That's very odd."

"We are an odd organization. We need private funding to stay off the Cabal's radar."

"Are they really that powerful?"

"Yes."

Harry enjoyed walking with Amanda; only a fool would not find such an experience appealing. She looked like she belonged here in the outdoors, in her simple jeans and boots; even the flannel shirt fit the stereotype.

He felt wary, knowing that she was more complex than any woman he had ever known. Her mystery didn't attract him—to be frank, that actually scared him—but her obvious intelligence, her self-confidence, and her beauty created a potent combination. He no longer felt the urge to tell her almost everything, as he had after they first met. Somehow he had kept the location of the artifact to himself, the only secret that remained sacrosanct. He did not feel giddy around her, perhaps the result of his years of experience. When he was a teenager or even in his twenties, he would have acted the fool around such an attractive woman, like a puppy happy for any trace of attention.

On the way back from the tennis courts, she showed him the interior of a large outbuilding that held carpenter's tools, metal-working tools, both hand tools and power tools, all arranged around work spaces. Though well kept, the smell of oil and wood shavings, along with the dirt that gets into the nooks and crannies of a workshop showed him that this was no collection of tools for unrealized ambitions, but a place for real work. There were even two furnaces, perhaps for smelting and for pottery work.

"The owner of this house likes to make things," Amanda

said.

They returned to the mansion. The logs of the exterior were all the same size, planed down to make them fit tightly, and two large chimneys of stone stood out on the sides of the mansion like rooks on a chessboard. Two lightning rods protruded up from the top of the chimneys—sentinels on guard.

The mansion had dozens of rooms, but the hallway on the ground floor that ran from the foyer to the great room caught his attention. Display cases lined the hallway. Amanda flipped a switch to turn on the lights, which lit up the contents of each display.

In the first case was a copy of the Declaration of Independence, yellowed and fragile-looking, yet without much wear. Someone had taken care of it. Next to it was a copy of the Constitution of the United States, all four sheets laid side by side. Both documents were hand-written with precise penmanship.

"Are these originals?" Harry asked.

"I don't know," she said. "Probably. Franklin doesn't care to keep copies or replicas."

"They must be worth a fortune."

"This is a well-protected place, as safe as any museum in the world. It has an electronic surveillance system and guards on the perimeter. The estate is over four thousand acres in size."

The next case was much smaller, holding a pair of old bifocals in wire frames. Other lenses rested on soft cloths. A sign above the case read, *Bifocal glasses. Invented 1760.*

The sign over the next display read, *Glass armonica. Invented 1761. Built by the London glassblower Charles James. First played by Marianne Davies in 1762.*

"What's this do?" Harry pointed at the horizontal metal rod laying on a stand, with a wheel at one end that allowed a person to rotate the rod like a lathe. Several dozen glasses lay sideways, with the metal rod running through the middle of each glass. The largest glass was on the left, with the smallest on the right, with descending sizes marching left to right in perfect order. The glasses were blown from different colors: a blue that was almost black, purple, red, orange, yellow, green, blue, and white.

"A musical instrument from the 1700s," Amanda said. "Have you ever seen a person play wine glasses by rubbing their moistened finger around the rims?"

"In the movies or on TV."

"They put water in the glasses, a different amount in each one, to vary the pitch so each glass makes a different note. This device before you does the same thing, but the glasses are different sizes to vary the pitch."

"So how was this played?"

"A person rotated the armonica while the musician placed their fingers on the glasses to produce notes. Unlike using water in glasses, you can use all ten fingers, but it's quite a stretch. Whatever chord you are making has to be close enough to allow your fingers to reach."

"What are the colors for?"

"To easily see which notes are which. If I recall correctly, red is C."

"An interesting invention," Harry noted. "Not much practical use. Which reminds me, tell me more about these helpers. When were they invented? Where? And how many people have access to them?"

Amanda jumped slightly, reached for her cell phone and glanced at the screen. "I have a quick meeting. Please, continue the tour on your own."

Harry remained in the museum hall after she left, chewing over her words in his mind. His skepticism gnawed at the idea of helpers, yet there he was, alive and hale. Nanotechnology was the stuff of science fiction novels. It was supposed to transform everything, making matter malleable and offering extraordinary cures, almost like magic. Just that spring he had read a whole issue of *Scientific American* on nanotechnology. He remembered enough to know that he should be dead and that nanotechnology would explain why he had survived.

The only problem as he saw it was simple enough: absent

some extraordinary recent breakthrough, no one had solved all the problems necessary to make nanobots really work.

CHAPTER FORTY-TWO

A decade had passed since she had seen Franklin, a stout man of medium height, but he looked as healthy as ever. He still affected a trim beard, perhaps because he enjoyed running his fingers through it as he talked to her. It may have been ten years, but Franklin's was the kind of presence that was always felt in her mind, even if he was half a world away. They had been lovers once, for a brief few years, more of a dalliance than a real commitment.

Franklin had not been at Raven's Nest when she brought the comatose archaeologist in. He had just returned and immediately summoned her and his closest advisor, Sam Bullard, to his study. Bullard was tall, muscular, and handsome, with an arrogance that radiated from him like an aura. She had no idea where the two men had been. Keeping secrets, even among themselves, had become a reflexive habit. She did not do it easily, but Franklin was a master at it. Regardless, she trusted him implicitly.

The study occupied a large room at the end of the second floor, with windows facing three directions. The evening sun streamed in from the west window, leaving many of the bookcases that lined the walls in shadow. A cast-iron stove, cold during the summer, sat on four legs next to the stonework of the chimney that ran from floor to ceiling. No roaring fire for this room, just the stove, and the central heating vents in the corner. Four large tables surrounded a center square of couches. Papers covered the tables in disarray, and woe to the fool that tried to straighten the mess, a quick way to get the normally placid Franklin fuming. One of the tables had a late-model computer on it, with two large monitors, next to a pile of buddies and other electronic gizmos.

"How is our guest doing?" Franklin asked.

"Completely recovered."

"Your medical helpers are truly marvelous. I wish that we all had them."

Bullard spoke up. "You shouldn't have brought him here."

She sighed. "Where else is safe right now? I made a decision and we have to live with it."

"He believes that you are a government agent and that this is a government safe house?" Franklin asked.

"That's what I told him, but he doesn't believe it," she said.

"What about your trust helpers?" Bullard asked. "Another one of those little treats that the rest of us don't have the privilege of holding."

She turned on Bullard. "I volunteered, you didn't. Leave it in the past."

Like an indulgent father, Franklin held up his hands as if to calm his children. "Back to the point. You used the trust helpers?"

"Yes, but the trust chemicals didn't work that well. Harry relics on his intellect and listens to his skepticism, not his emotions. He's not immune to trusting me, but he was wary. Besides, now that he has healing helpers in him, they keep the hormones in balance and my trust hormones have little effect, if any."

"That's unfortunate," said Franklin.

"Maybe it doesn't matter. I think that we should tell him the truth about us," she said. "It will make him more effective, able to make better decisions, since he doesn't believe the cover story."

"Oh, please, Amanda," Bullard rolled his eyes. "Our secret is too precious to just go throwing it before the rabble."

Her eyes hardened. "Really, Bullard, sometimes I wonder

if you are a Humanist at all. You sound like one of *them*, a Hedonist or someone who subscribes to the Chosen philosophy. You don't love Earthers as you love Alphas."

"No, Amanda, I don't love them," Bullard said. "I wish I were back on Alpha, but I have shown my loyalty to our faction ever since I came here."

Franklin spoke up. "Amanda, Bullard has shown his loyalty again and again. I trust him. I would like you to trust him."

"Very well. I bow to your superior wisdom." There was no tone of irony in her words. "But I still think that we should let Harry know the truth."

"Very well, I will trust you on this," Franklin said.

"Franklin, isn't it obvious? She's going sweet on him," Bullard smirked. "Like a little girl with a new puppy. All cute and cuddly."

"I've made my decision," Franklin said.

Amanda swallowed her irritation with Bullard and smiled sweetly at him before turning to stroll from the room. She wished that her trust chemicals worked on Bullard as well as they did on so many other people. Then she might be able to like him.

CHAPTER FORTY-THREE

John Johnson figured that his mother must have known that something was askew with him when she named him; otherwise, why would she have given him a recursive name, like he was his own father? He seemed normal enough as a child, but after he grew hair on his chest the voices came. As first they were only whispers, then a cacophony of conflicting advice. One demanded that he burn down the shed with the lawnmower in it, so that he wouldn't have to mow the lawn anymore, since without the lawnmower around the lawn wouldn't have a reason to grow longer anymore.

He obeyed the voice and burned down the shed. His mother wasn't mad, just sad. She cried a lot. The doctors wanted to send him to a bigger house, where other people heard voices, and where the nurses used pills to turn you into a stupid person. They had used the pills on him before. The voices couldn't reach his ears if he was a stupid person, with slurred words because his tongue felt too large, and a shuffling gait because it took too much effort to pick up his feet.

Mother decided that the bigger house wasn't for him. She took him to the island instead and left him in a smaller house. Only a kitchen, a bedroom, a bathroom with a toilet and a tub, and a living room. He had his books, his flute, and someone brought groceries every two weeks. Mother sometimes visited, though he found that she really didn't need to come by too much, since he liked to be alone. When he was alone and not having to figure out what was real and what was not real, the voices didn't bother him so much. Some of the voices, the nicer ones, even became friends with him.

He hadn't left the island since he was sixteen years old, and that had been over forty years ago.

It wasn't like he didn't have anything to do. His hands were quick with machines, and he maintained the pump house that brought fresh water from a spring to the other houses on the island.

During the winters, he was the only one on the island, living off a stockpile of groceries and propane. The winter storms lashed the shore with waves that left ice on the trees and he sat snug in his house, rereading the novels that brought him so much comfort. Stories of men on horses, castaways on deserted isles, young girls in love, mysteries to be solved, and spaceships seeking new worlds.

He was not a complete recluse. The other fourteen homes on the island were all owned by relatives, used during the summers, and sometimes he had visitors.

Like today.

* * * * * * *

"John, so good to see you," Brenda called out as they approached the small house where John the Hermit lived.

On his knees in garden, pulling weeds, the bearded man looked up and squinted. He stood up and waited for them to come closer. He didn't wipe his dirty hands on his jeans as most people would have, perhaps because he refused to shake hands. He had once told Brenda that he didn't shake hands because everyone else's hands were full of snakes and he didn't like snakes.

Her instinct was to join him in his garden and help him pull weeds, but she had learned as a young girl that wouldn't work with John. Only he could work in his garden, pulling weeds by an internal plan that only he saw. Other people working with him only agitated him.

"Brenda and Dirk," John said, speaking slowly, clearly articulating each word as if unused to having to talk out load. "It is good to see you. I heard that you were on an archaeological dig. In Arizona?"

"New Mexico, John," she said. "I'm back now."

"I would find digging up old bones very scary," John said.

"We aren't looking for bodies. We want to find other artifacts: pottery shards, tools, foundation stones, that kind of thing."

"You wouldn't find me digging up our graveyard." He gestured to the small hill behind his home.

The tiny graveyard held only five graves, but having a graveyard as a playground had led to many a spooky adventure as children. James Flannery was buried there, under a marble tombstone grown brown with the elements. His wife was buried next to him. She had waited long months as he made his fortune on trading expeditions to China. As everyone did at that time in the China trade, James Flannery dealt in opium. Profits from the trade allowed him to buy the island in 1864 for twelve hundred dollars and two barrels of Cuban rum. Dirk and Brenda liked to tease their father that they had such a nice vacation hideaway because of their drug-dealing ancestor.

"I think I'd skip digging up there, too," Brenda said. "Just some moldy old bones."

John shook himself, like a child trying to chase away a horrible image. "That'll haunt me in my dreams."

"I'm sorry, John," Brenda said. Even as a young girl, she had always liked John, finding him a fascinating window into an alternate reality. She also admired his courage, facing demons that he only occasionally hinted at when he said something odd. The words often chilled her, such as when he told her to watch out for the spider people who came out at night and grabbed animals and small children. She knew that there was no such thing as spider people, but lying in her bed that night, snug under the covers, she realized that the spider people were real to John. She respected him, that he kept functioning, not quailing before his fears.

The sister and brother talked with John for a while, drinking some punch that he mixed up for them. He told them about the pod of orcas that he had seen earlier that month, just off the island, only a few hundred yards away. He was a keen student of nature, sitting for hours and watching.

"Speaking of artifacts," Dirk said as they walked away from the hermit's home, "Harry told me about one."

"He did, huh?"

"Yes, the box that you found in the tomb."

"Did he tell you what he did with it?" she asked.

"No, he refused to let anyone else know where it was. He thought that the box was the reason that you were attacked and the others were killed."

Tears trickled down her face. "I hate that box."

He put his arm around her. "It's okay. It's not your fault. You just found the box, you didn't kill anyone."

"Harry did, though," she said. "Kill people, I mean."

"Only people that deserved it. Besides, Harry is a soldier and is used to that sort to thing."

"I don't think you could ever get used to killing people."

"Not 'used to'—I used the wrong word—but better able to adapt," Dirk said.

"Do you have any idea where Harry is?"

"I have no idea."

"Is he dead?"

"I don't think so," he said. "Harry is a survivor. Quite frankly, I was a bit chilled by how competent and clear-headed he was."

"That's Harry for you," she said. "Do Mom and Dad know about the box?"

"I decided to keep that information from them. Dad is not really in any condition to handle that sort of thing."

"What do you mean?"

"We found out about five months ago and they didn't know how to tell you."

Alarm rose in her chest. "Tell me what?"

"Dad has Alzheimer's."

CHAPTER FORTY-FOUR

Harry was still in the museum hall, carefully scrutinizing the artifacts, when Amanda returned to him. She carried a plastic box in her arms, the necks of wine coolers and beer bottles sticking out of a bed of ice. He sensed that her mood had changed. A certain wariness had disappeared.

"Let's go sit on the veranda," she said.

They found a pair of padded chairs overlooking the ocean. Amanda sat down the box of drinks down between them and settled down. She used a key to pop open a wine cooler and took a sip.

Harry sat down and looked at the drinks. Awkward situation here. "I don't drink alcohol anymore," he said, embarrassed to have to explain himself. "I'm an alcoholic."

"Not anymore," she said, taking another sip. "I love the strawberry taste of this one."

"What do you mean?"

She laughed like a schoolgirl about to reveal a secret. "You can't get drunk ever again. Your helpers think that alcohol is fuel for them and will metabolize it out of your bloodstream before you even get a buzz."

"Are you sure?" he asked, reaching for a beer. The green bottle was a Heineken. His mouth salivated at the remembered taste of dark beer. "Are you really sure?"

"I'm really sure."

He unscrewed the cap and took a taste. It was heavenly, a pleasure he thought forbidden for the rest of his life. A long swallow followed, a declaration of liberty against his demons.

"I can't believe I'm doing this," he said, settling back in the chair. "I can't believe that your helpers really work. The technology's too advanced. Yet here I am, healed from a gunshot wound, and drinking a beer."

"You're right, the technology is too advanced," Amanda said. She smiled at him, patted his arm, then let her fingers linger, burning awareness into him. He tried to look nonchalant as he smiled back at her.

"Let me tell you a story," Amanda said. "It's a long story and you need to listen to the whole thing, take it in as a whole. No interruptions, okay?"

"Okay."

"About 5600 BCE, there was a people who lived in the valleys and wetlands around a large freshwater lake in the area that we now call the Black Sea. The Black Sea did not exist then because the Bosporus Straits was a rock wall, holding back the water of the Mediterranean Sea. These people lived in a fertile area that was below sea level, yet had no idea of the danger they lived in. These people were humans, physiologically modern humans, just like you and me, evolved from earlier primates. They had discovered agriculture and had domesticated cattle, donkeys, the dog, and chickens. They grew grain that was like modern wheat and our rye. They lived in villages and had built towns that held up to two or three thousand people.

"They weren't the only people in the world that had made the leap to agriculture. There were the people at Catal Hüyük in Turkey, and Jericho at the West Bank, and maybe other places that archaeologists haven't found yet. But they had made some other leaps. They worshiped a complex set of gods that from our modern perspective were designed to keep the agriculture going. They had also invented writing, a primitive set of symbols on pieces of wood used to keep accounts and prayers to the gods. No literature yet, but they had a rich oral tradition.

"One day everything changed. An alien species came and grabbed thousands of them and transported them to a planet around another star. Whole villages and towns were uprooted—people, tools, animals, all at once."

Harry's eyes went wide and he restrained the words that leapt to mind. He knew that only recently had archaeologists discovered that the Black Sea basin had been dry land. Research submersibles had even found a village under hundreds of feet of water. But aliens? That was too weird—science fiction come to life. But what were the helpers in his bloodstream, if not science fiction come to life? He finished the beer and fished another one from the bed of ice.

Amanda continued her story. "We don't know who the aliens were, what they looked like, or what their motivation was. We never even saw them, just their machines. We called them the Movers, for the lack of a better term. The new planet was completely like Earth. We have determined that it wasn't always that way, but had been terraformed with species from Earth over a period of tens of thousands of years. Plants and animals from Earth, even bacteria, were brought there to make a new world. We called the new world Alpha.

"The world was different in that there was a smaller moon than Earth has, but still pretty big. That moon also didn't belong there. It belongs around one of the gas giants in the system, but had been moved to become the moon of Alpha. You can see that the Movers were capable of moving a lot more than just some primitive bipeds from Earth. A lot of Earth ecology requires the regular rhythms that lunar gravity creates, and depends on the reflected light of the moon for nocturnal activities.

"Only later did these people, who are known as Alphas, discover that they were located in the Alpha Centauri system. The Centauri system is the closest system to Earth, but still it's over four light years away. In the center of the system is a binary set of stars, named Father and Mother by the Alphas. The first is slightly larger than the Sun and shines with the same wavelengths as the Sun, though it looks brighter, and the other is smaller and its light is slightly more orange than the yellow that we are used to. Alpha orbits the Father. The Mother is far enough away that its sunlight doesn't make much difference, but during the closest approaches by Alpha to the Mother, nights have a kind of blue tint to them and you can see quite well, like twilight. I know that I am just getting into astronomical arcana, but I find my home interesting. There is one more star in the Centauri system, called the Little Brother by the Alphas. It's a red dwarf and is quite faint, even from the surface of Alpha."

Amanda finished her wine cooler and picked up a beer. "Maybe a few days, maybe a century—we just don't know—after the Alphas were taken from Earth, their homes on Earth were destroyed. The Mediterranean Sea, whose level had risen as a result of the melting of the Ice Age glaciers, broke through into the Black Sea basin at the Bosporus Straits. We have modeled what must have happened in computer simulations. At first the flow of water must have been a horrendous flood, carving a canyon into the earth as it ran to the lowest point, the lake in the center of the basin. Who knows how many people died in that initial flood. Maybe none, since we don't know exactly where the Movers took the Alphas from. Having formed this fast-flowing river, the water continued to pour in. We estimate the flow rate to have been about ten cubic miles per day, which raised the level of the lake by about a foot a day and added about an additional mile of shoreline each day, turning it into the Black Sea. Whoever the Movers had left behind would have had to move quickly to keep away from the rising water. It's not impossible to keep ahead of that much water, though finding food would have been hard during a trek that must have been hundreds of miles for some. All the freshwater fish and other organisms in the lake would have died off as the seawater changed their environment.

"The people from Earth on Alpha, the Alphas, quickly adapted to our new home. We continued their technological development, much faster than here on Earth. We don't know why we were so much faster. Some people think that it was because Alphas are just smarter than Earthers, but that can't be true because there are no significant genetic differences. Some think that perhaps the experience of being transplanted focused our society or perhaps the Movers subtly accelerated our technological development. Why would they do that? No one has a good answer for any of that. What matters is that after three thousand years a full technological civilization had been developed, complete with sophisticated computers, nanotechnology, and space travel.

"Nanotechnology changed everything. We developed the helpers, which every child inherits from his or her mother in the womb, and is given an extra dose of helpers after birth. Helpers give us effective immortality because they can keep us alive absent a catastrophic injury, like losing your head or being blown apart. Our helpers, not your helpers. Your helpers will not stop the normal processes of aging."

Harry raised his eyebrows, trying to wrap his thoughts around the idea of living such a long time, cheating old man death. He kept his mouth shut, not wanted to interrupt the flow of fascinating information.

"Immortality changed every aspect of our society. Children became a completely rare phenomenon in order to prevent runaway population growth. We became much more conservative, worried about accidents, and we changed how we viewed punishment. Sending a person to prison for life no longer made sense. The death penalty for murder seemed excessive, even though the murder victim had their life cut short. In a way we learned to respect life, especially our own lives.

"So we needed a new method of punishment. We settled on the idea of exile, but where to send these exiles? There were some different ideas and lots of arguments, including confining people to virtual worlds created by computer programs, but pretty soon most people agreed to the idea of sending criminals into exile back on Earth. The criminals were each put into a small spaceship, placed in artificial hibernation for a trip that took dozens of years, and sent back to Earth. Most of their helpers were disabled before exile, but the helpers to keep them alive, absent a catastrophic death, were left in.

"Of course, Earth is a much more dangerous place than Alpha, and many exiles have died. Accidents, starvation— even helpers need food—and injuries in battle, and such. Not only criminals were sent here. On Alpha, there are people who engage in reckless behavior, such as hang-gliding, surfing, and mountain climbing and such, taking risks in order to feel alive. They are considered mentally ill by others and many of these people are exiled because of this. In a way, exile became a ready solution to so many of our problems. It was too easy, sending people away, and of course, the consequences to the Earthers was completely ignored.

"Finally, to answer your obvious questions. I am an exile, born on Alpha. The man in the desert whom I shot and that you shot again in Colorado, Marshall Stone, is also an exile. He is part of an organization called the Cabal. I told you the truth about that. The expansion to the truth is that the Cabal is an organization made up of exiles, a nasty bunch of people."

"That's it." She picked up another beer. "Questions?"

Harry had been keeping the chronology straight in his head, an ingrained professional trait. "So you're telling me that you are four thousand years old?"

"Yes," she said. "Four thousand three hundred and ninety-two, actually."

"When did you come to Earth?"

"When I first arrived on Earth, they landed me in France in 1241 A.D. that is, or should I say C.E., though the term Common Era always seemed silly to me. You are still measuring the date system from the same event. As usual, the automated space-craft found a spot away from towns or villages. I was awakened when the craft entered the atmosphere and was still groggy when it dumped me. Some villagers found me and attacked me. I barely got away. They wounded me, and only my helpers kept me alive. Quite a rude introduction to life on Earth."

"What's this have to do with the artifact that I found?"

"The symbol on the artifact, the three triangles within a circle, is a common Alpha symbol. Part of our glyph system.

The tomb you found it in was probably the tomb of an exile."

"There was what looked like glitter all over the corpse," Harry recalled.

"That would be clumps of helpers, often found on one of our dead if enough time has passed for physical decay."

"You want me to give you the artifact?" Harry asked.

"We do," she said. "But we want to keep it out of the hands of the Cabal even more."

"What does the artifact do?" Harry asked. "What is it?"

"We have no idea. The Cabal is acting like they might know what it does, though they have a tendency to be extreme in whatever they do anyway."

"Maybe they killed those people just on pure speculation?"

"The people mean nothing to them. Exiles who join the Cabal are either Hedonists or Deists. Hedonists are constantly seeking pleasure. Back on Alpha they used drugs to help them forget experiences so that new experiences would seem fresh. They see Earth as a playground for their megalomaniacal fantasies. Deists are a form of a religion, except they worship themselves. They see Alphas as being gods, at least in comparison to Earthers. They like to have Earthers serve them as a serfs and playthings. They are similar to Hedonists in that they tend towards megalomaniacal fantasies. Either way, Hedonist or Deist, Earthers are just pawns to them."

"And what are you?" Harry asked.

"I'm a Humanist. We are part of a philosophical movement driven by respect for all human life and all other life. Some of us converted to humanism after becoming exiles, while others were Humanists to begin with. I was part of the latter group. Unlike most exiles, I didn't commit a crime or act mentally ill to go into exile. I volunteered."

"And you don't work for secret government agency?" The answer was obvious.

"No, I work with a group of exiles that are motivated by humanism. We are trying to protect Earth from exiles who want to harm you. In our own way, we are the anti-Cabal."

CHAPTER FORTY-FIVE

"Why didn't you want to tell me?" Brenda asked, trying to keep the irritation out of her voice.

The colonel sat in his easy chair in the living room, a chair that had been there and his alone ever since she could remember. Its cloth upholstery was worn and getting the ratty look of furniture found in charity stores. His face remained impassive as he looked at his daughter. She had been standing, but under his eyes, she took a seat on the couch. Her brother stood near the doorway and her mother watched from the kitchen table in the other room.

"A man only has two things to call his own in this world," Rusty Finnigan said. "Everything else either belongs to someone else, or he shares it with someone else, whether it be his family, his wife, his buddies, or even his dog. Those two things that a man owns are his reputation and his pride. His reputation is what other people think of him. His pride is what motivates him to establish and keep that reputation."

He cleared his throat. "This disease takes away a man's reputation. It takes away his pride. I didn't want you to know."

"I would love you just as much."

His eyes glistened. "A man wants more than love."

Her mother came into the room. "We all thought that it was for the best."

"Good grief," she said. "I'm twenty-one years old, not a child. It's not like it's cancer or something like that."

"No, it's worse," the colonel said.

As if to prove his point, his intense gaze softened and he turned to his wife. "Dear, what's for dinner tonight?"

"You've asked three times," she snapped, then her face softened. "We're having your favorite, beef stroganoff and candied carrots. And I've made rhubarb pie."

"I'm sorry. I forgot." He sounded like a compliant child being chastised.

A trivial exchange of words, but they chilled Brenda. She was losing her father.

Later that evening, her father came to her room, where she was reading in her pajamas on her bed. He stood at the doorway, like he had stood so many times before, a comforting presence in her life.

"I'm not afraid of dying, Brenda," he said, his tone matter-of-fact, even a bit reflective. "I made peace with that long ago, before my first battle. I just don't want to die of Alzheimer's." He paused. "It's not noble."

CHAPTER FORTY-SIX

Harry stood on the patio, staring up at the stars. A hint of the Northern Lights twinkled on the far horizon. He had occasionally seen the Northern Lights as a boy in Minneapolis, and they had drawn him to books and web sites on astronomy. Launches of the space shuttle had also fascinated him and he had decided that he wanted to be an astronomer and an astronaut. Those dreams thrilled him in his youth, but foundered on his lack of interest in mathematics. He traced the Big Dipper with his eyes, used the two end stars to find Polaris, the North Star, and traced out the Little Dipper. Other friends attracted his attention: the Milky Way, so aptly named; the Pleiades, a cauldron birthing new stars; the simple 'W' of Cassiopeia. Many of the other constellations, so painstakingly memorized as a child, were now just a jumble.

"Enjoying yourself?" Amanda asked from behind him.

He started, surprised that she had approached without him hearing her. The strain of the past several days had dulled his edge, and the seeming safety of Raven's Nest had encouraged him to drop out of combat mode.

"Yes. I enjoy the stars. They were particularly wonderful in Afghanistan, even clearer than here."

"I agree, though Tibet is even more amazing."

"You've been to Afghanistan?"

She came up to stand beside him, folded her arms, and looked up. He was intensely aware of her presence. "Yes," she said.

"When?"

"Many times."

"Why?"

"Missions of hope."

He always felt frustrated talking to her. She seemed to honestly answer his questions, but not by way of volunteering information that would let him better understand her. Too many of her answers were riddles.

"Do you know what Fermi's Paradox is?" she asked.

Harry sifted through his memory. The history of science had always attracted him, but one cannot remember everything. "Ah, something to do with extraterrestrial life, I can't quite remember the details."

"Simply stated: if extraterrestrial life exists, where are they? There are billions of stars in our galaxy, billions of galaxies, with untold numbers of planets. If intelligent life arose, why has it not spread everywhere, after the billions of years that the universe has been around?"

"Do you know the answer?" he asked with smile, teasing her.

"No," she replied seriously. "But I suspect that intelligent life is very rare."

"I guess you have solved the Paradox then, since your people have met extraterrestrials, and by the strict definition of the word, you are extraterrestrials now, also."

"No, we haven't solved the Paradox," she said. "Our very existence makes it even harder to understand the Paradox. One of the unknowns of the Paradox, as understood by Earth scientists, is that they don't know how many planets out there are capable of supporting life. We Alphas know that there are many, since we live on one, and have found several others around nearby stars. We also have another answer that the Earthers don't. We know that alien life really exists, that intelligence didn't just rise up on Earth."

"Okay."

"But the Paradox is still there. Where is everyone else? The galaxy should be teeming with intelligent alien life, yet we have never picked up their radio signals, nor seen evidence of them."

"The best questions are those that don't have definitive answers," Harry said. "A philosopher told me that once."

"Let me introduce you to another philosopher. Franklin wants to meet you. For a late lunch tomorrow."

They talked long into the night, combining stimulating intellectual and personal conversation, finding some deck chairs that they pulled together and lay down on to better watch the sky. Orion the Hunter marched across the sky. A few satellites moved past. Harry asked about the location of Alpha Centauri and was disappointed to find that it was only visible in the southern hemisphere. At some point in the early morning, he was surprised to find the two of them holding hands.

CHAPTER FORTY-SEVEN

Amanda found Franklin in his study. He was whittling away at a piece of wood, shavings falling onto his pants and piling around his ankles, as he read from a computer monitor. Occasionally he put down the wood and his knife and typed in some quick letters or worked the trackball with his fingers.

"How has he been taking your revelations?" Franklin asked.

"Very well, just as I expected." She came around to see what Franklin was up to. E-mail. Filtered through numerous cutouts, encrypted with the best software, the links that he used to run a vast network of spies, informers, and other exiles of like mind. "He has a quick mind and is very adaptable. I guess the combination of being an archeologist, soldier, and science fiction fan fosters those traits."

"You are enamored with him," Franklin said, looking up at her and smiling.

"I would like to deny it, but I can't." She tried to find something on the ceiling to look at, wanting to avoid Franklin's probing gaze.

"It's been a long time since you were interested in such things."

"Maybe too long," she said in a dry tone.

He laughed.

* * * * * * *

An hour later, she sat down at the dining table with Franklin and Harry. Subdued lighting showed off two paintings for effect—a Gauguin, from his naked women of the South Pacific period, and a Renoir of two children in a park, a piece not listed in any catalogs. A cook brought in sandwiches and soup from the kitchen. The staff that maintained Raven's Nest were all long-time employees, well paid and loyal; all Earthers, no exiles among them. To them, Franklin was just an eccentric rich man.

"How old are you?" Harry asked.

Franklin laughed. "You are quite direct. I like that. I'm about the same age as Amanda. Most of us are of similar ages, give or take a few centuries, because we were the generation alive on Alpha when the medical helper technology was developed."

"Why were you exiled to Earth?"

Franklin looked down at his plate and pushed the sandwich around a bit before he answered. "Let's just say that I engaged in a forbidden experiment. One that very much upset many people, so I was exiled."

"How long ago?" Harry asked.

"I was an early exile. I have been here for over three thousand years. I spent most of that time in the boonies. My pod dropped me in New Guinea, a wonderful, rugged island, with many different cultures. The deep mountain valleys create such barriers to communication that there was a wealth of different languages, totally different ways of living, and of course, you could see what was truly common among humans. An excellent laboratory for watching our fellow humans and learning about them. People and their psychological quirks had not really interested me that much up until then, but New Guinea made me into an anthropologist, a psychologist, a student of what it meant to be human. I was not a Humanist when exiled, but I became a Humanist there."

"Which means?" Harry asked.

"Put simply, I came to love Earthers as I love Alphas. I came to enjoy the companionship of many different types of people and found glory in the potential of each individual. Our Humanist philosophy arrived at these insights, as we were in so many things, long before your Enlightenment thinkers had similar insights."

"You're white. How did you blend into the population?"

"Our helpers can manipulate the melatonin in our skin, so racial differences do not matter. We can blend in."

"So you stayed on that one island for all that time?"

"It's a big island. Like many other Alphas, I was afraid of ocean voyages. Drowning can be very unpleasant when your helpers are trying to keep you alive, and the helpers can't help you get to dry land. Even so, I did take the plunge and go to Australia. Took centuries to tour that island. Truly remarkable how primitively the aborigines lived, especially compared to how I had lived on Alpha."

"Why didn't you just island-hop through Indonesia to Asia?" Harry asked.

"I thought about it. Like most exiles, I had memorized the geography of Earth and knew what was possible. But quite frankly, I found myself too fascinated with the truly primitive, humanity in the raw, hunting and gathering, using only the most primitive agriculture. Another fear also kept me on the island. There were only two other exiles on New Guinea that I was aware of. One of them was eventually killed when he annoyed a whole tribe and they cut him up into pieces. Helpers can't fix that. The other was a Deist and was quite happy to lord over his small tribe in his high mountain valley, treating the villagers as his personal toys. I left him alone and he left me alone, at least until I went back and took care of him about eighty years ago. To my shame, I never liberated those people from his tyranny for all that time. You see, many of the exiles sent to Earth would be considered clinically insane, and I had heard that some of them liked to hunt other exiles. Keeping a low profile was a good way to keep safe.

"That being said, when a European sailing ship landed in New Guinea near where I lived, I took the opportunity to go. I was scared, but finally bored enough to take the risk. That was in 1622, as I recall. I didn't go all the way back to Europe with them, just to what is now Malaysia. I toured the whole of Asia and didn't get to Europe for another fifty years. After some time touring Europe, I met Amanda in Prague."

"Yes," she agreed. "Sometime in the 1670s."

Harry took a bite out of his sandwich, ignored up until then. Listening to the casual way they talked about centuries was so surreal. In a way he envied them, cruising through history as tourists. But not always as tourists, he realized.

"You don't always try to stay in the background, do you," Harry said, a statement, not a question.

Franklin smiled. "No, sometimes we like to play in the limelight."

"I suspected as much," Harry said. "Though you don't look much like the portraits that I've seen, especially on the hundred dollar bill. You are Benjamin Franklin."

"Benjamin Franklin is dead," the young man said. "Perhaps it would be more accurate to say that I used to be Benjamin Franklin. I assume that my little museum collection gave me away."

"Yes," Harry said. "I knew that you had invented the bifocals and worked on the Declaration of Independence, but it took some web searches to see that you had invented everything else in the hall. There was also a letter in there, something about how wonderful the future could be."

Franklin laughed. "A bit of vanity there. If I might quote from myself, written back in 1780, 'We may perhaps learn to deprive large masses of their gravity, and give them absolute levity, for the sake of easy transport. Agriculture may diminish its labor and double its produce; all diseases may by sure means be prevented or cured.'"

"Why be so bold?" Harry asked. "Weren't you afraid anymore?"

"The quote is just a private joke for my own amusement," Franklin explained.

"Weren't you concerned that one of the other exiles might have read the quote and realized that you were one of them?"

Harry asked.

"That would have been a risk, of course," Franklin said. "Our anonymity protects us. But I wrote those words in a private letter to a fellow natural philosopher, so the risk was really quite small."

"Making all those inventions, and being such a prominent man, weren't you worried about being exposed?"

"I got carried away. At first I just wanted to be part of that grand experiment going on in America. There was a group of us Humanist exiles who were subtly encouraging the thinking that had blossomed into the Enlightenment. Individual rights, rational thought, skepticism, breaking the shackles of thoughtless religious conformity, science, new inventions—all were very exciting. I contributed my small part from Philadelphia.

"The real reason I became so prominent was to earn a fortune. I decided that the Humanists needed money to form a more effective underground network. Other than some historians, most people still don't realize how wealthy old Ben was, all earned from my many business enterprises. My science and inventions were just a part of the package."

"But you look old in your portraits," Harry objected.

"Not all of us have the same set of helpers. My helpers allow me age my body, getting fatter, sagging skin, going bald—the whole appearance—though my health and energy levels remain the same. I stayed in the role as long as I could, eighty-four years, so much longer and more vigorous than other people of that time. I had to end it eventually, though. An exile named Dulkin actually came and tried to kill me. I escaped and hid for a long time."

Franklin took out his cell phone and looked at it. He frowned and tapped in a message. "Not good news, I'm afraid. We have been monitoring Cabal communications. They have no idea of how far we have penetrated their technical network. We've just intercepted a message. The Cabal is going to escalate the situation by kidnapping Brenda and using the threat against her to get you to give them the artifact."

Harry shot to his feet, tipping back his chair to the floor with a loud clatter. "We must go."

"Yes, quite so," Franklin said. "I have summoned a helicopter. A jet will be waiting for you at the airport. All the equipment you will need is being gathered." He looked at Amanda, "You will go with him?"

"Of course."

CHAPTER FORTY-EIGHT

The room stank of testosterone.

Six men sprawled on couches and chairs, all concentrating on a big screen television on the wall. Each had a controller in his hands and they twisted back and forth, blasting aliens and hunting each other in *Halo VI*.

Gretel stood at the doorway. She didn't want to be here. She wanted to be back in New York, at an upstate estate, nursing Stone back to health. His body was well enough now, and the physical structure of the brain rebuilt, but the neural connections took a lot longer to reconstruct. Much of it was lost forever: memories, skills, aspects of his personality. She grieved for what had happened to him, but also saw it as an opportunity

He remembered who she was and his fondness for her. She loved him too, but sometimes she got so sick of him that she left him for years, once even for a full century. She always came back. Now she could nurse his mind back to health, making him loyal to her. No longer would he chase after other women; he would find passion only for her. A perfect mate.

One of the men shouted, dissing on the man he had just blown away. The man took it quietly, other than a terse description of the first man's mother as an expletive. He re-entered the game and hunted his adversary.

The six men were all ex-military and had served together as a team for the Cabal for the past four years. She wished that Stone were here; this is what he liked to do.

Gretel cleared her throat, a quiet sound that one would not

have expected to hear. The men instantly reacted. One paused the game, another hit the mute on the television, and all six pairs of eyes turned to her.

"Go through the drill," she said.

The men spoke by turn, as if chanting a devotional in a monastery.

"2300, gear up and police the safe house, leave nothing behind."

"0130, leave for the airfield."

"0200, embark in the helicopter."

"0220, or thereabouts, land helicopter in a clearing on the south end of the island. If there are obstructions, use alternate landing site on the west of the island. If further obstructed, rappel from the helicopter. If rappelling, return to refuel before going back for extraction, otherwise the chopper will wait."

"0300, two teams will canvass the island, searching each home, looking for the girl."

"Name is Brenda Finnigan."

"Red hair, big tits."

Gretel frowned and the men hurried on.

"Capture her alive at all costs."

"Extract before dawn."

"Leave no witnesses."

Gretel looked at each man in turn, following the methods that she had learned from Stone. All this military posturing, running around with guns, hurting people, held no interest for her. She did it because the Cabal asked her to do it.

"Make no mistakes," she said, and left them to their game.

A seventh man sat at the kitchen table, looking at his pornographic magazine. Jack Hull was an ideal operative who always followed orders and never asked questions. She despised him, which wasn't much of a surprise, since she despised most Earthers.

"We've got a job to do," Gretel said.

The house had only been rented the day before, chosen because of the two acres of land and numerous trees that provided concealment. Walls on each side also helped. Gretel sat in the passenger seat, giving instructions to Hull from the GPS unit in her cell phone.

Jonesport sprawled along the coast, protected from the long waves of the Atlantic by Beals Island. First they drove across the bridge to Beals Island and along the road that circled the island. This island joined Wass Island. Near the end of the road, on a hill, a cell tower loomed. Hull stopped the car and Gretel rolled down her window.

From her large purse, she removed a black wand, a foot long and two inches in diameter. A small LCD on its face showed an image of what the wand was pointed at. Rotating a knob on the rear of the wand caused the image to zoom in or zoom out, like a camera. She brought the cell tower and the small building at its base into focus. She pressed another button and the image blinked.

A directed blast of electromagnetic energy fried all the electronics in the cell tower. The box used technology not yet invented by the Earthers. In a few years, they certainly would have the ability. Making advanced technology was not a matter of going into a lab and just making it; you needed an entire technological civilization behind the efforts, making all the parts. The Earthers could make all the parts, and factories in Taiwan, Indiana, Germany, and Israel had all contributed their share; all the Alphas knew was how to put the pieces together. The melted electronics would bewilder the telephone company, one of those mysteries that scientists occasionally ran across that had no explanation.

"Next one," she said.

Her psychological profile back on Alpha said that she was lazy. That word always annoyed her. What the psychologists saw as laziness, she saw as prudence. So what if she enjoyed laying in the sun all day? What was the point of running about, helter-skelter, all the time? She was immortal; she had a lifetime to get things done.

Even so, she could move with decision when she needed to.

That decisiveness had gotten her in trouble back on Alpha. A love triangle—herself, her sister, and a handsome man—ended when she struck back at them for betraying her. Her sister died, but his helpers were able to keep him alive; she would have preferred the opposite outcome. The punishment had been exile. Stone believed that Gretel had chosen exile to be with him, and she allowed him to think so.

The Cabal was all abuzz over this effort to recover the box in New Mexico, even though they had no idea what was in it. That eagerness had come close to taking Stone from her. The very thought of the possibility of losing him forever stabbed into her heart. The Earthers lived such quick lives that death meant little compared to the pain that an Alpha felt when someone died. She even still missed her sister, after thousands of years.

The other two cell phone towers were back on the mainland, both on hills. The first was among luxury homes, each with a pool and at least four garages. She fried that tower. The last tower was located near a neighborhood of close-packed row houses, from a time when Jonesport had been a fishing village, not the summer destination of the wealthy. Gretel fried the tower. Opening her cell phone, she saw that there was no signal. Jonesport and the nearby islands were now in a communications blackout.

Gretel opened the wand to a wider setting and waved it along the row houses, with their peeling paint, children's bicycles, and cars more than three years old. She smiled. No more televisions, computers, microwaves—anything with electronics or electricity running through it.

CHAPTER FORTY-NINE

A twin-engine Learjet raced across Canada, leaving a streak in the late evening sky, eating up 510 miles an hour, fighting a bit of a headwind. Around nightfall they landed in Winnipeg to refuel. Harry sat in the cabin, watching a woman in a soiled shirt and pants attaching a hose from the fuel truck. He wished she would hurry. Past experience had taught him that he should sleep, catching winks whenever he got a chance, but he was too nervous to relax.

"I've been so enchanted with Raven's Keep and my recovery that I haven't been thinking straight," he said in a low voice. Only Amanda was in the passenger cabin with him. "I've failed in my responsibilities. I should have been thinking about Brenda. If the Cabal is willing to hurt her, they are willing to use any lever they can get hold of. What about my ex-wife and son? I think they live in Chicago."

Amanda smirked at him. "You're not sure?"

He damped down a surge of irritation. "I screwed up that part of my life. I have my son's cell number, so I don't really need to know where they live."

"I'm sorry, that was uncalled for," she said. "I understand that sometimes things don't work out the way we hope."

"I love my son. My wife just doesn't want me in their lives. I'm worried about them, though."

"We already took them into protective custody two days ago, so to speak, and are hiding them," Amanda said.

"Since you have no government authority, that means that

you, in effect, kidnapped them."

"Yes." She looked embarrassed. "It's for their own good."

"I bet that really pissed off my ex."

"So I've heard," she said. "You might want to call her and calm her down."

"What cover story are you using?"

"That you are working for the government and got the wrong guys angry with you. They might come after your ex-wife and children, so we are protecting them. We have them in a safe house up in northern Michigan."

"I should call them," Harry said.

"I'll arrange it."

A few minutes later, she handed her cell phone to Harry. "Just press send to dial her number."

He took the phone and paused, his finger poised over the green button. "So where does she live?" he asked. "The child support payment is taken out my pension by the Pentagon, so I really don't have any reason to contact her."

"She lives in Minneapolis. She moved there seven months ago to become a director in an accounting firm."

"You certainly did a lot of research on me."

"Information is power," Amanda said. "It's the only way that we successfully fight against the Cabal."

Harry pressed the button.

"Hello." The voice was neutral, like a cat wondering if it wanted to go outdoors.

"Maria, it's Harry."

Her tone downshifted. "What kind of trouble have you got us into?" she demanded. Her voice contained that bitterness that always made him feel guilty. He had heard no other emotion from her for ten years. Sometimes he sought memories of when she had sounded sweet, but those memories only increased the guilt. Most divorces have two sides to them, a sharing of responsibility, but the collapse of his marriage lay only at his feet. She had struggled for so long, cried, forgiven, tried to make it work, and he had repeatedly fouled it all up, driven by alcohol and a libido that knew no rules. Now the alcohol was gone, and the libido tamed by age and discipline, and the relationship too poisoned to be anything other than bitter.

"I can't go into the details. This really has nothing to do with you, but the bad guys are pissed and might try to get to me through you."

"How long is this going to last?"

"I don't know. Maybe only a few more days, probably a lot longer. Are they taking good care of you?"

"Yes, just wonderful care." Her voice dripped sarcasm. "Harry, I have a life I have to get back to. People depend on me. I have forty employees in my office that need me to be there."

"I can't help that right now," he said. "It's better to be alive than inconvenienced."

"My life is not an inconvenience." He could hear razors in her voice. "I know you always thought it was an inconvenience. That I was an inconvenience. That James was an inconvenience. I thought that we were rid of you, but here you are back, screwing up everything."

"Maria, I didn't ask for this to happen. It wasn't my fault. People have already died. Too many people, some of them my friends. They weren't soldiers, they weren't ready to die. It was just murder."

There was a long silence on the other end. "I'm sorry, Harry."

"It's not your fault. I'm trying to fix things."

"Is this more black ops kind of stuff?"

"Yes."

"You were always good at that. I will pray for you."

"Thank you," he said. She had returned to her Catholic faith in a big way after he had hurt her so much, with a strong mixture of New Age mysticism. "Can I talk to James?"

"He's already asleep."

"A teenager who goes to bed early?"

"He's asleep," she said stubbornly.

"Okay. Tell him I love him and hope to talk to him soon."

"I will. Bye."

"Goodbye." He spoke to a closed connection.

Harry handed the cell phone back to Amanda. "That really sucked," he said. "I really wish that I was part of my son's life. I'm just like my dad, absent without permission."

"Maybe things will change in the future," Amanda said. "We all make mistakes; what matters is if we try to fix them. That's the wisdom from an old gal like me."

"Yeah, but it's easy to put off fixing it when the ex hates your guts."

The aircraft took off. Harry had never even met the pilots, who were in their cockpit before takeoff and remained there. Didn't the guys need to pee?

Amanda handled Harry a bundle of papers. "This is the new you. New ID papers, passports, driver's license, credit cards, library card, everything to make a new cover. Your name is now Harry Rivera and you live in Fayetteville, North Carolina. We picked a place that you would be familiar with.'

"Stationed at Fort Bragg for nine years."

"I know."

"More of that information-is-power thing?"

"Of course." Amanda pointed to two chests in the back of the airplane cabin. "There's more. We have gear that you should be used to from the Army."

Harry opened one of the trunks, like a child opening a present on Christmas morning. Inside on top was an M4 carbine with a folding stock, with a flashlight mounted below. Beneath, packed with foam squares and cloths were more toys: night goggles, bulletproof vest, extra magazines, boxes of ammunition, the long tubes of silencers for the M4 and his Beretta, flash-bang grenades, two smoke grenades, even three pineapple-shaped fragmentation grenades. Radio with an earpiece and throat mike, knife, GPS unit, flares, and everything else that the competent special operator would want. Harry had only brought along his cell phone and his pistol.

Now he had something to distract his mind. He field-stripped the M4, cleaning every clean piece, and put it back together tenderly. He began to load the magazines with ammunition, feeling a sense of satisfaction with each bullet that he slid into place.

Amanda opened her trunk and removed her sniper rifle. The barrel had been unscrewed to make it fit in the trunk.

Harry glanced in her trunk. "You didn't bring any night goggles?"

"No need for them. I can see in the dark was well as the best night goggles."

"A nice advantage," Harry said. "The helpers do that?"

"No, advanced genetic engineering. All the bad genes have been removed and certain advantages added in."

"Quite a neat trick."

She nodded as she stripped her rifle apart and began to clean it.

"Why did you come along?" Harry asked.

"You need help."

"You said that you don't like to kill," Harry said. "What if we have to kill people in order to protect Brenda and her family?"

"No one likes to kill," Amanda said. "Well, no one who is not a psychopath or completely deranged. Don't worry about me. I will kill if I need to. I won't let innocents die because I felt queasy."

"You said you knew that Stone was an exile when you shot him," Harry said. "How was that? Did you know Stone?"

"No. Back on Alpha our helpers could talk to each other, sort of as if we were all nodes in a large wireless network. That ability is burned out of us before we are sent to Earth, but if we run into enough exiles, we pick up sort of intuitive hunches of who might be an exile. The way that a person carries himself, how symmetrical someone is, how attractive. Most of us are too vain to not be as attractive as the helpers can make us. That FBI agent looked too damned good, so I shot him."

"Do you think that there will be exiles trying to kidnap Brenda?"

"I don't know, maybe," she said. "Why?"

"I just want to know if I should go for head shots."

Amanda gave him a strange look that he interpreted as a mixture of respect and fear. No disgust, at least.

It was midnight when they landed at the airport in Banger and taxied over to a private hangar. Harry and Amanda carried their gear in large duffel bags over to a Jeep Cherokee waiting for them, keys in the ignition.

"Who left this here for us?" Harry asked. Amanda drove while he used the GPS in his cell phone to navigate.

"I have no idea," she said. "Franklin contacted someone. He is very well connected. Sometimes it is an operative that he has, sometimes a government official who thinks he's getting orders from a legitimate source, sometimes it's a criminal gang. We try to stay away from the criminals, because they aren't professional in their behavior and sometimes try to double-cross you, thinking they will get more money. But sometimes you have to use what is available."

"Does the Cabal use the same type of resources?"

She turned onto the freeway and accelerated to the speed limit, but no more. "The Cabal is much larger than us. You have to remember that most of the exiles committed criminal acts back on Alpha. They also have a lot more full-time employees, who think that they just work for an organized crime gang. If necessary, the Cabal uses mercenaries or other criminals."

Harry looked at his cell phone, memorizing the map of Flannery's Island and the surrounding water. It was only about two miles from Jonesport, with other islands nearby. Harry burned the contours of the islands into his brain. The middle of a quick-moving battle was no time to look at maps. He tried to call Brenda, but received an out-of-service signal. He must have tried to call her two or three dozen times already, always getting the same result.

As they approached Jonesport his cell phone beeped at him and complained that it could no longer find a signal. Harry suspected that this was all the Cabal's doing and that worried him. He set his cell phone to not make any more audible alerts and placed it inside a plastic bag, sealed it, and then slipped it into his pocket.

There were several marinas in the quiet town. Amanda drove to the municipal marina and parked in the mostly empty parking lot. As they got out of the car, carrying their duffel bags, Harry checked his watch. 0210. The air smelled of salt. Only a few houses on the other side of the street had any lights on. A few streetlights illuminated intersections and a small light illuminated the sign "Jonesport Marina." Harry noticed that two of the streetlights had traffic cameras on them. They were certainly being recorded on a hard drive somewhere; not much they could do about that.

A chain-link fence provided anti-theft protection for the moored boats, with a gate secured with a chain and padlock. Amanda drew a set of bolt cutters from her duffle bag and offered them to Harry to do the honors. He had always marveled at the ability of bolt cutters, which looked like shrubbery shears, to cut through metal. He cut the chain and pulled it aside.

"Which boat are we looking for?" he whispered.

"The *Mary Jane*," she whispered back. "It's supposed to be at the end of the second-to-last pier to the left. Slip 41."

They found a middle-aged man sitting on a chair, with his legs crossed, on the dock next to slip 41. He wore a jacket to ward off the night chill and was smoking a cigarette, its red tip glowing in the dark. The moonless night was only illuminated by the stars and by stray light from the houses in Jonesport and on the large island across the small sound.

"You folks looking for a boat?" he asked. The voice was gruff from too many years of smoking.

"Yes," Amanda said. "We rented it. Are you the owner of the *Mary Jane*?"

"Yep, there she is," he said. Harry could make out the twenty-six-foot cabin cruiser, painted white. "All fueled up, key in the ignition, just like you asked."

"We appreciate you making it available on such a short notice," she said.

Harry placed his duffel on the dock. This delay was starting to annoy him.

"Why not?" the man said. "You offer five times my going rate, plus a deposit equal to the value of the boat. That's a cool two hundred grand. I took the money, but then I got to thinking."

"Thinking what?" Amanda demanded, steel in her voice.

The boat owner was not intimidated. "I'm thinking that I wanted to meet the kind of people who want to rent a boat in the middle of the night."

Neither Amanda or Harry said anything in response.

"You're not drug runners, are you?" the boat owner demanded.

"No, of course not," Harry said. "Who runs drugs off New England?"

"Running illegals? You picking up some of those Chinese trying to sneak into the country? Taking jobs from good Americans?"

"No, none of that," Harry said.

"Then why want a boat in the middle of the night?"

"We have an itch to go fishing," Amanda said.

"Bullshit."

"Do you ask all your charters this many questions?" Amanda asked.

Before the boat owner answered, Harry shushed everyone. He listened intently. There it was again, coming on the breeze off the water—the sound of a helicopter. He felt a chill run through him. Choppers didn't usually run at night. It must be the bad guys.

"We gotta go," Harry said, picking up his duffle bag and passing the sitting man to get onto the boat.

"Hey!" The boat owner stood up. "What if you don't bring my boat back?"

Harry placed the duffle bag on the deck and reached for the small of his back, where his pistol rested. He was not going to listen anymore, every second counted.

Amanda stepped on the boat, holding her hand out at Harry, and he paused. She turned to the man on the dock.

"We will bring your boat back," she said. "Even if we didn't, and we will, you will be able to keep the deposit."

"What if I don't trust you and want to keep my boat?" the owner asked.

"You signed a contract," Amanda said as Harry climbed the short ladder from the back deck, the cockpit, to the flying bridge. He pulled out a small flashlight with a red filter over the light, and flashed it across the control console.

"There's no key in the ignition," Harry called out.

"I don't want this charter anymore," the owner said. "I don't like other people taking my boat anyway."

"You accepted our money," Amanda said, her tone increasingly urgent.

"I'll give it back."

Harry bounded down from the flying bridge. Any more seconds wasted was too much time. Jumping up onto the dock, Harry grabbed the man's upper arms around the biceps with his hands. He had intended to draw his pistol, but a lower-key approach seemed workable.

The man was about his height, with a layer of flab over muscles that tightened under Harry's fingers. He had probably been a fisherman when he was younger, before the commercial fishing business evaporated and only taking out sports fishing charters remained. Fishing was a hard business, making tough men, but Harry had no doubt that his skills were enough for this annoying man.

"You will give me the keys now and honor your contract," Harry hissed into the boat owner's face.

"Release me or I'll call the police." The uncertain voice turned shaky in just those few words.

"The keys, now!"

The owner took a few more precious seconds to make up his mind. "Let me go and I'll give you the keys."

Harry stepped back, flexing his fingers into fists by his side and releasing them with a deliberate effort.

The keys came out. Harry grabbed them and tossed them to

Amanda. She caught them, even though Harry was sure that he wouldn't have been able to see well enough in the dark to do so. She hurried up to the controls and a moment later the engine growled to life.

She returned to the cockpit. "It's got full tanks. Let's go."

Harry ran along the edge of the boat, releasing the tie lines, then jumped onto the boat and went to the controls. He heard Amanda cajoling the boat owner to keep his contract. If he called the police, payment would evaporate because of a breach of contract.

Harry eased the boat out of the slip, squinting in the darkness. Amanda appeared next to him. "Let me drive," she said. "I can see better."

"Okay. Head to the left, there's a buoy marking the outer edge of the marina."

Harry went to his duffel for his night vision goggles. While there, he decided to put on his bulletproof vest and other rigging. A throat mike went around his neck and the earpiece of the radio into his left ear, all attached to a radio in a pocket on the front of his left shoulder. He looped the M4 carbine across his back and pulled the goggles on his forehead. He would rely on Amanda as much as possible before using the goggles. Looking through the goggles, which turned the night into shades of green and flattened everything always gave him a headache before too long.

He returned to the flying bridge, bringing her duffel back with him.

"Now where?" she asked.

"We are heading right, between the large island and that island over there. See the houses on it? There's a buoy with a light on it in the middle of the channel."

Amanda throttled forward and the boat leaped into high speed, thirty knots. Clearly against the navigation rules, dangerous even in daylight. Harry swallowed and trusted her.

He looked at his watch. 0218.

After the channel buoy, they turned seaward. The long swells of the ocean rolled here and the boat skipped over them in a regular jarring rhythm that shook their bodies with each bounce.

He held the wheel while Amanda put her gear on. When the boat hit a wave and came down hard, spray hit him in the face.

Flannery's Island was visible ahead, visible even to his non-enhanced eyes as a hill in the ocean. He pulled down his goggles and scanned the green mass. Not much information. He switched to thermal imaging, seeing everything in shades of black and white. The heat of the helicopter stood out. It looked like had already landed, but then the image inched down just a bit, indicting that it had just settled onto the ground.

"Dammit," Harry exclaimed. "The helicopter is landing now."

"Let me drive," Amanda said.

Harry took out his cell phone from the plastic bag and keyed for Brenda. The phone had a short-range transmitter, maybe a mile, that didn't rely on the cell network. He keyed in a text message, knowing that the letters took up little bandwidth and would go further than an attempt to use voice communication.

BRENDA BAD MEN IN HELICOPTER JUST LANDED GET OUT OF HOUSE HIDE NOW I'M COMING HARRY

CHAPTER FIFTY

Brenda jumped when her cell phone beeped on her night-stand, waking her. The cell network had been down all day. She had sent messages to Harry, but he had never responded. She had told her phone to alert her if Harry tried to contact her—otherwise it would have remained quiet. She was not one those people who needed to answer every call, no matter what the hour.

She read the message. Fear jolted through her, settling on her chest and her arm, memories of the last time that bad men had come into her life. She read it once more, inserting punctuation to help the words make better sense.

She flung back her covers. Her pajamas had unicorns all over them. At fourteen she had still had enough of a soft spot for mythical animals to ask for the pajamas. They were her pajamas just for the island, kept there in the sea chest at the foot of her bed. Still holding onto the cell phone, she grabbed her jeans and sneakers from the floor.

Only one other bedroom was on the second floor. She burst through the door. "Dirk, Harry says bad men are on the island, we gotta hide!"

Her brother tumbled out of bed behind her as she scurried down the stairs. She opened the door to her parents' room. The house was eighty years old, built back when bedrooms were small, and the queen-sized bed that her parents insisted on took up so much room that the door banged on their bed when anyone opened it. "Mom, Dad, bad guys are on the island, we gotta hide!"

Brenda backed out of the room, dropped her shoes, stripped off her pajama bottoms, and pulled on her jeans.

A nightstand light came on. "What's going on?" her mother asked, groggy and concerned.

"No lights!" Brenda screamed. "Off, off, off!"

The light went off. Brenda pushed her feet into her sneakers.

"Are these some of the same people who hurt you before?" her father asked. His calm voice settled like a warm blanket on their fear.

"Yes, probably, I don't know," Brenda said. "Harry texted me and told me that they're here on the island. Came in a helicopter."

"We have to get out of the house," her brother said from behind her. In the dim light, Brenda saw that he had something in his hand. He moved to one of the windows and peered out.

"I can't find my clothes," her mother said from the bedroom.

"Liz, just take your bathrobe," her father said, again so calm that it was frightening. "It's on the hook. You need shoes too. Just grab your slippers. They're pretty rugged."

Rusty Finnigan emerged from the room, already dressed in his jeans and flannel shirt. He had a pistol in his hand.

"The best place to land a helicopter is Jerry's lawn. That's south. Head north, go to John's house and get him. There's no one else on the island. Hide in the cemetery, it will give you a good vantage point. And a good field of fire. You got your gun, Dirk?"

"Yes, sir."

"Don't shoot blindly. Make sure of your targets because your fire will draw them like flies to fish guts."

"Yes, sir," Dirk said.

"Is Harry on his way?" her father asked Brenda.

"Yes, Dad."

"Good man."

She felt a surge of pride; yes, Harry was a good man.

"Okay, I'm ready," her mother stumbled into the living room.

"You have your pistol?" her husband asked.

"Oh, no, it's in the drawer. I'll get it."

"No time, get out of here, all of you."

Dirk opened the kitchen door, peeked out with a quick bob of his head. "I think it's clear," he said.

"Go, now, go," her father urged, pushing against the two women, propelling them towards the door.

"Aren't you coming with us?" her mother said, as if struck by a sudden insight.

"No," he said in a voice so conversational and matter-of-fact that Brenda didn't immediately catch the implication. "You guys go. I'm staying. I'll slow them down."

"No, Dad, come with us," Brenda said, her voice bordering on desperation.

"Someone has to stay. Now, you obey me and get out of here. I love you." The words came out in a rush and she felt his urgent hands push her out the door. Dirk was across the yard near the large bayberry bushes, a shadow among shadows, but she saw his hand motioning for them to hurry.

Brenda and her mother hurried over. Dirk grabbed his mother's hand and led the way, while Brenda held her mother's other hand and formed the caboose. They started up the trail that led north. Brenda and Dirk had played enough night games to easily find their way around the island, even with only starlight from the bright swath of the Milky Way light the way.

Her mother's robe was dark blue, covering up her white pajamas. Brenda realized that her father had made the right choice, not doubt deliberately, so that her mother would not stand out like a bright ghost at night.

She still had her phone in her hand. Like most kids of her generation, it was attached by an invisible umbilical cord. She tapped in a message by feel.

HARRY HIDING AT THE CEMETERY DAD STAY-
ING IN HOUSE

CHAPTER FIFTY-ONE

As he read the text message, Harry felt a sense of relief so profound that his knees went weak. Brenda was safe, at least for the moment. The fog of fear clouding his mind lifted and clarity of thought came through.

"They'll hear the engine and know we're coming," he shouted to Amanda.

"What do you suggest?" Amanda shouted back

Harry scanned the island with his goggles. The helicopter was clearly visible. Two smaller stick figures moved next to it. The rest of the island was darker shades of green, no other obvious bad guys. There must be more, though, probably shielded by trees and folds in the ground.

Amanda throttled the boat to a stop, picked up her sniper rifle, and scoped the two men near the helicopter. "No way am I going to hit a thing," she said. "They're bouncing all over in the scope. The boat is too unstable."

"I've been trying to think of a plan that has some finesse," he said. "But we don't have enough intel. I say we just go straight to the dock and get off this damned boat."

"Great place to be ambushed," Amanda said.

"Yes, but at least we know that we can approach the island at the dock. We'd probably hit rocks somewhere else, unless you can see rocks in the dark."

"Not easy, unless the rocks are big enough," she said.

"We just can't chat about this. We need to go straight at it. The bad guys aren't expecting opposition and they might think that we're just some drunken twits. Let's go for it."

Amanda applied power to the engine and twisted the wheel. They moved in towards the pier that protruded out from the shore for about fifty feet. It was a faint image in Harry's goggles, just a suggestion of solid matter in the motion of the sea.

"When we get ashore," Harry said, "we should split up. I'll head for the cemetery to find Brenda and you go take care of those blokes at the chopper."

"Sounds good," Amanda said, peering intently into the black night.

"I figure we're facing four to six bad guys," Harry said. "A bigger chopper is just too unlikely."

"I'll check out the number of seats when I get there," Amanda said.

Working the throttle, she eased closer to the dock. "Get down there and tie us on when we land," she said.

Harry went down to the cockpit. He bumped into the fighting chair, used to secure a sports fisherman and his rod and reel while he wrestled to land his catch. He found a rope with a large loop spliced into it.

The boat bumped against the pier. The tide was just right, the planks of the pier almost level with the boat deck. Regularly spaced pilings jutted up like fence posts. Harry tossed the loop over the nearest piling. There were undoubtedly cleats in the dock where he could secure the boat, but they would be hard to find in the dark. This way at least the boat wouldn't drift away.

Amanda cut the engine, creating a silence that seemed eerie after listening to the engine for the last ten minutes.

Harry perked his head up, like an animal alert suddenly alert, hearing the cough of distant gunfire. Not the machine-like regularity of an automatic rifle, but the irregular chatter of someone pumping the trigger with their finger.

The regular sound of an automatic weapon started up. Much closer. Bullets smacked into the boat, especially up on the flying bridge, where Amanda was.

"Amanda!" Harry called out in alarm.

CHAPTER FIFTY-TWO

Rusty Finnigan rifled through the drawers, throwing clothes on the floor, before finding his wife's pistol tangled among her underwear. Even after all these decades, the touch of his wife's panties still sent a tingle of anticipation along his fingers. The Tomcat pistol felt too small in his hand; still, he might need the extra firepower.

Liz had put the gun away as a way of declaring that they were safe on the island. Rusty knew that safety was an illusion and had kept his clothes stacked next to his bed and the pistol nearby, ready for action.

He grabbed the two extra magazines for his own pistol that he kept on his nightstand. Not that he expected to need them. The men coming would be using night vision goggles, thermal imaging goggles, or the new goggles that combined both into one apparatus. While the newest model was restricted to the military, the older types of goggles were too inexpensive to not to buy them for night operations, especially if the enemy could afford a helicopter. The bad men had the all the advantages, so Rusty picked up the TV remote when he went into the living room.

The old man pulled the couch away from the wall and crawled behind it. They had owned the couch for twenty-two years, having bought it just before Brenda was born. Liz had sewn a cover for it when the cloth upholstery had started to wear out, and she washed the covering every spring. It was a familiar friend, still comfortable after all this time. He hoped the couch would serve one last time and block his heat signature.

Rusty pulled back the slide on his pistol, made sure there was a bullet in the chamber, then did the same for his wife's pistol. Both were ready. He lay on his back, feeling the hard wooden floor through his shirt, his arms crossed, a pistol in each hand. The TV remote lay on his stomach.

It had been just a few minutes since his family left. They should be halfway to the cemetery by now. It was not uncommon for the island to be empty on a weekday, even during the summer, so only the Finnigans and John the Hermit were on the island. Everyone else had to make a living. He was grateful that no other relatives were at risk, for the Finnigans had most certainly brought this trouble here, thinking the island a refuge, not a trap.

His thumbs slid the safety off and he waited.

He had told his kids many stories about the Army and even about his time in Nam, but one story never got told. He had been only nineteen years old, a young and eager recruit, already a corporal in a career during which each rank came naturally. Three of the other guys in his unit had actually gone through basic training with him: Harvey, a Jew from New Jersey; Reese, a black man from Oakland; and Coyote, a Hopi from Arizona. Coyote wasn't his real name, just the name he wanted to have, a trickster in the Army. With Rusty being an Irish Catholic from Boston, the four amigos were living proof of the melting pot of America.

Outside Cai Khe, a small village in Phuoc Tuy province, on a muggy morning, their platoon was ambushed. The lieutenant had muttered that something might be up, even as green as he was, because the village was empty when they passed through it. Most of the time the Vietcong just hit you with a mine or a few shots and then ran, but this time they wanted to fight and arranged their forces in an inverted V, creating a kill zone. The second lieutenant who had commanded them for two weeks died in the first scythe of machine-gun fire zipping through their ranks. Everyone went to ground, trying to form their own personal foxholes by wiggling frantically in one spot.

The sergeant took over, ordering everyone to withdraw to a ditch several dozen meters behind them. Normal tactics was to attack into the ambush, but the nasty cough of two heavy machine guns told the soldiers that forward movement would just make the VC's job easier.

The ditch was an outdoor latrine, full of urine and human feces, maybe some even dropped from the asses of the VC out there. The Americans squirmed along the ditch, heading for the village. Most of the homes in the village were just huts, useless for stopping 12.7mm bullets, but there was a small Catholic church made of wood and small cut stones brought in from a mountain quarry for a foundation. It even had glass windows, although the panes were not stained glass and most were broken. Still, someone had paid a lot of money to bring Christianity to the village, or maybe the villagers had built it as a measure of their devotion.

By the time the soldiers made it to the church, they stank, and had lost eight men, and six of the remaining twenty-five were wounded. Reese had been hit and was dragging his right arm like it was a burden. Blood streamed down from his shoulder. The medic bandaged him up, pushed a vial of morphine into him and tried to make him comfortable with the other wounded at the base of the altar. There were no pews, just a barren floor, empty except for dust.

Sarge put everyone else at the windows and called for the radioman. But the kid from Wyoming was where he was supposed to be, at the side of his lieutenant, cut down by the same swath of bullets. Backup radio? Didn't work, no juice in the batteries.

They were up the river, desperately looking for a paddle. Sarge told everyone that the company knew their route and would send a rescue platoon real soon now. Maybe use those new tanks that had been assigned to the base. About time those tankers got their tracks dirty.

The VC closed in, chipping pieces of wood from the sides of

the church with their smaller AK-47 fire. By noon, the enemy had brought up one of their heavy machine guns and started to poke holes through the church like the vengeful fingers of demons from hell.

The Americans scrambled around like trapped rats, trying to find shelter. Two men went down. Rusty suggested that they rip up the floorboards. Knives came out, levering the planks up. They were worn smooth from years of knees and feet. Beneath the floor was about foot of space atop hard ground. Ponchos were laid over the ground to protect the wounded and each of the hurt men placed down there, stacked on each other. The floorboards were piled around to provide as much protection as possible.

As the heavy machine-gun bullets continued to riddle the church, all the able-bodied men wanted to huddle down in the hole with the wounded. Sarge allowed this, as long as four men were out and standing watch, one posted in each direction. What Sarge feared appeared soon afterwards when a young man in tattered black clothes snuck forward with a satchel in his hands.

Rusty shot the man.

A few minutes later, Sarge went down, a soft moan escaping his lips as a half-inch-wide bullet left him with no heart. Harvey died right after that. Rusty was the only corporal left. He dragged the bodies over to help form the barricade around the nest of wounded. It felt sacrilegious, but he knew that they would want to keep protecting their buddies, even in death.

Another heavy machine gun opened up from a different direction. Splinters and chunks of wood littered the floor. The Americans darted back and forth, stealing quick looks out of the windows, occasionally loosing bursts of fire to keep the VC from organizing an attack.

Rusty was leaning on the wall and peering out of a window, the glass long gone, when the wall exploded next to his left hand. He cried out and fell to his knees. A large splinter protruded from his hand and red flowed everywhere. He staggered back to the medic and crawled down in the nest with him.

The medic's hands were already soaked with the blood of other men. He wiped his hands on Rusty's sweat-soaked shirt, since his own clothes were already too covered with blood. Without even warning Rusty, the medic yanked out the splinter. Rusty almost passed out, not from the pain or the blood, just the idea of what was happening before his disbelieving eyes. There were more splinters in there, dark slivers among the blood. The medic wrapped a bandage around the hand, tied it tight, and Rusty went back to the battle.

He fired his M16 with one hand easily enough, supporting the stock with the back of his other hand, but it hurt a lot. His hand throbbed, dulling his senses.

The next hours were a blur, running from window to window, driving back the sappers and their presents of explosives. The heavy bullets continued to perforate the church. More men went down. Coyote died.

While dragging another wounded man to the nest, Rusty saw that Reese's black face had gone grey. He was no longer breathing.

The four amigos were gone. Only he was left. No time for tears; just get back to the windows, run the drill, keep those sappers away.

Then Rusty noticed that he was the only man still running around, and that pissed him off. Where was his help? He rushed over to the nest. The two piles of bodies that helped protect the wounded, stacked in the directions of the two heavy machine guns, had become slippery, misshapen masses of hamburger and fatigues. Even so, some bullets still got through, and the medic lay with his charges, eyes glassy from the bullet that had shaved off the top of his skull.

There were seven wounded men left, only two of them still conscious, and Rusty.

He ran again, firing bursts out of each window, warning the enemy away. He had long ago raided the dead and wounded for their magazines of ammo.

That evening, with the sun dropping towards the green mountains in the distance, two tanks rolled into the village. Rescue.

Three more of the wounded died.

The second platoon of Baker Company had lost all but five men. After the operation on his hand, digging out splinters, and sewing him back together, Rusty took two months to recover. Another two months in rehabilitation got his hand working almost as good as new, though the scar tissue on his palm sometimes got in the way.

He volunteered for another tour. He couldn't explain to anyone why he went back, not even himself. His friends were back there, even if their mangled bodies had been shipped back to the United States. Their spirits were there.

A sound brought him back to the present. Someone had opened the front door, slowly turning the knob, but that knob was always noisy. Of course the door wasn't locked. No one locked their doors on the island.

Rusty lay still, straining to hear. His hearing was still excellent, oddly enough, despite all the abuse that he had subjected it to. The door opened. Footfalls as someone entered the room. More footfalls. Two of them?

A cough tugged at his throat. Rusty put down his wife's pistol and pressed on his Adam's apple. It felt odd, even wrong, but the old trick suppressed the urge.

The two men were not moving, perhaps straining to hear, just as he was.

Now was as good a time as any. Rusty pushed the remote button for the television.

The television lit up the room with its flickering glow, blaring out a late-night infomercial.

Rusty grabbed his wife's pistol and rose up on his knees, the remote sliding to the floor. In a flash he saw the two men, each clad all in black, both wearing night vision goggles, two eyepieces merging into a single eye. They carried small submachines and were obviously up to no good.

One of the men shot at the TV, the household appliance spraying sparks as it died. Rusty opened fire with both pistols, one at each target. He was no Wyatt Earp, able to accurately fire that way, so he concentrated on the .45 Colt in his right hand, aiming at the afterimage of the man in his retina. The .32 Tomcat in his left hand was for suppressive fire on the other target.

The flashes from the pistols blinded him and the sound was deafening in such a small room. Fire spat back at him and he felt himself take hits in the chest. He slumped to the floor.

The Tomcat slipped from his limp fingers. He thumbed the release for the magazine on his Colt. It dropped out. He put down the pistol and pawed for an extra magazine in his shirt pocket. The first was dented from a bullet, but the next felt okay. He struggled to insert it into the pistol, an awkward movement with only one hand. Images flashed through his mind: his wife kissing him, his son graduating, his daughter playing in a new dress, nights in Saigon with his friends, the four amigos together again. The images rushed by too quickly to catch, a kaleidoscope trying to grab the highlights before it was too late.

He heard a man swearing. "Sam, I'm hit. You get him, Sam?"

Sam didn't answer and Rusty smiled at that. One dead and one wounded, or so he hoped. It was the best he could do for Brenda. Oh, Brenda, the little girl who had grown up to be a fine woman. Really his favorite.

Then there were three pale shadows: a Jew, a black man, and an Indian, urging him to join them.

The four amigos together again.

CHAPTER FIFTY-THREE

The automatic weapons fire continued, spraying all over the boat, punching holes into the fiberglass. Harry was tickled by the thought of the boat owner's reaction to the damage.

Harry found a smoke grenade on his webbing, pulled the pin, and tossed it out onto the dock. He hoped the smoke would interfere with the night goggles of the enemy. He climbed up onto the flying bridge and found Amanda lying on the deck.

"I'm hit in the leg," she said, her voice so completely calm and normal that he had to replay the words in his mind to make sure that he had heard her correctly.

"Does it hurt?" he asked, crawling past her and setting his other smoke grenade on the control panel next to the steering wheel. He pulled the pin.

"Of course, but my helpers are damping it down," she said. "I'll be able to move in a couple of minutes."

The incoming fire stopped. The grenades must be working—for the moment.

Harry slid down next to Amanda. He felt that he should comfort her, but it felt awkward to touch her too intimately, so he settled for a hand on her arm. "Do you need me to bandage the wound?"

"No," she said. "My helpers have closed the wound and are repairing the muscles right now."

"What about the bullet?"

"They are forming a cyst around it. Later I can have them expel it or break it up."

"You can talk to your helpers?"

"Not talk. I just know what is going on, like you know where your hand is."

"Will my helpers do that if I get shot?"

"Much more slowly and you can't tell them what you need," she said. "So don't get shot."

"Right."

"So what do we do now?"

Harry thought for a moment. The grenades didn't last long and the smoke was dissipating. The weapons fire had not resumed yet.

"I shouldn't have used the smoke grenades," he said. "It was just instinct. Now the bad guys know that whoever is on this boat has some military ordnance. If we had just hunkered down they might have thought we were just tourists or lived on the island."

Amanda licked her finger and held it up, reaching high enough to catch the breeze. "The wind is coming off the island, driving the smoke over us. They may not smell it or even realize that the fog in their goggles is smoke."

A bulkhead about three feet high surrounded the flying bridge, except for where a safety rail at the rear stopped people from tumbling into the cockpit. The bulkhead was perforated with bullet holes. Harry pulled his goggles over his eyes, wiggled over to the bulkhead, and ran his fingers across the torn-up fiberglass, wincing at the slivers of fiber that jabbed him. He found a bullet hole about an inch in diameter. He positioned the center scope of his goggles behind the hole and found that he could see the end of the dock well in the green landscape.

The smoke had all drifted away. Two men stood at the end of the dock, facing each other as if talking. They obviously didn't fear anything from the boat. Still, they were professionals, and one began to walk down the dock while the other moved about twenty feet down the shore and knelt. A good position to bring down fire on the boat without hitting his comrade. Harry couldn't see the weapons. He switched to thermals and found that the weapons didn't glow with enough heat, but he knew they were there.

"Amanda, can you move?" he whispered.

"Yes," she whispered back.

"You got your sniper's rifle?"

"Yes."

"Okay. Your target is approximately twenty yards away, on the shore, about ten degrees to the left of the dock." It was always hard to estimate distance in the goggles, which flattened everything to two dimensions. "He's kneeling and aiming at us, I think. When I give you the word, I want you to pop up and drop him. Okay?"

She moved next to Harry and touched his shoulder with her hand. "Okay," she whispered.

She left her hand on him and he felt its warmth. Harry forced himself to not be distracted and keep track of the other man, who slowly walked down the pier. As the bad guy drew closer to the boat, he crouched down, making his profile smaller.

Harry slid the selector on his M4 to full auto.

"Now," Harry whispered urgently. He stood up, bringing his M4 to his shoulder, and fired all thirty rounds at the man on the pier. Firing a rifle with night vision goggles was different from the normal method, because you couldn't aim along the sights or use a scope already on the rifle. Long practice with a weapon taught him where his shots would go by just pointing. Still, he swept back and forth to make sure.

Magazine went empty and he dropped down and reloaded with a magazine from his webbing. Amanda joined him, crouching with her rifle out in front of her. He had barely noticed the sharp report of Amanda's rifle.

Harry twisted around, found his hole and looked through. The man on the pier was a crumpled heap, and Amanda's target lay on his back, his legs splayed out.

"Let's get out of here and follow the plan," Harry said. "You got the chopper. I got the cemetery."

"Radio check," she said, her voice a tinny echo in his ear.

He pressed his own throat mike and said, "Got it."

"I hear you," she said.

Harry slipped his assault rifle selector to three-round bursts as they moved down to the cockpit and then climbed onto the pier. "You see anything?" Harry asked.

"No. Looks clear."

They ran down the pier, feeling awfully exposed. As they passed the crumpled man, Harry put an extra burst into the man, just to make sure. They were making lots of noise. Should have screwed the silencers onto their weapons, but no time for regrets.

At the end of the pier they parted without a word. Harry passed Amanda's target and again made sure with another burst. As he moved off the beach of gravel onto a trail that led to the northern end of the island, he replaced the magazine in his M4. He wanted those extra six bullets.

CHAPTER FIFTY-FOUR

Walking along a path that led south to the helicopter, Amanda strained her eyes, her pupils as large as dimes. The trees and bushes to the left of the path could hide an entire army, except for their heat signatures. To the right was the coast, a rocky drop to where water lapped against the shore. Across the water she could see faint lights on the mainland and other islands.

The trail forked. She paused. Think like the enemy, she told herself. If they were smart, and no doubt they were, they would have laid an ambush along the trail as soon as they heard the gunfire and could no longer reach their two buddies by radio.

Amanda followed the fork inland and soon came upon a house with darkened windows. She hoped that no one was home. Moving across the lawn, she circled the home and came to another trail that led south. The island was a maze. Only a few feet further on she came to a small bluff that looked down over the end of the island. She melted to the ground.

Ahead of her was the bulk of the helicopter, only fifty feet away. A man stood next to it, a stubby assault rifle in his hands, just like the weapons that the other two men had carried.

Amanda had already killed one man today and that was too many. This commando was not doing anyone any harm just yet. Perhaps he would even get scared and fly away, abandoning the rest of his team. She hoped he was enough of a coward to do that.

She waited.

The thrill of the hunt did not excite Amanda. Her empathy

for other life, even the lives of bad men, was too keen for her to enjoy the game that led to ending a life. She would kill only in defense of others or in self-defense, because she valued her own life. She was not immortal, just long-lived. A bullet in the brain could mean the end or make her an imbecile.

An informal rule existed among the exiles to avoid killing each other. She appreciated the rule, which had saved her life several times, but was ashamed of it as well. The rule implicitly valued the lives of Alphas over Earthers. The men she hunted were almost certainly not exiles. The Cabal usually preferred to use hired muscle, not risk themselves.

She once had a lover named Wilson, a fellow exile. He had really been a Hedonist, but was trying to do better, so he had linked up with her and tried to be a Humanist. She convinced him to help her try to get some of the Jews out of Germany as the Nazis raged across Europe. He loved the danger and excitement, while the thought of being captured made Amanda ill to her stomach.

In 1944 they got an old tramp steamer filled with refugees, bribed all the right people, and made a run across the Baltic Sea for Sweden. The leaky engine sprayed steam that turned the engine room into a furnace which only Wilson could tolerate, shoveling coal into the burning maw. They barely made four knots. Amanda stayed on deck, making sure that captain kept his nerve. He was a sorry sort of man, ravaged by syphilis, perhaps even half mad, working only for the money.

She never knew which side the submarine was on. A Soviet boat, prowling for German prey, or perhaps a German U-boat sent by one of the bribed officials to cover up his crime? No matter. The torpedo broke the ship in half. Amanda frantically tried to organize the lifeboats, but only got two launched. Desperate hands capsized Amanda's boat. Gasping in the cold water, she tried to keep others alive while she clung to the overturned boat. The refugees didn't last long in the water, deprived of adequate food for too long, their hopes for escape dashed.

After only an hour, Amanda was alone, sitting on the hull of the overturned boat, flecks of white paint on her soggy clothes. The boat hadn't been painted for a long time. The other craft held nineteen Jews, nervous as the waves lapped at their over-loaded boat.

Wilson never appeared. She assumed that he had been trapped in the boiler room when his half of the ship went down. Even an Alpha couldn't survive drowning in his own coffin. Well, not quite; back on their home world, some Alphas had helpers that formed gills, making them into mermen or merwomen. Such helpers had been burned out before exile.

Wilson never told her what his crime had been. She had never asked. Oddly enough, there was a sort of exile code of ethics that suggested that the past on Alpha be left behind and replaced by a new life on Earth.

A fishing trawler found them in the morning and brought the survivors to Sweden. She was grateful for the lives of the Jews that had survived, knowing that only a few days at sea would have killed them. She herself could have lasted much longer, drinking seawater and eating fish, or whatever else she could find.

She missed Wilson. He would have loved being here right now and would have had no qualms in killing.

Another man emerged from the woods and walked over to talk to the first. She strained her ears, but could not hear anything.

She shifted her rifle, taking aim. *Please fly away*, she silently pleaded.

* * * * * * *

There were two schools of thought on night movement. One prescribed moving as slowly as possible, blending into the land-scape; always hard to do if your enemies had night vision equip-ment. The other school argued for moving as fast as possible without making undue noise, hoping to surprise the bored or distracted enemy.

Harry chose the latter tactic, following a trail that led up into the middle of the island. He stopped after only a minute, shook his head, wondered if he was losing his touch, and returned to the beach. He found the radio on the dead commando on the beach, a similar setup to his own, with earpiece and throat mike. He placed the earpiece in his unoccupied ear and listened. Nothing. The bad guys weren't talking to each other. That confirmed to him that they were professionals, only talking when necessary, not needing chatter to keep up their courage. He wrapped up the radio and placed it in his pocket. He would have liked to keep the earpiece in, but he needed all the hearing he could get.

He returned to the trail, moving quickly.

Even though Brenda had texted him that she was heading for the cemetery, Harry decided to check out her house; it was on the way, and she had texted that her father was remaining there. His internal map of the island matched the trail before him. He passed two houses, both of them dark and quiet, then slowed his pace as he neared the Finnigan home.

Pushing away a throbbing headache, Harry crouched and approached slowly, taking advantage of a row of bushes along the front of the home. He paused and slowly scanned the entire house, letting the goggles collect all the light possible. Everything seemed dark, though a green sliver on the ground attracted his attention. He crept closer and found a body sprawled on the grass.

Pulling up the goggles, he blinked and rested for a few minutes, waiting for his eyes to adjust. He crawled forward, the smell of freshly cut grass in his nostrils, and placed his hand on the body. He felt webbing similar to his own. Good, one of the bad guys. He reached around and touched the clammy skin of the neck. No real need to check for a pulse, but he did anyway. There was none.

He pulled the goggles back down over his aching eyes, switched to the thermal sights, and wiggled across the lawn to the front door. It was wide open and inside he could see a bright shape on the floor, though not bright enough to be a human still generating his full body heat. The air smelled faintly of gunfire. Harry crawled inside, scattering shell casings on the floor. They tinkled together. He froze.

All was silent and still. Reaching out, he felt the other man over. Military webbing again, wet with blood, growing sticky as it dried. He found a wrist and felt for the pulse. Dead.

Getting up in a crouch, Harry explored the rest of the room and found a body behind the couch. No military rigging on this man, though his fist still clutched a pistol. From the feel of the bulky weapon, Harry decided that it was a Colt .45. He remembered that the colonel favored such a weapon.

Harry risked using his red-lensed flashlight for a moment. Yes, it was the colonel. He must have hit both men in the front room, killing one and mortally wounding the other, who made it out to the yard before expiring.

He keyed his mike. "Amanda, we have another two down. What's your situation?"

Amanda clicked her mike twice, not wanting to talk, and Harry went away for the moment. The two men in front of her finished their conversation. One of them walked over to the helicopter, and hope bloomed that he was preparing to leave. No such luck. He took the keys and rejoined his companion. They moved towards the trail, holding their weapons at the ready, men determined to complete their mission.

She shot the front man, a clean hit in the head, and fired a snap shot at the other man as he dove for cover. No such luck. She buried her head into the ground as he blindly emptied his magazine towards her, trying to suppress.

Moving a hand down to her webbing, she pulled out a fragmentation grenade. Her mind was a mask of self-discipline, intellect over emotion, doing what had to be done.

She tossed the grenade and covered her head with her arms.

It exploded and she was on the move, wiggling down the slope as fast as she could, snaking around two bushes, leaving her rifle behind as an awkward impediment. She stopped, listening intently.

The sound of gurgling. She pulled out a flash-bang grenade, closed her eyes tightly, tossed it forward, and clamped her hands over her ears. A bright flash and sharp crash, with decibels high enough to disorient a normal person.

She was no normal person. Pulling out her pistol, she rushed forward, her enhanced eyes sweeping the ground. She saw the man lying there and put four bullets into him.

With both men down, she went over to the helicopter. Its windshield was pocked with shrapnel. She counted the seats.

Fingers at her throat, she activated the mike. "Two more down. Only six seats in the chopper—no way more than six fully equipped men flew in. They'd have to squeeze Brenda in between them to just fly her back."

Harry voice: "Confirmed. I count two at the boat, two at Brenda's house, and now two at the helicopter. Is that your count?"

"Yes."

CHAPTER FIFTY-FIVE

When dawn peeped over the flat line of the Atlantic Ocean, Brenda felt the chill of a world gone cold. She stood outside her home tightly hugging Harry, sure that she would never let go. Her father was dead, lying in the living room under a blanket. Only her brother had mustered up the necessary resolve to go see the colonel. He had brought back out a pair of kitchen chairs and now sat with their mother, holding her hand.

One of the evil men who had killed her father was lying under a blanket also, staining the grass red. John stood outside the bushes, a low keening coming from him. It was like a funeral dirge from some ancient people, yet she also suspected that he was frantically trying to hold onto some sense of sanity, for now the demons of his schizophrenia had come out into the light.

Harry had been thoughtful enough to pull off his vest of weapons, bulging with ammo magazines and grenades, so that she could feel his heart beating against her ear. The last time that she had seen him—while waiting for a helicopter to take her to the hospital after being shot at the dig—seemed a year ago.

"Why did he have to die?" she muttered into his shirt.

"Because bad people wanted to hurt you," Harry said softly. "He died to save you. Always remember that. He has given you a gift that you must honor by living life fully."

"I want him back," she said, a fresh torrent of tears starting again.

"We all want him back," Harry said. "I'm so sorry that all

this happened."

"Why is this happening?" she asked, words that came out burbling.

"Because of that artifact we found."

She looked up at him, her face streaked with tears. "Really?" She wanted to ask more questions, but right then she just didn't care. Nothing seemed important.

The woman that had come with Harry came up to them. "Cell service has been restored. I just talked to Franklin."

Brenda turned her head to look at this new woman, still keeping her arms around Harry. The statuesque blonde was so beautiful that her very presence made Brenda feel uncomfortable and inadequate. She also casually carried a rifle, as if it was a familiar tool.

"What's the plan?" Harry asked.

"We need to extract ourselves," she said. "The helicopter needs a mechanic to go over it before it would be safe to fly. I've already checked the boat. It's still in running condition. Oh, and the police have received a report of a stolen boat."

"That little twerp," Harry said.

"Yes. Franklin is arranging for a car to be brought to a little cove just up the coast." She looked at her cell phone. "I have the coordinates."

"Harry, just who is this woman?" Brenda asked. Harry had come to the cemetery, calling out loudly so that they wouldn't shoot him, and led them back to the house, explaining that he had help with him.

"Brenda, this is Amanda," Harry said. "Amanda, this Brenda Finnigan. And that is Dirk and Liz, also Finnigans."

The blonde put out her hand and Brenda took it, expecting it to feel like a hand of a celebrity. Just a normal hand. "Where did you come from?" Brenda asked.

"I know you," Dirk interrupted. "You were the medical technician at the hospital in New Mexico."

Amanda turned to him. "Yes, I was there."

"Why were you at the hospital?" Brenda asked.

Amanda looked at her for moment, as if deliberating about what to say. She reached out and touched Brenda on the arm, her hand warm and caring. "You needed fixing. Harry was so worried about you, it almost made him sick."

The blonde woman touched Harry on the arm also and gave it a quick squeeze, an act of intimate familiarity. Brenda felt a stab of jealousy. Harry belonged to her. The thought surprised her and she mulled it over for a moment, glad for the distraction from the pressure in her head that came from knowing her father was gone. She liked Harry, loved him, felt protected by him, but he had always been like a father to her, not a potential lover. She choked and started to cry again. Her father had died, and she had already found a substitute for him; she felt like a traitor, betraying the colonel.

Amanda went over and shook Dirk's hand, then held Liz's hand in both of hers. She even went out beyond the shrubs and shook hands with John. The hermit looked at her with a mixture of horror and undisguised lust.

Amanda returned to Brenda. "We need to leave the island and get you to a safe place."

"What about my father?" Brenda asked.

"The police will be here soon and take care of the bodies," Amanda said. "I know that it sounds blunt, but we need to get moving."

"I will not go," John said, still standing outside the line of bushes. "This is my home. You go. I am going back to my house."

Amanda looked surprised at this disagreement. "But I want you to go," she said. "It's safer away from here."

"This is my home," he repeated, his jaws clenched and his eyes staring into the distance. "I have lived with fear all my life. This will not be different." He looked at Brenda. "I will miss your father. He was always nice."

"He's not part of this," Harry said. "Perhaps we can leave him behind."

"The Cabal may not agree with you," Amanda said.

"Taking someone who doesn't want to cooperate could complicate everything," Harry said. "As much as I want maximum safety for everyone, we have to get moving and can't stand here having a discussion."

Amanda shrugged.

The five of them followed the trail down to the boat, leaving the hermit behind. He waved back when Brenda waved farewell to him. She worried that she would never see that sweet man again.

Brenda turned away from the dead man on the beach and held onto Harry's hand tightly, with her eyes closed, as they stepped over the man on the pier. The pockmarks all over the boat showed her that her father had not done all the fighting.

Amanda drove, skipping over the waves with the throttle full open, as the sun brought the full light of day. Brenda noticed a streak of blood on the deck of the flying bridge. Her innate curiosity made her wonder why there was blood up there. She noticed dried blood on the thigh of Amanda's jeans and a torn spot that looked like a bullet hole. She kept her questions to herself and returned to the cockpit, where Dirk huddled with her mother. She put her arms around her mother and had a good cry.

A few minutes later they pulled up to a private dock. The mansion on the bluff above them looked silent. Harry had been putting the weapons and gear away in large duffle bags. He jumped off the boat and tied the bow and stern lines.

"Who lives here?" Brenda asked when Amanda came down from the flying bridge.

"I have no idea," the tall woman said. "We just need a place to tie up. The owner of this boat may want it back, though I think he will take the money instead. Do any of you have buddies or other networked equipment?"

Brenda and Dirk did. They turned them off as instructed, then followed Amanda and Harry, carrying their duffle bags up the lawn. It was only about six in the morning; apparently everyone in the house was still asleep. A dog barked, urging them to quicker steps.

A green minivan sat on the side of the road, keys in the ignition. Harry drove, with Amanda giving him instructions from her cell phone. They headed inland, passing houses nestled back among the trees and joggers taking advantage of the morning. They came to the lakes region, small farms mixed with vacation homes among hundreds of glacial lakes, scrapped into the land by the last ice age.

Brenda sat with her mother's head on her shoulder, holding her hand. Even thinking about her father brought tears to her eyes. Still dressed in her pajamas top and jeans, with her face flushed and streaked, she thought that she must look a fright. She watched the interaction between Harry and Amanda: quick words, no extraneous talk, still acting like they were on a combat mission. They made her feel safe. She was happy for Harry, she decided. This was a good woman for him.

* * * * * * *

Amanda stood on the edge of a dock that reached out into a lake. Trees came down to the shore and other docks poked out into the blue water. It was late enough that fishermen had gone home, but too early for water-skiers. Two airplanes with pontoons circled above the small party. Already the day promised a hot day for New England.

She had used her trust hormones on the Finnigans and the hermit, and while she was glad that the family cooperated, as expected, the resistance of the hermit had surprised her. Perhaps his brain chemistry resisted the hormones. She had wanted to use her trust hormones on the boat owner, but previous experience had shown her that the nicotine in cigarettes mixed with the hormones and made them useless.

"We will part ways here," Amanda said. "Brenda, Dirk, and Liz will be flying to a safe house in Michigan. There are men there that will protect you. It is important that you not contact anyone or turn your electronics back on. You could be traced that way."

Harry raised his eyebrows, the question unspoken, and Amanda nodded briefly. Yes, Brenda would be meeting his ex-wife and son.

"Where are you and Harry going?" Brenda asked.

"We have to find a way to end this," Amanda said.

Harry nodded his head. "We need to go get the artifact and finish this."

CHAPTER FIFTY-SIX

Two hours in the float-plane brought them to Lake Ontario. Any other time, Harry would have found the flight a fascinating adventure, something that he had never done before. Like a good soldier, he slept. After landing amid a bouncing burst of spray, another car was waiting for them with keys in the ignition. Harry wondered what would happen if some opportunistic thief stumbled on one of these cars and took it for a joyride. On such chances do the best-conceived plans founder.

The Learjet waited for them at a small airport. The pilots remained in the cockpit again, but had left two boxes of food and drink on the passenger seats. After the jet took off and turned southwest, Harry chewed on an egg sandwich and sipped a beer. Alcohol with breakfast suited him just fine.

Amanda tapped at her cell phone. "Franklin has sent a file for you to read. Let me beam it over to your cell."

Harry held up his phone. "What is it?"

"It's an old Alpha journal. I read the original a few days ago in Franklin's library. He won't let anyone take it out of the room. The pages were thick and stiff and had actual handwriting on them. The faded black ink was still quite legible. This file is translated into English from the original Alpha."

Harry was still groggy from not enough sleep and the decompression that came from combat, like his body was applying all the stress held at bay during the fighting. It was a familiar feeling. Her description perked him up enough to look at the file and read.

Record of the Historian Alger, 1543:

On May 30, 1498, I left Sanlúcar, Spain aboard one of the seven ships under the command of Lord Admiral Cristóbal Colón. This was his third voyage to the New World. In my previous report, I documented my suspicions that other exiles were involved in inspiring Colón to seek out the new world. In brief, we know that it existed and that he would find it if he sailed far enough. His silly notion that the world was much smaller than it really is, which would make it possible to sail directly to China, has always bewildered me.

I deserted when we made landfall on the new continent. What a marvelous place. I am on the southern continent, a land of plentiful water and the lush vegetation of the tropics. Even Colón had come to the conclusion that he had found a new continent, not just some islands off of Asia. I did not put those ideas in his head. In fact, I took care to not even talk to him, since I prefer my role as an observer, always watching, never interfering, except as necessary to preserve my own life.

The people live here in small villages, living off of the small fields that they cut and burn out of the forest. Of course, the soil is poor, and they quickly deplete its ability to grow crops, so they are constantly moving their villages. The rivers and ocean provide fish. A group of hunters attacked me and I was forced to kill four of them. They lack the compound bow, so their arrows are small things designed to deliver a poison. They were quite astonished that the deadly toxin had no effect on me.

About four hundred years ago—I don't have the exact date because my records are safe back in Spain and Ireland—the exile Khrusli told me that before he was exiled, he had gotten a look at the most recent imagery from Earth. He had noticed an advanced civilization on the western coast of the southern continent, extensive settlements on the neck of land between the two continents, and a rising civilization along the great river in the northern continent. I wanted to see these places.

Traveling through the jungle proved a challenge, as always, and sometimes I went hungry. My helpers earned their keep. After three months, or so (I had lost track of the date by then) I made it to the Inca Empire. What a curious people. The Incas have managed to create a large empire between the mountains and the sea, with rigid control and a remarkable system of roads. They have done this without having any animal labor, since this New World has no horses, donkeys, or oxen, only dogs and the contrary and weak-backed llamas.

Only three or four generations ago, the Inca began to expand and create their empire. They have a most curious royal and religious system. The ruler conquers new territories to build up his estates. On his death, he is mummified and buried in an elaborate tomb, accompanied into the afterlife with the sacrifice of hundreds of servants. All of his estates are dedicated to maintaining his tomb and to sustain a cult of worship. The next ruler must be the offspring of the ruler and his full sister, a result of royal incest. The taboo against incest is so strong on most of this world, and rightly so, but royal families become so preoccupied with their supposed special genes that they turn to believing that only their own family is worthy of creating the proper offspring. The Egyptian pharaohs believed this, though I don't see much evidence that the Incan idea came from them. Independent creation, I say.

Because the dead ruler takes all his lands with him, so to speak, the next Inca ruler must expand the empire in order to acquire his own estates. When he dies, his estates are then bound to his cult, and the new ruler must conquer yet more territories for his own use. It always amazes me how these Earthers can come up with systems that are clearly not sustainable. Their short lives make them short sighted.

I stumbled across another exile, quite literally. He is Mannik and I tripped over him because he was lying in the road, his mouth slack and a silly smile on his face. He is a Hedonist who has been in the same area for about fourteen hundred years, according to my reckoning, since he was exiled in the year 6,023. His sin was the accidental death of his brother. They were both experimenting with a new memory-erase drug of their own design, seeking ways to remove the memories of the past so that new experiences would have an intense freshness to them. I had heard of this back on Alpha, but had not met anyone who tried it. I personally treasure my memories too much to purposely erase any of them.

The locals have a drink called chicha, made from fermented maize. Mannik came up with a bit of his own innovation to make it stronger, and often combined his drinking with powerful hallucinogens from plants ground up into dust and either ingested, smoked, or snorted straight up his nose. He has ordered his helpers to not prevent inebriation or any of the other effects of the drug. I am surprised that he had not been killed or died of an accident. Isn't his behavior just a form of a slow suicide?

I spent three days with Mannik, trying to encourage him to find something of interest beyond mere pleasure. He isn't even interested in the girls. I have no knowledge of what has happened to him since I left. In

1816, I sent an observer to try to find him. No traces were found.

After this, I headed north. I arrived in the land of the Maya during the rainy season. There are many stories of cities lost to the jungle, built of stone, with steep-sided pyramid temples and great plazas. I saw two of these cities. Around the campfires in the villages, I listened to the stories of people who remembered when they used to be greater. One story is of more interest than the others. Hundreds of years ago, a ruler named "Sky Witness" took over the throne of Kaan. His origin and motivations are obscure. Sky Witness wanted to destroy the state of Mutal and its client cities. Using assassination, wars, intimidation, treaties—anything that worked—Sky Witness asserted control over all the surrounding cities and their lands, and isolated Mutal. When he was finally ready, the Sky Witness led his armies against the Mutal, defeating its armies, killing its king, and sacking the city. The war continued for centuries, until the two peoples eventually collapsed in exhaustion and their cities became ruins in the jungle.

This is not an uncommon type of story on this world, but the name of Sky Witness stuck with me. I can't prove it, but I suspect that this ruler was an exile. I don't have enough information to identify which faction he belonged to, if he survived, or anything else. Such frustrations are the lot of a historian who doesn't want to resort to writing fiction.

I moved north again as part of my grand tour. The great city of Tenochtitlan, the center city of the Aztec empire, impressed me. This is one of the great cities of the world, built on an island in a shallow lake, with causeways leading out to the city. My rough count shows that about two hundred thousand people live here. In the center of the city are great plazas and temples. Two aqueducts bring fresh water to the city, and a dike, maybe ten miles in length, divides the brack-ish water from the fresh water in the lake, since there is no outlet to keep the water flowing properly. They remind me of the Romans, but so much more impres-sive because they have only humans for labor, no draft animals.

On one of the streets they have tens of thousands of skulls, religious trophies of the many captured en-emy soldiers that they have sacrificed to their sun god. They practice a curious form of warfare where it is a greater honor to hamstring an opponent with their war clubs, edged by obsidian chips, than to kill him. A captured enemy can be sacrificed, a dead man cannot. I don't see how they can sustain this religious practice, which requires a state of regular warfare with their surrounding vassal states so they can obtain captives. I have never seen a people so obsessed with human sacrifice and so keen to continually keep the practice going, day after day. Most civilizations that practice human sacrifice reserve it for funerals of important people and for extraordinary religious occasions. For the Aztecs, desperate to feed their sun god, they have made it mundane.

I found two other exiles in the city, a brother and sister, Gine and Genoia. No doubt many will remem-ber when they were exiled because it was so unusual. For their joint crimes, they were some of the first ex-iles, some three thousand years ago. They live as man and wife and are a respected priest and priestess to the sun god, Huitzilopochtli. They welcomed me into their home and provided me access to meeting the elite of the city. While their habits and inclinations are anath-ema to me, I found them good company, perhaps be-cause they were on their best behavior, having not met another exile for some six hundred years. I asked Gine if they had been the ones to introduce human sacrifice to the Aztecs and their precursors, the Toltecs. He just smiled.

Among some of the peoples that I have met, the direction of north is considered the direction of evil. That odd idea intrigued me. As I have moved north, beyond the Aztec lands, I have noticed that the levels of technology and political organization are falling. I also found more traces of a story common to many peoples. They tell of a long-lost brother or god, a bearded white man, who will return one day. The Aztecs called him Quetzalcoatl. Many of the names for this figure can be translated as One from Across the Water. I wonder if this is the memory of an exile whom I have not identified. Curious though, that an exile would chose to have white skin among a land of brown skins; perhaps he didn't have the proper helpers to alter his skin color.

I came upon a river valley with small villages. In the valley were larger buildings, now abandoned, which used to be temples and apartment houses. Ruins always fascinate me, with their aura of former greatness and unfulfilled hopes for permanence, so I stopped and learned the local language and their stories.

Apparently the larger buildings had only been abandoned two generations ago and some of the older people actually lived in them when they were children. A disease came and decimated the population, killing nine out of ten. The buildings fell into disrepair due to a lack of people to maintain them.

These people call their valley Paquime. They told me that their people had come from the north, following a direct line that they measured from hilltop to hilltop, until they found a fertile valley to settle. They had once lived in a canyon in the desert, where a man called the Master led them. He lived for twelve generations before he was assassinated. He taught their people how to make buildings and the art of worshiping only him. According to their poems, which I listened to late into the nights, this Master lived for ten generations before he founded their people. After his death, they moved directly north to another settlement. Drought forced them to abandon that settlement and they moved directly south.

I suspect that this Master was an exile. Obviously a Deist. He may have even been a full-blown megalomaniac, which Deists are inclined toward.

After leaving Paquime, I crossed a desert and came to a great steppe of grasslands that stretch all the way north to the tundra. What must be millions of buffalo range across this grassland. Beyond the grassland was the great river that I sought. The locals call it "Father of Waters." The civilization that I expected to find is no longer there. Only their mounds remain, overgrown with grass or trees.

Such is the fate of civilizations, to rise and fall.

I found no other exiles, though my travels covered only a small fraction of the lands. After about four decades of wandering, I had a pack full of written observations. I made my way back down to the Aztecs. The Spaniards had arrived more quickly than I would have expected and had taken the empire for their own. This was to my benefit, for I was able to take a ship back to Spain.

I could find no trace of Gine and Genoia.

* * * * * * *

Harry put down the cell phone and rubbed his eyes. He still felt exhausted. The story had intrigued him, though.

"The place called Paquime still exists as an archaeological site in northern Mexico," he said to Amanda. She put down her sandwich to listen. "We call it Casas Grandes."

"Is it connected to Chaco Canyon?"

"There is a theory, not accepted by many of us—archae-ologists, that is—that Chaco Canyon, Aztec Ruins, and Casas Grandes were each occupied by the same culture in turn. Oddly enough, the central tenant of the theory is that all three sites form a direct north-south meridian."

"Aztec Ruins?"

"They are north of Chaco Canyon, named by the locals," Harry explained. "They have nothing to do with the Aztecs of central Mexico."

"So the stories that Alger recorded match the archaeological record?"

"Yes, though this story of the Master is nowhere else to be found."

"Back on Alpha, we knew him as Gilgal the Proud, of the Harlee Clan," Amanda said. "The account you have just read is a record of the memories of him. The Chacoans knew him as the Master. He was from the Deist faction. They're a small faction, natural allies of the Hedonists."

"Other than the obvious implications of that name, what do they believe?"

"They want to be gods. They say that this is the answer to our technological and cultural stagnation on Alpha. They want to reveal us to Earth and start to exploit the people of this planet in order to get science and technology going again, but keep immortality to themselves, allowing themselves to be quasi-gods. They would maintain control of Earthers, as quasi-slaves, by placing helpers that can be remotely instructed to kill their hosts in all humans."

"Could Gilgal control the Chacoans?"

"Not with helpers, since such specialized helpers were not put in him before he was exiled. But he did manage to take something with him. He smuggled down a small box, embla-zoned with the Alpha symbol—three triangles within a circle."

"What's in the box?"

"No one knows. There are lots of rumors and speculation, but no one knows."

"How do you even know that the box exists?"

"A later Exile, Fereki the Cunning, of the Harlee Clan, told us about it. He was a Hedonist who visited the Chacoans, and Gilgal told him about it."

"Did this Fereki actually see the box?" Harry asked.

"No, the only reason that they probably even talked was because they were both of the same clan and knew each other back on Alpha."

"What's this clan thing? Does it match what faction Alphas belong to?"

"No. We all have only one name, and often a title that is given to us in our youth, on our one hundredth birthday. We don't get to pick the title; it is given to us by a vote of the clan. We are born into our clan, but we choose our faction as a political point of view. The factions are very organized. They used to be more fluid, but the lines hardened as time went by."

"What is your full name?"

"I am Amanda the Soft and Kind One, of the Harlee Clan."

"So you knew these men, Gilgal and Fereki?"

"Slightly. The Harlee Clan is large, tens of thousands, but anyone who is exiled is usually well known."

"Your world is so surreal," he said.

She smiled and reached out to put her hand on his knee. "It's your world now, too."

"I'm no exile," he said.

"But you know about us and you have helpers in your blood, making you highly resistant to disease."

"They are not as good as your helpers," he said.

"True, they won't halt aging, but you will be extraordinarily healthy for another forty or fifty years."

He liked that idea.

CHAPTER FIFTY-SEVEN

"Now you know what we know," Amanda said. "We never really followed up on this report. It was so long ago. Now we are very interested."

"Something else is kind of interesting," Harry said. "There is a Navajo story about Chaco Canyon, which is that a person named the Great Gambler came from the south, enslaved the local people, and forced them to build the great houses in the canyon. They tricked him into leaving."

"Sounds like an echo of the real story."

"Does the Cabal know about this story that you showed me?" Harry pointed at his cell phone.

"We didn't think so. We thought that only we had the records of Alger, but they must have known something." She held up her phone. "Franklin sent me a message while you were reading. He investigated the foundation in New York that funded your archaeological dig. It's pretty obscure, just a PO box and phone number. He did track down the lawyer to who set up the foundation, and while he didn't contact him, since we want to remain in the background, this lawyer has done work for Cabal cutouts and phony corporations in the past."

"So we were all just pawns," Harry said. "Even Dr. Bancroft. The Cabal wanted to see what we would find."

"So it seems."

"And everyone is paying for it with their lives."

"That's how the Cabal works," she said. "The life of an Earther means nothing to them."

"But you don't believe that because you are a Humanist?"

"That is what makes me and the other Humanists different."

"Are there more Humanists back on Alpha?" he asked.

"We are a strong faction," she said. "Or at least we were when I left. It seems that the exiles stopped coming about four hundred years ago, perhaps because my faction became strong enough to stop the practice. That was always one of our goals. We believed that Earthers should develop on their own, not as pawns in a playground for Alpha criminals."

He mulled this over. It was hard for him to swallow that there was a secret history that paralleled the history which historians and archaeologists and other scholars had worked so hard to create. He felt violated by what the exiles had done, and by how they had made so much scholarship only a pale shadow of the truth. So many scholars had devoted their lives to understanding the past and these exiles had come from another planet to muck everything up. In Chaco, the Master had driven everything, negating all the fancy sociological and anthropological theories that had assumed that only humans (correction, Earthers) had been the actors.

"Tell me more about Chaco," Amanda said, looking intently at him, a student ready to absorb data. "Tell me everything. I want lots of details."

He laughed. "That would take years. There have been dozens of books, dozens of dig reports, and hundreds of articles published. What I know only scratches the surface. Besides, so much of what we thought we knew isn't true because we had no idea that you Alphas existed."

She looked exasperated. "There is still truth in your learning. Tell me some of the strangest things about Chaco that you know. Maybe we can find something to help us."

"The whole canyon is strange, filled with mysteries and unanswered questions," Harry said. "But okay, here's what I think about. There are thirteen great houses at Chaco Canyon, out of a total of about 150 great houses in the greater cultural area of the Pueblo peoples. Most of these have never been excavated, at least not properly by archaeologists. Clearly Chaco was clearly the center of a larger trade network that they may have controlled through religious symbols and ceremonies. Eighty-five percent of the pottery found at Pueblo Alto from the time period—that is, at the height of the Chaco culture, the late eleventh century—came from outside the canyon.

"At Chaco, Casa Bonito is the largest great house. It's the largest great house anywhere, built of sandstone blocks in the shape of a D, and has about eight hundred rooms. Casa Bonito was started about 850 and abandoned about 1140. All the other great houses in Chaco had already been abandoned or were abandoned at that time. The building has an orientation line towards the equinox; other buildings are also aligned that way."

"How many people lived in Casa Bonito?" she asked.

"We constantly argue over that. It could have been as few as a hundred, but during religious ceremonies the population may have swelled to thousands. We just don't find much in the way of household garbage, not nearly enough to make us believe that many people lived in that building.

"But there were so many rooms."

"The builders just added rooms over the years, like adding Lego blocks, and sometimes they even closed off rooms so that no one could access them. They were constantly adding rooms and rebuilding rooms, making it a nightmare for us archaeologists to accurately reconstruct what happened. Unlike the modern pueblos of the Hopi and Zuni, in some ways the great houses in Chaco weren't very practical. Even building Casa Bonito where they did was foolish."

"Why?"

"Casa Bonito was built near what we called Threatening Rock. The rock leaned out from the cliff behind Casa Bonito, like an iceberg ready to calf off from a glacier. It weighed 30,000 tons, if I recall correctly. It's always struck me as odd that the Chacoans didn't build Casa Bonito further away from the cliff or off to the side, since they obviously feared the rock. Early archaeologists found the remains of a masonry wall that the Chacoans had built to help prop it up and they found prayer sticks, called pahos, in the crevices between the rock and the cliff, probably put there as part of religious ceremonies to encourage the rock to stay upright. After Casa Bonito was reconstructed by archeologists in the 1920s, it was partially destroyed when Threatening Rock finally fell. That was in 1941, the same year as Pearl Harbor."

"Hundreds of years after the canyon had been abandoned," Amanda said.

"Yes, about eight hundred years."

"If the people who built these places didn't live in the great houses, where did they live?"

"Villages and smaller buildings. They are scattered all over the canyon."

"Why build the great houses, then?"

"Chaco Canyon was obviously a religious center. I know that we archaeologists often say that when we find something that doesn't make sense any other way, but the force of religion is something that we don't appreciate sufficiently in our modern world. There are fifteen great kivas in the canyon, each of which can hold over four hundred people, and over one hundred other kivas, which might have been able to hold fifty to a hundred people at a time. Of course, some of the kivas are too small to hold that many. Kivas are not the only evidence we have. For instance, we estimate that they had to bring 220,000 timbers from the mountains over fifty miles away to serve as the roof timbers for the structures in Chaco Canyon. We actually recovered one of the pine logs used to support one of the larger kivas. It measured over two feet in diameter and was over thirty feet long. Think of hauling those logs over roads that amounted to trails—no beasts of burden, just human power."

"What did they do in the kivas?" she asked.

"Religious ceremonies. There are kivas in modern pueblos, though the Pueblo people are very secretive about what goes on in there. We know that there is a great variance from kiva to kiva. The great kivas usually had masonry benches around their edges. In some of the modern pueblos, no one sits there because that is reserved for the ancestors; everyone else sits on the floor. Each clan probably had its own kiva. Maybe the way to form a new clan was to build a kiva. We just don't know."

"And you think that all these great houses were primarily religious in nature?"

"Not all great houses, but the ones in Chaco definitely were. They are filled with kivas for worship. There is even one building called Casa Rinconada that is one massive kiva. That's it, no other rooms. Many of the great houses were laid out in such a way that they match the lines from the summer or winter solstice, or even patterns from lunar orbits. There is a spiral shape on the top of Fajada Butte that is obviously designed to match certain astronomical events. Three rocks are carefully positioned in front of it so that sunlight shines through the rocks on different days and creates a shape of light that is called a sun dagger on different edges of the spiral."

"Very intriguing."

"Building religious monuments in sync with patterns in the sky is common around the world, though Chaco is pretty impressive. While many cultures have used the cycles of the sun to orient their buildings, Chaco Canyon is the only known culture to also use the lunar cycle. The solar cycle takes place over a year, and the lunar cycle takes place over an eighteen-and-a-half-year cycle."

"That's almost a generation," she said. "And would take some good record-keeping."

"Yes. This culture did not have writing or mathematics, so somehow they kept track, probably with marks on sticks or a piece of wood, indicating when the moon was where on the horizon or the sky. They had to keep track which marks meant what. A real challenge over that many years."

"Is that how they did it?"

"It's pure conjecture. We have never found any traces of how they did it, like pieces of wood with marks that we can say have astronomical significance."

"So there is no writing at all?" she asked.

"There are petroglyphs, usually of unknown meaning, or at least the meanings are disputed. Most of them are probably just graffiti or have religious significance. There is one exception, a group of petroglyphs at the far end of the canyon, near Peñasco Blanco. It has three symbols: a human hand, a crescent shape, and a star. Interpreting petroglyphs is always challenging. The crescent is probably the moon and the star has been interpreted as the famous supernova of 1054, which formed the Crab Nebula. There is a Hopi oral tradition that when this event occurred, they called it the blue star, and everyone traveled to Chaco Canyon for a religious observance. Lots of what-ifs in that interpretation, though it makes a great story, but I have always been skeptical."

"What eventually happened to the Chacoans?" she asked. "Drought? A plague? Starvation?"

"Even though it is high desert, one of the reasons that they must have settled Chaco Canyon is that the summer rains are remarkably consistent. They reached the carrying capacity of the land, supporting their population by growing as much food as the land could support. Tree ring data shows a lack of moisture for forty years, which would depress crop yields. You can image the entire economic system collapsing, like dominos falling as the Chacoan people watched their children starve."

"That would be hard," she said.

He nodded. "By 1150 most of the canyon had been abandoned. We find evidence that when they abandoned Chaco, they burned the kivas and destroyed other things, like metates. The Chacoans already had a character trait that led to this. There are mounds of shattered pots that we think were destroyed deliberately as gifts to the dead or for purification purposes. What I wouldn't give to interview a Chacoan for a couple of hours."

"History gets lost, memories are lost, we all live with that," she said. "The people must have gone somewhere."

"There are oral traditions," he said. "The surrounding native peoples, the Navajo, the Hopi, the Zuni, other contemporary

Pueblo peoples, all have religious traditions which associate different clans with different great houses in Chaco and elsewhere. Some of those connections are certainly real, from when clan members left Chaco and settled elsewhere, but some are obviously not. The Navajo didn't even come to the area until after Chaco Canyon was abandoned, so they must have adopted earlier clan traditions from the locals or made up their own. At least that is the traditional historical interpretation, which assumed that the Navajo migrated down from Canada about four hundred years ago."

"Canada?"

"Yes, the Navajo language is part of the Athabascan language family. Most of the other groups in that language still live in the Athabascan region, with the Navajo a thousand miles south. The Apache language is also Athabascan. But as I was saying, there has been some recent work on the ruins of some old Navajo hogans, using dendrochronology, and it looks like the Navajo may have come earlier, maybe even early enough to have been present during the occupation phase of Chaco Canyon."

"Tell me more."

"The roads are particularly fascinating. They are so irrational, not like regular roads. These roads run straight across the landscape, not following topography, always thirty feet wide. They don't go to other settlements. They obviously weren't used for travel. In other words, of no use except for some religious or ideological purpose."

"What were the roads made of?"

"Just cleared ground, though stairs were cut into cliffs or rocks that were in the way, so that you could actually walk along the roads. I know that sounds strange, but remember that these roads were obviously for ceremonial use, not actual practical travel. Sometimes they made ramps to get over obstacles or constructed berms to mark the edges of the road. Calling them roads doesn't always make sense either, because it is apparent that many of the roads had sections missing, where they hadn't completed the work or were satisfied with a road that was like a dashed line, not continuous. In a couple of spots the roads have parallel segments that start and end at no rational place. There are often borders to the road, sometimes complete berms of earth, or small masonry walls, and other times just rocks evenly spaced along it.

"It seems obvious that religion processions may have followed the roads, though what seems obvious now may not always be true. We are moderns and have a tough time getting into the heads of other peoples and other times."

"How long are these roads?"

"They vary a lot. If I recall correctly, the total of all the road segments that have been surveyed so far is something like four hundred miles. A lot of the roads are only visible through aerial or satellite photography, showing up because of differences in vegetation or soil disturbance."

Amanda perked up. "Really? Show me."

CHAPTER FIFTY-EIGHT

Amanda pulled a laptop out of a compartment in front of the cabin. She popped it open and they were connected to the Internet. Harry searched for archaeological sites that had maps of the roads radiating out from Chaco Canyon. A friend of his at Utah State University maintained the best site, with raw satellite and aerial photos, as well as a comprehensive map showing all the roads. He brought the map up.

"Sweet Mother Julia," Amanda gasped. "It's a glyph."

"A what?"

"An Alpha glyph. It's a symbol, like a letter or logo. This is a personal glyph—for whom, I don't know. Back home I would just ask the Cloud who it represented."

"The Cloud?" Harry asked.

"Sort of like our Internet here, but so much more," she said. "It also has the symbol for *land here*. See those three loops and that line?"

"You're kidding."

"I kid you not," she smiled. "I wonder what the so-called Master was up to? Was he trying to get other exiles to land at Chaco Canyon?"

"Do exiles get to choose where to land?"

"No, it's random, though they place us where it is somewhat safe. You know, not in the polar regions or down in the middle of a desert someplace. The ship's computer is also supposed to pick someplace near people, which means a village or a city."

"So why have a glyph saying *land here*?"

"I don't know. It's forbidden for any Alphas except for exiles to come anywhere near Earth, you know, to prevent the friends of exiles from rescuing them."

"What if someone slipped a change into the program of a ship's computer so it would survey the Earth and find that glyph and follow the instructions?" Harry asked.

"Interesting idea," she mused. "Not impossible to do, though the computer is supposed to be self-repairing. Maybe they also subverted that protection feature. But I don't see the point."

"What happens to the ships after they drop off an exile?"

"They return to Alpha to be reused again. They take a lot of resources to build so we just don't throw them away."

"Have any never returned?"

"I don't know. I would suspect that some have been lost. Space is a pretty big place and interstellar space has many hazards. The ships are going pretty fast and could encounter a dark mass or clump of strange particles."

The airplane banked and Harry looked out the window. It was midday and he recognized the rough terrain of southern Colorado below them. The airplane banked again and he saw the town of Cortez, a quaint farming community turned tourist attraction because they were at the entrance to famed Mesa Verde National Park, where the Anasazi cliff dwellers had lived.

A Toyota FJ Cruiser waited for them, again with keys in the ignition. As Harry opened the door to the bright yellow all-wheel off-road vehicle, he felt like a pawn in the game being played by two factions of demigods. Cars and equipment appeared when needed as if the gods on Olympus had opened the sky and placed them on the game board. As he had come to expect, there was food and water in the car, and plenty of vitamins and alcohol.

They placed their duffel bags in the back seat and Amanda took the wheel. The woman obviously loved to drive. He regretted that he hadn't taken the opportunity to clean his weapons, but sleep and the research had demanded his time instead. He knew the weapons were probably okay, but the salt air might have been hard on them. What a strange thought: he had been on the Atlantic Ocean just that morning. He had traveled enough in his life to not be disoriented by such rapid changes, but this time it felt different. The whole world was different. The woman beside him was the most extraordinary person he had ever met, and she changed everything. But, really, did she change anything?

"I have genital herpes," he blurted out as they drove out of the airport.

Amanda looked at him with a quizzical expression that made him want to crawl away and hide.

"I had an episode of stupid," he continued. He felt his face getting flushed, something that hadn't happened for years, maybe even decades. He was a grown man, experienced in the ways of the world and did not readily feel embarrassed. He couldn't remember the last time.

"Don't worry about it," Amanda said. "The helpers in you have surely taken care of that little problem."

"That's nice to hear," he said. "Sorry I brought it up."

"No, that's okay," she said. "I like you, too, and we will be exploring that when all this nastiness is over."

Harry's mouth dropped open. He fumbled for words. "That's good." His face felt even redder; he must be tired or something, wearing his emotions on the surface. This was completely unlike him. Must be the relief over rescuing Brenda.

"Could you hand me those vitamins?" she asked, and he was grateful for the change of subject.

She twisted open the bottle and started to pop them in, one at a time, like candy. They turned onto US Highway 160, heading south for Shiprock. Beyond was Farmington and Chaco Canyon.

"You really like those vitamins," Harry said. "Should I be eating some?"

She gave him a handful. "That should do. Your helpers have already fixed you—they are just in maintenance mode now. My helpers are seriously depleted in numbers. I gave an awful lot of them to you and I have to make more. I also gave some to Brenda, though much fewer."

"How long before you have enough new helpers?"

"It could be another week before I am up to my usual healthy self. I love these things." She popped two more multivitamins into her mouth. "Before this century, it was hard to get the right minerals that my helpers needed. Sometimes I even ate dirt."

"How'd it taste?"

"Like dirt."

"Have you healed many people?" Harry asked. "Like you healed Brenda and me?"

"No, I haven't," she said. "I'm no saving angel, at least not in that way. Before multivitamins came along, it wasn't even a consideration, since it would take me too long to recover. Another reason that I haven't done it much is that I didn't want to attract attention. There are other Alphas who are up to no good, not like the Cabal, who have some sort of agenda. These Alphas are crazy, for lack of a better word; they hunt Earthers and they hunt Alphas. They really like to kill Alphas—it's like the Most Dangerous Game multiplied by ten."

"So you actually hide as much as you can?"

"Yes, we all do. Those who don't end up dead," Amanda said. "There's something else that you should know. I am the only exile that I know of that can heal others. It was an ability left in me because I volunteered for exile. Very few other exiles know about it. I don't know what might happen if other exiles knew. They might want to take me prisoner so that they could force me to use that ability."

"You're secret's safe with me."

"I know." She smiled at him. When a woman smiles, it completely transforms her entire countenance, making them into a new, more appealing person. Harry smiled back and turned to look out the window, feeling awkward.

They passed a pair of white crosses on the roadside. Someone had placed wreathes of plastic flowers on them, their bright colors now grown pale from the sunlight. Harry liked the idea of putting crosses at the roadside where fatal car accidents occurred. It reminded other drivers of their mortality.

It reminded him of his own mortality.

He had always wanted to die a noble death, a romantic ideal that he had never abandoned, acquired from his youth of reading adventure and science fiction novels. To die without purpose, just because the physics of the universe came together and terminated him—the idea truly terrified him. He had seen enough of war to know that most deaths were not noble; they happened just because a bullet or a bomb intersected with a body. There was no meaning there.

The exiles seemed to have the same fears. Amanda may be thousands of years old, but inside she was just like him, just as afraid and seeking meaning in her life. He knew that the intensity of the last few days had bonded them together, and that raw physical attraction was driving his libido in frustrating directions, but they might have something special together. What could she see in him? Such doubts were not part of his normal makeup, but what would a woman of that caliber see in a forty-four-year-old archaeologist?

"What's our destination?" she asked.

"Just drive to the Chaco Canyon." He looked at the map on his cell phone. "I figure that we have another two hours before we're there."

"Okay," she said. "Stay alert. I'm sure that we're being watched."

"What?"

"They have a lot of resources and I'm sure that they have this area covered, but I don't think that the Cabal will make a move before we get the artifact. After that it will be us trying to keep one step ahead of them."

"That's a cheery thought."

She looked at him and grinned. "I'm a cheery person."

CHAPTER FIFTY-NINE

Keith Russell liked being a criminal. When he was a kid and read comic books, he always rooted for the criminals. The Joker was so much more hip than Batman, and Lex Luthor was brilliant compared to Superman. Magneto was the cool guy compared to that bald cripple, Charles Xavier. He loved how they flaunted the rules and made up their own. Money, women, and power were theirs for the taking.

Ironically enough, he joined the Army, an organization that was all about rules. He had to get out of that small town somehow and the recruiter told a good story. The Army and he didn't get along, but he learned how to simulate obedience and he learned weapons. His high aptitude score got him slotted into a signals specialty and he learned to run surveillance equipment. The War on Terror kept him in the Army even though his officers wanted to discharge him, though finally an incident with a prostitute in Manila resulted in a court-martial. He was stripped of his security clearance, which would have made getting a civilian job much easier, and cast adrift.

Four months later he was convicted for shoplifting, bizarrely enough. He normally went for more serious stuff, and the police had no idea how many felonies he had committed. After serving three weeks in a Sacramento jail, mostly for telling the judge to use his anatomy in ways that were probably physically impossible, a strange man in a suit approached him on his release. The man had a copy of Russell's psychological profile from the Army and offered him a job on the spot.

He called the organization he worked for the Machine, since his employers never gave him any name for themselves. Sometimes he thought that they were a rogue branch of the government, other times he thought maybe the Mafia. Finally he came to the conclusion that the tight-lipped people who paid him so well were just eccentric rich people who liked to commit crimes. Four days ago the call came for him to get himself and his equipment to Albuquerque as quickly as possible. As usual, budget was not a problem.

Other agents already in place pointed him to their base, just a little south of Bloomfield, near a group of oil derricks. US Highway 550 was only half a mile away, but a fold in the land hid the derricks from the road. Russell set up camp in a rented motor home, placing his antennas atop the vehicle. Chaco Canyon was only forty miles away as the hawk flies, and Russell had two hawks and an eagle.

His birds came on the same charter flight into Albuquerque. He unpacked them, still marveling that his employers had been able to obtain the latest military hardware. The Pentagon only sold these unmanned aerial vehicles to their closest allies, like the British and the Israelis. He attached the wings to the eagle, an unmanned aerial vehicle. With its twelve-foot wingspan and pusher propeller, the eagle could loiter for over a day, its sharp camera eyes relaying a steady stream of data back to Russell. Two small missiles, mini-Hellfires, were snugly attached to bottom of the aircraft. The eagle also acted as a data relay for the hawks.

The hawks had wingspans of three feet, with spinning fans in their centers that gave them lift like a helicopter. They could stay aloft for about twelve hours.

All the UAVs were painted a pale blue-grey that helped them blend in with the background. Russell had heard of a model with chameleon paint, which changed to match the background, but he had never seen that—maybe it was just a fantasy that surveillance specialists told each other.

From his three laptops, arranged in a row on the table before him, Russell flew all three birds remotely. He flew the two hawks down to Chaco Canyon and landed on the tall butte to the southeast of the canyon, where they soaked up power from the solar cells on their backs, and waited for further instructions. He picked the butte because it was high and hard to get to, so a hiker wouldn't stumble across them.

The eagle roamed freely and Russell was happy. The air conditioner of the motor home blew a stream of dry cool air down on the back of his neck. Beer in the fridge and a stack of microwaved taquitos completed his bliss.

In the early afternoon, the sound of helicopters disrupted the calm. He set the eagle on autopilot and went to the door.

Two UH-1 Huey helicopters landed, Vietnam-vintage aircraft, with the logos of an oil field services company on their doors. Ten men got out of each chopper, armed to the hilt and wearing tan desert camouflage.

A woman in camouflage also got out, her long blonde hair wrapped into a bun. She carried a pistol and nasty expression on her face. He recognized her from a previous operation in Brazil, which had involved the assassination of a slew of government officials and labor leaders. Gretel. One of the bosses.

"Good afternoon, ma'am," he said as she came up to him.

"There is a yellow Toyota SUV leaving Bloomington as we speak." She handed him a cell phone that had a real-time data scrolling on it. He recognized it as coming from a military satellite feed. How had the Machine gotten hold of that?

"You want me to follow this?" he asked.

"Of course," she said in a tone indicating that she thought he was a fool. He bit back an angry retort, remembering that she paid the bills. Or at least her superiors did, whoever they were.

Russell went back to his laptops and sent the eagle after its prey.

CHAPTER SIXTY

Harry pointed at the small road that led south from the grav-eled road which connected the highway to Chaco Canyon. Amanda turned and they raced down the narrow road, trailed by a cloud of dust. She slowed only occasionally to dodge large rocks.

After three miles, Harry motioned for her to stop near a rocky butte. They strapped on their holsters and Amanda followed Harry out into the desert of small sage and rabbit brush, with small clumps of grass dried by the sun into a brittle brown that was a lighter shade than the soil. The heat beat down, leaching sweat out of his skin in the short walk.

Harry looked around as they walked. No other cars on the road. He saw only the contrails of a jetliner heading west and a bird so high above that it was little more than a dot. He found the small marker rock where he had expected it, next to the sandstone wall of the butte. Moving the rock, he burrowed with his hands down into the soft sand. A piece of plastic caught on his finger.

Rather than just pull the plastic and the artifact straight up, Harry excavated around it, as a proper archaeologist should, then pulled the plastic-wrapped artifact out. He motioned for Amanda to withdraw over next to the butte, where an overhang provided several feet of shade.

Harry took the artifact out of the plastic, four inches long and two inches wide, with the symbol on the surface that had attracted all the attention. He blew across its burnished surface, more from habit than because he saw any dust. This artifact had so far been directly responsible for the deaths of over a dozen people in the past week. How many others had died during the harsh, self-indulgent rule of the Master eight hundred years ago?

He offered the artifact to the blonde woman. She took the box, balanced it on her left hand, and gently caressed it along the edges with the fingers of her right hand.

"It's a gift box, used to hold small messages or presents," she said. "I haven't seen one since I was exiled. Normally only the person for whom the box was intended for can open it, because the box checks for their helper signatures. I'm seeing if this box will recognize me as an Alpha and open anyway."

The artifact made a small noise, a tinkle of musical notes, and Amanda drew her finger back. The top of the box opened on invisible hinges. The cavity inside was full of sparkling dust.

Amanda wet her little finger and dipped it into the sparkles, removing a fingertip covered with the glitter, and put it into her mouth. Pulling her finger from pursed lips, she closed her eyes as if contemplating the joys of a piece of fine chocolate.

Harry waited and after a minute she opened her eyes.

Her eyes glistened and she smiled. "They're forbidden helpers."

"Forbidden? Why?"

"We had many different types of helpers on Alpha that were removed before exile. These are some of them. Somehow he had these smuggled in."

Amanda stroked the inside of the box's lid and it expanded, like a fan opening. Inside were glyphs inscribed into the metal. "It's in Alpha," she said. "I'll translate."

Gimus,

If you are reading this then by some chance I am dead and you have had to break into my tomb. The starskiff came as planned and I hid it at 542,123,432,876. Take

care, brother, we from the same womb, and take revenge for me.

Gilgal

"I assume that Gilgal is the Master who ruled Chaco that you told me about before," Harry said.

"Yes, it's an unusual name, even for an Alpha."

"Who's Gimus?" Harry asked.

"Gimus must be his brother, since they came from the same womb. It sounds to me like they were both exiled to Earth and planned to escape. For some reason, Gimus never found this. Perhaps he was killed, or never came to Earth."

"So you don't know who Gimus is?" Harry repeated.

"Not a clue."

"The starskiff is a spaceship?"

"Yes. It's probably still here."

"Can you translate those coordinates into something that we can use?"

Amanda held up her hand. "Just a moment. This is all more than I expected to find." She was silent for a moment, her eyes closed. "Let's get going."

Back in the Toyota, she took out her cell phone and brought up a calculator to help her work larger numbers. "I just can't believe that there might be a starskiff around here."

"What's a starskiff, exactly?"

"It's one of the spaceships that bring each of the exiles to Earth. We need to go find it."

"We have the artifact that the Cabal wants," Harry said. "Shouldn't we just bail out?"

"This is so much bigger than I expected. I have to see if that spaceship really exists. It's just too important." She paused for a moment, tapped twice more on her phone, and handed it to Harry. "That's where the coordinates point to."

Harry looked at the GPS coordinates on her phone and tapped them into his own phone. His personalized map, filled with archaeological data, came up.

"That's Casa Ketl," he said. "It's about twenty-five miles west of Chaco Canyon. It's never been excavated."

She started up the engine. "Can we drive there?"

Harry traced the back roads for a moment on his cell phone. "Yes, we can. Head back the way we came."

They rejoined the road to Chaco Canyon for a few minutes before Harry told her to take a right turn. They would loop around to the north of the national historic park, staying on BLM land.

"So what do these new helpers do?" Harry asked.

"I'm still trying to find out," she said, eyes on the road. "Back on Alpha I had command helpers that could simply query a new helper and learn what it could do. I don't have command helpers anymore so my helpers have to sort of experiment with the new helpers. It could take a few hours for some types of helpers or even days or weeks. At least, I think that's what will happen. We have never had any new helpers as far as I know."

"This could change everything," he said. "Give the Humanists an edge in their struggle with the Cabal."

"I hope so."

* * * * * * *

An eagle followed them.

CHAPTER SIXTY-ONE

Casa Ketl had never been an impressive great house—only two stories, with perhaps a hundred rooms. As time had worked its inexorable influence, the rocks forming the upper walls had collapsed, creating piles of debris along the lower walls. Large parts of the site were completely covered with dirt, forming a small hill. A few of the interior walls remained, valiantly resisting gravity and entropy. Such an isolated great house was not uncommon, and fragments of one of the Chaco roads ran in this direction.

Directly behind the ruin was a large hill that rose five hundred feet off the desert floor. Small cliffs and steep draws marked its rugged terrain. Small clumps of juniper grew in folds of the earth, marking where enough ground water existed to sustain life. One fold had willows growing there and a solitary cottonwood, so there must be a small spring, even if it never surfaced as open water.

This was part of the Navajo Reservation; a Bureau of Indian Affairs road ran near the great house—really no more than a faded track through the sagebrush. They passed a solitary abandoned hogan about two miles before reaching the ruin. To the west Harry could see the hazy outline of the Chuska Mountains.

Amanda brought the Toyota skidding to a stop in front of the ruin, allowing the cloud of dust that had trailed them to settle down on the car. They both got out and found that the heat of the day had not yet started to abate, even though it was after five in the afternoon. The contrast to the air conditioning in the car quickly brought a layer of sweat to Harry's skin.

Harry looked at his phone. "How accurate are those coordinates?"

"They should be very accurate."

"Then our goal is five hundred and twenty meters west, about halfway up that hill, I would say."

Amanda pulled her duffel bag from the back seat. "We should gear up," she said. "Trouble could show up anytime."

Harry pulled on his flak jacket, the webbing, and a small backpack holding a gallon of water along with any of other goodies he could find. Franklin had equipped them well. He even found two cubes of C4 explosive, along with a set of blasting caps; the off-white cubes and bright red plastic caps went into a pocket of the backpack. He picked up his M4 and checked it, working the slide, blowing inside the chamber just to be sure. Extra magazines went into his webbing, along with the remaining grenades.

Amanda set the pace, her sniper rifle over her shoulder, moving with an eagerness that forced him to hurry to keep up. They circled the ruin. Pottery shards were scattered around the remains of a midden near the front, where the ground rose in a gentle hump. Harry saw three beams still sticking out of one of the walls—a good source for dendrochronology dating of the site. A large kiva anchoring the end of the ruin was no more than a circular-shaped depression in the ground with a large sagebrush growing in the center, taking advantage of the inner slopes to bring moisture when any rain came.

A draw led up the hill behind the ruin. A dry runoff channel cut down its center; pockets of sand and soft dirt had formed anywhere that the draw flattened out. The two climbed up the draw, with Harry occasionally stopping to consult his phone. Ravens lived in the cliffs on one side of the draw, their caw-caw calls objecting to the intruders. They came to a small cliff a dozen feet high that blocked the draw. Centuries of runoff had eroded the center of the cliff, forcing blocks of limestone to fall into a jumble that formed a sort of staircase. They scrambled up and over. Harry saw from his phone that they were only ninety meters from the coordinates.

He looked back down the draw to Casa Ketl and out across the rolling folds of the barren land. He could see perhaps twenty or thirty miles to the horizon. Chaco Canyon was out there; if he squinted, Fajada Butte stuck up like stubby finger.

"Where now?" Amanda asked, breathing quickly through her nose.

"Up there and to the left."

They found another draw that branched off to the left, and as they approached their goal, Harry's practiced eye traced the straight lines of masonry built into the side of the draw. It was odd. Initially he thought that it had been a granary, used to store the corn grown on the flat spaces before Casa Ketl. Now it looked wrong though, built on a slope forming the side of the draw, about twenty feet long and ten feet high.

They reached the wall and Amanda ran her fingers across the stones. "Are we here?" she asked.

Harry checked his phone. The margin of error from the satellite signals was only two meters. "This is it."

"We need to get inside, and fast," she said.

"I don't see any sign of an entrance," Harry said, walking back and forth. He tugged at one of the stones. "It's still in excellent shape. Take at least several hours to get through."

"Blow it," she said.

"Excuse me?" Harry was certain he hadn't heard her correctly.

"I saw you take the C4," she said. "Blow a hole in it."

"I'm an archaeologist," he objected. "I don't blow things up. I excavate, with a brush and trowel if necessary. I've even used dental tools before."

Amanda visibly restrained herself and looked at him with bright eyes, her pretty face streaked with sweat and dust. "We have to move quickly. I need to know what's in there. Please."

Harry grumbled to himself as he pulled off his backpack. She was the expert in exile matters, and it was her responsibility to make the call. Using his knife, he managed to pry one of the stones in the center of the wall out, nicking his knuckles and drawing a thin trickle of blood. A sacrifice to the gods of archaeology for the sin he was about to commit. The resulting hole was the size of his fist. Harry took the two cubes of C4, tore off the protective paper, and pushed them together like modeling clay. He formed a rough cone and pressed it into the hole in the wall, creating a shaped charge.

"Please move further up the draw and get behind that boulder," he instructed Amanda.

There was a variety of blasting caps. He picked one that had a one-minute timer built into it. Normally he preferred to lay a wire and use a battery to set off the explosion, but he only had these single caps. Pushing the red plastic nub into the C4, he twisted the end, activating the timer.

He scrambled up the draw to join Amanda. They both covered their ears and opened their mouths.

* * * * * * *

Gretel watched as Russell touched the joystick and tapped on the keyboard, bringing the cameras on his UAV into focus. He had instructed one of his smaller surveillance UAVs to head west from its resting place on Fajada Butte, but it flew more slowly and would not arrive for another half hour. She would have to make do with the camera on the larger aircraft.

The man and woman were quite visible. When the ground next to them erupted in dust, Gretel blinked in surprise. They had used explosives. Her instincts told her that this was the moment she had been waiting for. No more watching; now she wanted to be there.

"Keep me informed of developments," she ordered. "And pipe that feed to my cell."

She left the motor home. Her men were sprawled in any scrap of shade they could find. "Mount up," she called. "We are moving now."

Two minutes later the two Hueys took off, heading southwest

at 120 miles per hour. Gretel sat in the back among the merce-naries, their automatic weapons balanced vertically on their barrels and held between their knees. A headset plugged into a comms jack muffled the harsh throbbing of the rotors and kept her in touch with the pilots.

She squinted at the screen on her cell phone.

CHAPTER SIXTY-TWO

Amanda was moving even before the dust had settled. She pulled off her webbing and flak jacket, keeping only her flashlight. The dark hole was a good half-meter wide. She moved towards it, but Harry's hand on her arm stopped her.

"Wait a minute," he said, setting his rifle aside.

He went up to the hole and tugged at the masonry stones on the sides, pulling a few free. Then he tugged on the stones above the hole, putting his full strength into it. One of them proved to effectively be a keystone and he leaped back as the wall above the hole collapsed. She saw through the dust easily enough. Now there was only bare rock above a much larger and safer hole.

Amanda pushed past Harry and scrambled over the fallen stones and into the dark. She switched on her flashlight and blinked at the light that reflected back at her. Running her light back and forth showed her a bright mirrored object that filled most of the cavern.

"Oh, the divine creator be praised and let us be reconciled," she said aloud, reciting a prayer remembered from long ago on Alpha. "I can't believe it's a ship! A real ship, here!"

Harry joined her with his own flashlight.

The starskiff was about fifteen meters long and five meters high, shaped like a teardrop, entirely covered with a reflective metallic surface. The Master—Gilgal—had maneuvered the spaceship into a cavern and then covered the entrance. She could imagine how it must have landed on the plaza before Casa

Bonito, another manifestation of the Master's power, astonishing his wide-eyed people. For whatever reason—waiting for his brother, enjoying being the master of his people too much—he had not immediately used the starskiff. Instead he had hidden it here.

* * * * * * *

Harry felt like he had walked into a science fiction novel. He crept around Amanda and looked at the cavern. There were still scrape marks on the ceiling from the primitive tools the Chacoans had used to make a cave large enough to hold the spaceship. They had plastered the walls, and the colors of a geometric design were still brilliant, like on a piece of pottery, shades of green and blue drawn in squares.

At the base of the wall to his left were mummified corpses, piled haphazardly, still wearing clothes made from rabbit skins and yucca sandals. Harry assumed that they were workers slain by the Master, either as a sacrifice or to keep them quiet about the cave and its marvelous treasure, or both. Others who had sealed up the final hole in the wall had probably also died.

"What were those words you spoke?" Harry asked.

"It's a prayer."

"Do you believe in God?"

"Of course I believe in a divine creator," she said as she placed her hands on the surface of the ship. "Most of us do. To suppose that there are not more advanced beings, who might have something to do with our evolution and development, is pure hubris. Look at us Alphas; we have been profoundly changed by the Movers. Some of us back on Alpha—not me—actually worship the Movers, though they left us no indication that they wanted to be worshiped."

"But do you believe in a supernatural god?"

She smiled at him. "There is no such thing as the supernatural—only things that we don't yet understand."

Harry wanted to continue this intriguing conversation, but

the hint of a familiar sound drew him back out of the cave. He walked far enough down the branching draw to look back out over the ruin of Casa Ketl and the panorama of the New Mexico desert.

Two helicopters, old Hueys, had settled had landed on the BIA road behind the Toyota, their engines off and the rotors spooling down. Some twenty-odd men, wearing desert camouflage and carrying the distinctive hard lines of weapons, had spread out and were approaching the ruins. One of the group was obviously a woman, even from this distance. Women walk differently.

Harry put down his M4 and scrambled back up the draw. He grabbed Amanda's sniper rifle and called out to the cave entrance, "We've got lots of company, and they look ready to rumble."

CHAPTER SIXTY-THREE

Harry got back to the top of the main draw, found a comfortable space atop a boulder, and sighted through the scope of Amanda's rifle, tracing the outline of Casa Ketl. He didn't want to fire down into the ruin; he had destroyed enough archaeological sites that day, though the marks from the bullets would do less damage than the centuries of weather.

Where were they?

He pulled back from the scope and looked down the draw and over the ruin, blinking furiously to get the best focus possible. The soldiers were gone, but the helicopters were still there. He looked through the scope again and moved slowly, taking time to focus. There was one of them. The soldiers had gone to ground. Why? Did they know he was watching?

A loud crash ripped through his hearing and Harry gasped with sudden pain.

* * * * * *

Amanda had just emerged from the cavern when an explosion knocked her back on her butt. She rolled to her side on the hard edges of the masonry stones. Her ears rang for a moment, like a bell still echoing, but her helpers took care of that problem pretty quickly. Her cheek stung and she reached up to explore, finding a sticky mess. A trench about three inches long and the size of a pencil had been plowed out, exposing her cheekbone. The helpers could handle that, too.

She stood up, blood pouring down her neck and staining her chest. The blood had a faint silvery sheen to it.

The explosion had come from down the draw. As she stumbled down, she saw a piece of silver metal on the ground that she recognized as the tail fin from a small missile. She jerked her head up and squinted. Something that looked like a bird was thousands of feet in the air above, but coming closer.

A crater the size of a watermelon had been gouged out of a large rock ahead of her. Harry's legs protruded from the far side of the boulder. A knife thrust of fear went through her, sorrow and loss combining to make a debilitating stew. She clamped down, having her helpers control her brain chemicals, taking the fear away, giving her frontal cortex complete control over the more basic emotion centers deeper in the brain.

She kept looking up at the aircraft, hoping to catch a flash if it launched another missile. Scrambling around the boulder, she found the unconscious archaeologist. Half of his face was caved in, his right arm looked like shredded meat, with the white of bones exposed. His blood had the same metallic sheen as her own. His flak jacket had protected his torso, though his right pants leg was shredded and the leg ground up like his arm, but not as severely. The missile had hit the boulder right next to him.

She checked his breathing. It came in ragged gasps. She pulled at his body, adjusting him so that his head was further up the slope and gravity would be less inclined to help his body fluids leak out.

His helpers were keeping him alive.

She looked down the draw and saw dun-colored figures climbing up. Moving quickly, keeping the boulder between her and further downhill, darting glances at the descending aircraft, she reached her pile of gear and pulled on her flak jacket. It had been foolish to take it off. She grabbed Harry's backpack and looked for her rifle. It was not where she had left it, nor was Harry's assault rifle. He must have taken both weapons, intending to use them.

Back down the draw, scrambling with all four limbs like an inept monkey, feeling like the aircraft was a dagger poised to strike. It seemed content to circle ever closer. Maybe it only had one missile.

She reached Harry, pulled open his bloody mouth and dribbled some water in. He swallowed, and she knew that his helpers were in charge, having detected the water, and wanting more. She poured half the gallon jug into his mouth, found some vitamin pills in her pocket, broke them up, and dropped them in.

She looked down the hill. The Cabal mercenaries were moving fast and were now halfway up the draw.

* * * * * *

"You want me to take her out?" Russell asked in Gretel's ear.

The blonde woman stopped and pressed the send button on the radio attached to her webbing at her shoulder. "That's still a negative. Just keep telling me what she's doing."

Gretel figured that the woman was an exile. She had blonde hair, so she wasn't the redheaded archaeology student who had the family in Maine. Another woman running around with the male archaeologist would probably be from some other exile faction. The Cabal was not the only group of exiles interested in the artifact.

She had no intention of killing a fellow exile today.

Unless she needed to.

* * * * * *

Amanda had to make a fast decision. Her chemically induced clarity helped her look at the alternatives. She wanted to keep Harry alive, but she couldn't carry him quickly enough to escape that many soldiers, especially with an eye in the sky to follow her over this damn barren terrain. Even if she was willing to sacrifice Harry, and she wasn't, she couldn't leave the starskiff to be captured by the Cabal. Who knew what they would do with such a prize? Even if they didn't want to send someone back to Alpha, which would take decades, they could strip advanced technologies from the spaceship. That would give them advantages that she didn't have time to imagine, but were surely bad for the Humanist cause.

She made up her mind and left Harry for a moment, scrambling back up the draw. When she entered the cavern and saw her reflection in the dim light of the setting sun that leaked through the hole in the masonry wall, she felt homesickness sweep over her. She could leave now and go back home. Of course, she was an exile and would have to hide on Alpha, otherwise the justice authorities would send her back. Perhaps everything had changed on Alpha; after all, they apparently weren't sending any more exiles. On the other hand, nothing ever changed on Alpha—the curse of immortality.

She placed her hand on the reflective surface of the starskiff. It felt cool and exotic, like the surface of the gift box. She spoke in Alpha, her tone one of command, even though that was unnecessary. "Ship, do you hear me?"

Nothing happened. Of course, the ship was trying to talk to her helpers, and she didn't have those helpers. It should still be able to listen to audible instructions.

"Ship, I am giving you a direct command. You are to disassemble yourself, as quickly as you can without causing an explosion. Please acknowledge this command with an affirmative glyph displayed on your external hull."

Twin intersecting globes, representing the twin suns of her home world, appeared on the ship in front of her.

Amanda choked back a sob. It seemed so sacrilegious, so wrong, to destroy this link to home. She stepped back to the entrance that Harry had created for the cavern. Already it was becoming unusually warm in there.

Before stepping into sight of the aircraft above, she pulled the gift box from her pocket, opened it, and poured the contents into her mouth. It was like drinking sand. She had to choke down on her gag reflex.

She crawled out of the cavern, already soaked in sweat from the heat generated by the starskiff. Built of nano-sized components, the spaceship was methodically taking itself apart on the microscopic level, which created a lot of excess energy that had to be bled off as heat.

Amanda went back down the smaller draw, and as she peeked around the corner to look down towards the ruin, she saw one of the mercenaries, not more than a hundred feet away. He yanked his rifle to his shoulder and she jerked back out of his line of sight.

"I surrender, I surrender," she called, shouting as loud as she could, ending with a cough because her mouth was so dry.

With hands over her head, she stepped out into full view. There were six of them now, coming close, keeping their weapons trained on her.

* * * * * * *

Gretel followed her mercenaries, trying to keep close to them. These aggressive men annoyed her, constantly rushing from place to place, having no sense of relaxed pacing. They were always either going full speed or stopped in place, playing a video game.

The news of the woman surrendering came over her radio and spurred her to move more quickly.

CHAPTER SIXTY-FOUR

"Is he your lover?" the exile woman from the Cabal demanded.

The two women stood over Harry. Amanda knelt down, gently pulled on his chin, and poured more water between his parted lips. "Yes, he is."

Not a complete lie—more of a hope.

"As you can see," Amanda continued, "he is like us." She didn't speak more plainly because of the mercenaries that stood around, their weapons no longer pointing at her, but ready enough. Her own weapons, and Harry's, had been taken. Her sniper rifle had been found in front of the boulder, riddled with rock fragments.

"Yes, I can see that," the woman said. She stood with her hands on her hips. Amanda had no idea who this exile might be.

The sparkling sheen in the dried blood on both Amanda and Harry showed that they were different than normal humans.

"All of you," the woman said. "Withdraw back one hundred meters. I want some privacy. Keep this place surrounded and keep sharp—help may have been summoned to rescue these two."

After the soldiers withdrew, the woman knelt down. "You have the artifact?"

Amanda drew the box from her pocket and handed it over.

"It's a gift box," the exile said in obvious surprise. She caressed the surface and it opened. She read the inscription and looked up.

"The box was empty?" she asked.

"Yes," Amanda said, her helpers making sure that she betrayed no inadvertent hint of her deception through some form of subtle body language. "The gift was the words, I guess."

"Is it true?" the exile asked. "Is there really a spaceship here on Earth?"

"There was, but I destroyed it so that no one else could have it."

"Where is it?" The woman corrected herself. "Or, where was it?"

Amanda pointed up the draw.

The woman moved away and Amanda focused her attention on Harry. He needed more water, which she poured into his mouth, then she took some for herself to wash down the sandy taste of helpers in her mouth. She found the last of her vitamin pills and a protein bar in her pockets and crushed them into his mouth. More water washed down these supplies for his helpers.

The Cabal exile returned. "It's just a black sludge now," she announced. "I didn't want to leave Earth, anyway, though others might have wanted to do so."

"What are you going to do?" Amanda asked.

"I have someone I want to get back to. He needs me, just as your man needs you. I've got what I was sent to retrieve, so I'm just going to leave."

"You feel no need to kill us?" Amanda asked. She shouldn't have asked the question—it might give the other woman ideas—but she needed to know the answer.

"No," the exile from the Cabal said. "Maybe we'll meet again, but not as adversaries, and I may need a favor. You know, we Alphas have to stick together. We've only got each other on this world."

"Just each other," Amanda agreed; *And all the Earthers*, she added to herself.

The mercenaries led the way back down to the helicopters. The unmanned aerial vehicle above gained altitude and flew off towards the northeast.

Half an hour later, the other exile waved up at Amanda. She waved back and watched as the helicopters left.

* * * * * * *

Amanda sat on the ground with the head of her archaeologist in her lap. The sun was setting behind her, warming her back. She absently stroked his brow, then ran her fingers through the fringe of his hair. The hair was cropped short, obviously a way to compensate for the bald spot running from his forehead to his crown. She liked bald men. Of course, it didn't matter; the helpers would bring back his hair if he wanted it.

When he was better she would ask him to comb her hair for her. She loved it when a man pulled a comb through her tresses, feeling his fingers on her scalp, all very intimate and pleasing.

After night fell, as the stars came out, promising wonders that she could not touch, she felt him stir. With wide, dark pupils, she looked down at him. His eyes fluttered open.

She knelt down and kissed his forehead.

"Welcome back," she whispered.

AUTHOR'S NOTE

There are some excellent books on Chaco Canyon that I recommend for readers who want to learn more about that fascinating city in the desert of New Mexico:

Kendrick Frazier, *People of Chaco: A Canyon and its Culture* (Expanded edition, W. W. Norton, 2005).

R. Gwinn Vivian and Bruce Hilpert, *The Chaco Handbook: An Encyclopedic Guide* (University of Utah Press, 2002).

Brian M. Fagan, *Chaco Canyon: Archaeologists Explore the Lives of an Ancient Society* (Oxford University Press, 2005).

Stephen H. Lekson, *The Chaco Meridian: Centers of Political Power in the Ancient Southwest: Centers of Political Power in the Ancient Southwest* (AltaMira Press, 1999).

ABOUT THE AUTHOR

Eric G. Swedin is an Associate Professor in History at Weber State University. His publications include numerous articles, six history books, several science fiction novels, and an historical mystery novel. His *When Angels Wept: A What-If History of the Cuban Mystery Crisis* earned the 2010 Sidewise Award in Alternate History. Eric lives with his family in a house built in 1881. His website is:

http://www.swedin.org/

www.ingramcontent.com/pod-product-compliance
Lightning Source LLC
Chambersburg PA
CBHW021320250626
47155CB00002B/560